EXILED QUEEN

THE THIEF'S TALISMAN: BOOK THREE

EMMA L. ADAMS

I vy Lane rested one hand on her faerie talisman's hilt as her gaze flickered from me to Cedar. "I was told to speak to someone called Raine Whitefall—that is, Lady Whitefall."

I cleared my throat. "That's me."

I could hardly believe Ivy Lane herself—the only pure human with faerie magic I'd ever heard of—was in my living room. After the whirlwind of death and betrayal I'd experienced in the last few hours before my escape from Faerie into the mortal realm, I'd hoped to find my human father here and ensure he was safe. Instead, he'd disappeared without a trace, adding yet another dilemma to my growing heap of problems, which started with me being heir to the Whitefall family and ended with me being a wanted criminal. Ivy's sudden appearance was the last straw—and my last hope.

"And you are?" She addressed Cedar next to me, not taking her hand off her sword.

"My name is Cedar Hornbeam," he said. "Ivy Lane? I've heard that name."

"You might say I have a certain reputation," Ivy said. "For killing rogue Sidhe."

Cedar stiffened. "Rogues? You mean exiles?" Technically, that's what *we* were. Cedar had chosen to come with me rather than stay with the surviving members of the Hornbeam family, thus painting himself as a traitor in the eyes of the Summer Court if they worked out we'd run off together.

"Exiles, rogues, murderers," Ivy said. "A half-blood showed up on my doorstep telling me to find you. He said it was important."

"Who?" Surely not Robin. But when I could count my allies on one hand and most were in this room, there weren't a lot of possibilities. "If it's someone who can go to the Grey Vale and tell my deranged mother not to destroy the Courts, it'd save us a lot of trouble."

"Lady Whitefall—your mother. Ah." Understanding flashed across her face. "I *can* walk into the Grey Vale, but I can't find a Sidhe who doesn't want to be found. And I've never been good at persuading them to do anything."

I blinked at her. She was being serious. She might be a formidable force with a reputation amongst half-bloods for being a ruthless killer, but I'd half thought it was an exaggerated rumour that she could actually walk into the faeries' realm on her own power. Ivy Lane was a living legend, here in my dingy living room, talisman and all.

"You're half-Sidhe, then," she said, not perturbed by my silence. "Both of you?"

I nodded. "Yeah. You might say we have major family issues."

Her mouth twitched, almost a smile. "It seems to be a running theme with every half-faerie I've met lately. No offence."

"None taken," I said. "It's pretty much true."

"So you can explain," Ivy said. "I've heard second-hand accounts of what she did, but I'd like to hear it directly from you."

"Why? Are you planning to help us?" I asked.

"Yes. As much as is in my power, anyway. I have the Sight and can use magic, but there are some things you'll only be able to handle yourself. Especially as she's your mother. I might have their magic, but I'm still human."

"You're entirely human?" Cedar repeated, sounding as surprised as I was.

"One hundred percent."

"Then how did you come to be involved with the Courts?" he asked.

"Long story," said Ivy. "Let's just say the Sidhe and I started out on the wrong foot and went downhill from there."

A human with the Sight… but that wasn't all she had. Her faerie talisman was engraved with unfamiliar symbols, and its bluish tinge told me her magic was of the Unseelie variety.

I took in a breath and gave her a run-down of the last few months, starting with my unexpected invitation into Faerie to collect my inheritance, and finishing with the discovery that my mother wasn't dead but building an army in the Grey Vale to invade the Courts.

Ivy's gaze remained on Cedar and me as she considered my words, and her hand on her sword's hilt. Maybe she thought we'd attack her. I looked too much like the faerie mother who'd faked her death and ruined my life. Slender but athletic frame, icy-white hair, eyes bluer than any human's could ever be, a crescent-shaped birthmark on my face. My family's mark—which *she'd* put there, to mark me as hers.

Ivy pursed her lips. "So she planned this years ago, and

faked her death rather than being exiled. The Sidhe really don't do things by halves, do they? Have you spoken to the Court at all?"

"Well, the Unseelie Court helped me fight her, then ran off when she escaped. The Seelie Court, though—they sort of want me dead for murder."

Ivy opened her mouth then closed it again, shaking her head. "*Which* murder?"

"Lady Hornbeam. She tried to steal my magic and kill me in the process."

Ivy swore. "Your chances of getting cooperation from the Courts are slim to none anyway, but a murder accusation—"

"Yeah, I know I'll be killed or exiled for it," I said. "They won't hear my story. I'm half-blood, which means they'll automatically come out on the side of the Sidhe. Even a monster like Lady Hornbeam."

Ivy sighed. "That puts a wrench in our plans. I'm not blaming you, and heaven knows it's tough to wrangle any kind of commitment out of the Sidhe. They barely tolerate me most of the time. I can't stop them hunting you, but I can misdirect them if you'd like me to."

"Can you help me find my father?" I asked. "He's mortal. I think the faeries took him, like they did before I was born. Well, *she* did."

"I can do that," Ivy said. "I'll ask the leader of the local witch coven for a tracking spell. If I were you, I'd lie low until I can find out what's going on in Faerie."

"But you *can* go there?" asked Cedar. "How?"

"I stole the magic of an exiled Sidhe—it's a long story. Technically, I can't walk into the Courts themselves without an invitation, and for some reason, they go out of their way to avoid giving me one unless it's for a tedious meeting. But if I find anything in the Vale that might point to her whereabouts, I'll let you know."

"Thank you," I said. "There's one more thing. My mother used a different type of magic when she had us prisoner. She used this word—she called it an Invocation. A powerful word that made everyone kneel. Have you heard of those?"

"Unfortunately," Ivy said. "Invocations are the language of the gods. The Sidhe's gods." Her hand went to her sword's hilt, and the symbols etched there. "The Sidhe use them when they want to make a blatant display of power. Say, when they exile someone, or wipe their memory. But they're too powerful for anyone without a Sidhe's magic to handle."

Oh. That's how she did it. No wonder I'd always suspected there was a realm of faerie magic off limits to me. A forbidden language only the Sidhe knew.

Without warning, a sudden air current hit us from in front, sending me stumbling back a step. Cedar, too. Ivy, however, turned to the side, a smile curving her lips as though she'd expected it.

A man had appeared in the corridor. Tall, broad-shouldered and clearly human, he wore a smart suit and a long black coat. He walked into the flat, coat shifting in the breeze stirred up by his arrival.

He just teleported? I'd say he's a mage...

Oh shit.

The head of the Mage Lords frowned at the pair of us, then turned to Ivy. "I was told there was only one half-blood."

"Yeah, so was I. This is Lady Whitefall..."

"Best call me Raine," I said. "Seeing as the other person with my name isn't friendly. This is Cedar."

"Pleasure to meet you," Cedar said with the sort of flourish he usually reserved for members of the Courts. *Right. The Mage Lords are sort of the equivalent of the Sidhe here in this realm.* I'd never met him before, but this guy was the reason most of the dodgy magical schemes my former best friend Denzel had come up with had backfired and ended up with someone getting arrested or threatened. I really hoped he didn't make the connection. I looked a long way from the thief I'd once been, even here in the mortal realm.

The Mage Lord gave us a nod of acknowledgement. "You've come to an agreement?" he asked Ivy.

"Sort of," said Ivy. "You know how slippery the Sidhe are. Basically, we're looking for a missing human. Her father. Also, you'll need to station a guard by the Ley Line again. This time there's a Sidhe who can hypnotise people who might come over looking for mortals to ensnare."

He raised an eyebrow. "Hypnosis?"

"Apparently. Can't have a dull moment, huh." Ivy grinned slyly at him. "I'll check back with you tomorrow, Raine. Is there anything I can take for a tracking spell? It works better with hair, or blood."

My throat went dry. There was no blood in the flat, but a wave of dread rushed over me all the same. I ran to Dad's room, finding the furniture overturned and everything that wasn't nailed down scattered on the floor. Shakily, I grabbed a comb with several of Dad's hairs still tangled in it, left the bedroom, and handed it over to Ivy.

"I'll come back tomorrow," said Ivy, nodding to the Mage Lord.

As one, the pair of them disappeared. Curtains of dust fluttered down in their wake.

"Wow. Apparently we're royalty in this realm, too," I said.

Cedar turned to me. "She only said she'd try to help. No guarantees. She's human."

"She also has faerie magic," I said. "What's their problem with you?"

"Isn't it obvious?" Cedar said. "They hate the Sidhe. Ivy Lane does, anyway."

"And I look exactly like my power-crazy mother." Not for

the first time, I wished I'd taken after Dad instead, but faerie blood usually won out over human. Cedar's dark shoulder-length hair and elegantly carved features were fairly typical, but his light hazel eyes made him look different enough to his faerie mother that I didn't see her staring back at me when our eyes met. Thank the Sidhe for that.

Heat crept into my cheeks when I realised he saw me looking. "No," he said. "You don't look like her."

I blinked. "I've no idea if that was a compliment or not, considering she has everyone dancing to her tune. Aspen worships her."

"Aspen worships power." His jaw tightened. The resemblance between him and his half-brother was a more superficial one, not enough to be obvious unless they were standing right next to one another.

I cleared my throat. "Right. It's too late to call the mercenaries, but I'll do it tomorrow. And talk to the neighbours. Someone must have seen what happened." My throat closed up. There was no chance my mother could have done it in person, because I'd been with her at the time and he hadn't been in her castle. Maybe Dad had run away, but surely the mercenaries guarding him would have noticed.

Cedar nodded. "What do you suggest we do now?"

"Clean up and get some rest." I scrubbed a hand through my hair. Like Cedar, I was covered in blood and debris from the fight. "Do you want to sleep in my room? Dad's room's in a state, but I can sleep on the sofa."

"No, I will," Cedar said. Was I imagining things, or did he sound disappointed? My dad was missing. I couldn't forget it, not with the evidence all around me.

Nor could I forget that I'd got both of us exiled in the first place.

I'd always been terrified the faeries would come back and hurt my dad. But in the end, all my efforts to put up barriers between myself and Faerie had crumpled the instant I'd answered their call and followed them into their realm.

When I found him, this time I'd have to let him go. At least until I dealt with my mother. However painful it might be. The Sidhe would never take away anyone I loved again.

2

The beeping tone of a phone ringing somewhere nearby woke me from sleep. I slid out of bed and stumbled around looking for it before realising the noise came from outside my room.

Cedar was sprawled on his back, legs dangling over the sofa's side. He looked up as I walked in. The ringing came from under the rug I'd tossed over the bare floorboards by the door where hellhound drool had eaten through the carpet. Dad must have thrown it underneath. Lifting the rug, I retrieved the phone.

"Hello?" I asked.

"Raine Warren?" asked a tremulous voice I recognised as belonging to one of the mercenary kids I'd had guarding Dad before they'd taken off. *Good. Ivy spoke to them.* I'd planned to read them the riot act, but the kid sounded terrified anyway. "I—Ivy Lane came here. She said you... she said your father's been kidnapped."

"Yes. You're under this... Larsen Crawley, right? Can I speak to him? I'd like to know who told you not to guard him anymore."

"Mr Warren himself did."

I pressed the phone to my ear. "That can't be right. Can you put me through to your boss?"

"Are you sure? He won't be happy with me for disturbing him at this hour."

"It's urgent. Put me through."

The phone beeped. "Hello," snapped a male voice.

"Is this Larsen Crawley?"

"Yes," said the same irritable voice, which sounded like it belonged to someone in the death grip of a hangover.

"I'm Raine Whi—Warren," I corrected. "I hired several of your mercenaries for bodyguard duty a few weeks ago, and they left before the job was complete. There's a possibility some magic might have been used against them. Harold Warren. Ring any bells?"

He snorted. "Nice try. If you're trying to get out of paying for services, Miss Warren, then you're not fooling anyone."

"I'm not trying to get out of paying for anything." Who the hell was this prick? "I'm pretty sure I paid in advance. Your people never finished the job."

"Harold Warren told us he needed to discontinue the service as they were no longer required."

I stared at the phone for a moment then put it to my ear again. "Okay. That's… Er. Did he sound okay when he said it? Not drunk, or…"

"No, he sounded perfectly lucid."

I frowned. "And it was definitely him?"

"Are you mocking me? He came into the office in person."

Still might have been a glamour. Humans—except for Ivy Lane—didn't have the Sight. It couldn't be more obvious that this Larsen character wanted rid of me, but he wasn't exactly the most reliable bystander. Still, I needed to be sure he wasn't fobbing me off.

"No, I'm wondering if magic was involved," I said to him. "I'll have to inform the Mage Lords if nobody can confirm it."

"Naturally." He swore quietly. "There's been no magic. I do have people who specialise in supernatural nonsense to make sure nothing magical gets near my mercenaries."

"Are you absolutely positive?" I asked. "Because I spoke to Ivy Lane, and she planned to question the others at the guild very closely if it turns out there's any discrepancies. My father is missing, Mr Crawley. I'll hire any help I can to get him back."

"Lane." I heard him shuffle around swearing under his breath. "Of course she's involved."

"You didn't answer my question."

"Look, I'm not magical, okay? I can't see through your faerie charms and shit. Four people told me the job was done. If your old man's missing, I sure as hell don't know where he is."

"Right," I said, resigned. "Did they see anything else? Or— have you been called out on any other faerie-related cases lately?"

"No. Client info is confidential, besides."

"Nothing involving hypnosis?"

"Hypnosis?" He snorted. "What crap are you into? That'd be Ivy Lane's area."

And he hung up.

Cedar yawned and sat up. "Who was that?"

I scowled at the phone. "Mercenary. Or drunkard. Whoever he is, apparently my dad covered his tracks well. Or the person who captured him did."

Cedar swung his feet over the sofa's side, running a hand through his silky dark hair. "I don't suppose you have any spare clothes?" he asked. "These are covered in blood."

He indicated his shirt, which was torn to ribbons. Of

course—we'd fought a war yesterday. It already seemed a million years ago.

"I can use magic," I said. "Any preferences?"

"A similar outfit will do. I can glamour it."

My hands glowed blue as I directed my magic at his clothes, and a fresh outfit replaced the bloodstained one. I did the same to the ragged shorts and T-shirt I'd slept in. There was no point in dressing as a human now. I was all faerie or nothing, as Robin had once said. He might be a deceiving liar, but he'd been right about one thing: when you set foot in Faerie, it never truly left you.

Cedar eyed my armoured coat. "That ability of yours is certainly useful."

"Yeah, it's helpful when you're a fugitive," I said. "I'm going to question the neighbours about Dad. Someone must have seen him leave." Of course, considering we lived in a mostly-human area, nobody except me could see through glamour. I had to start somewhere, though.

"Do you need me to come with you?"

I shook my head. "Better not. They already think I'm going to hex them."

I walked to the door, then hesitated. Maybe I should have dressed as a human after all. But I didn't have the patience to put on an act for the people who'd probably be indifferent at best to Dad's disappearance.

Putting on my coldest Sidhe expression, I opened the door and nearly tripped over a pair of hooved feet.

"Raine." Denzel looked at me in astonishment, as though I'd wandered into his house, not the other way around. We hadn't spoken since an argument shortly after I'd been named as heir to the Whitefall family, when he'd been offended that I no longer wanted to spend time around thieves. We'd parted on the mutual understanding that if we stayed friends, he'd probably end up trying to steal my talisman at some point, which wouldn't end well for him.

"What are you doing here?" I asked. "I don't suppose you've seen my father?"

"Actually—yeah, I did," Denzel said. "He went into half-blood territory two days ago. Why?"

"What the hell was he doing over there?" Denzel stumbled back a few steps at my tone, fear flashing in his eyes. "Is that what you came here to tell me?"

"No. Never mind." He attempted to clip-clop away, but I reached and grabbed his coat, pulling him onto the doorstep. His arms flailed feebly for a second, then he looked at me in meek resignation. "I don't *know*, okay? You were off playing faerie queen, and I assumed he was supposed to be on half-blood territory. He didn't look lost."

I swore. "Is there nothing else you can tell me? I put him under twenty-four-hour guard and some faerie spell must have got through to him anyway."

"Uh, it didn't look that way to me." Denzel managed to pull his coat out of reach as the door opened behind me, and Cedar poked his head out. "You'll have to ask someone else. I don't know why he was there, honest."

He hobbled away then broke into a gallop, his hooves pounding against the pavement. I didn't bother to follow him. "Dad went to *half-blood* territory? I need to tell Ivy."

"Who was he?" asked Cedar. "Another thief?"

"Yep. One of my former light-fingered acquaintances." I went back into the flat, and put the kettle on, just for something to do.

Cedar hovered behind me. "That thing heats water up?"

"Yeah. Don't you—right, Faerie has magic as a substitute." Being here must be weird for him, even if he'd been walking between the two worlds for years. "I'm going to make breakfast, and hopefully Ivy won't take too long."

I poured dry cereal into two bowls, since the bread had long since expired. Dad had been gone for longer than a day. Of course, thanks to Faerie and its time inconsistencies, for him, it'd been weeks since we'd seen one another. If I hadn't put Faerie before him, he might have been spared—but stopping Lady Whitefall's quest for domination had to come first, at whatever cost. If I'd left her to her own devices, we'd be a hell of a lot worse off.

Cedar broke the silence by saying, "When was your father on half-blood territory?"

I ate a few mouthfuls of dry cereal. "Two days ago. Probably too late for Ivy's tracking spell to find him."

"How exactly does this spell work?" he said.

"No clue. Tracking spells are witch spells, so if he's in Faerie, it won't work either." I put my half-empty cereal bowl aside.

"So he left of his own volition?" asked Cedar.

"Even if he did, this is Faerie we're talking about." I groaned. "If the Seelie Court come here, their first stop will be half-blood territory. But I need to know if anyone there has seen him."

"Then I'll go," said Cedar. "I can use glamour to hide myself."

I frowned at him. "It'd have to be a damn good one to fool them."

"I haven't needed to use a full glamour for a while," Cedar said. "But I'm told it's convincing."

The air shimmered around him. My eyes picked out two images, superimposed on top of one another—at the bottom, the real Cedar, and on top, a blond half-faerie wearing torn jeans and a white T-shirt. Humans, and most faeries without strong magic, would see only the top image, and Cedar himself would remain hidden—unless he ran into someone who could see through powerful glamour. Which covered most Sidhe, but they weren't here. *I hope.* Even if they were, as long as he didn't draw attention, he'd be able to get away with it. I was the one with a price on my head.

The instant the door closed behind him, I regretted not following. I paced the room, fidgeted, skimmed through my contacts on my phone and finally sank onto the sofa, exhaustion from yesterday lying heavily on my eyelids. Now I finally had the chance to break down, I didn't have the energy for it. Cedar's scent lingered, and wrapped around me like a comforting blanket. My eyes closed, and I drifted off.

I woke to a hideous growling noise from outside. Grabbing my knife, I made for the door, easing it open in case an ambush waited.

Outside the front door, Cedar circled a beast the size of a wild boar. A second hellhound nipped at his ankles. He couldn't fight one without taking his attention off the other, though he did his best to engage both of them at once. He'd dropped his glamour and pulled out a knife from somewhere —not iron, but a faerie-made one.

"Hey!" I yelled at the monster, giving Cedar the chance to lunge forwards. His blade sank into its neck, blood sprayed, and its heavy body slumped onto the pavement.

Blue light shone around its corpse and the second hellhound grew, expanding to fill half the road. I'd forgotten they fed on death energy, like some other Grey Vale beasts. Wishing I'd grabbed a weapon, I backed up to the doorstep.

Before the beast could move, a sword came down, severing its head. Ivy Lane stepped aside, letting the second hellhound fall, her sword dripping blue-tinged blood. Glyphs flashed up and down its hilt, and its ancient, restrained power made the air tremble. Ivy had moved faster than I'd ever seen a human, lit up in the sheen of blue faerie magic usually afforded to Winter half-bloods only.

"So much for not bothering the neighbours," I said,

unable to take my eyes off the shimmering glyphs on her talisman. The thief part of me wanted a closer look, but I pushed the covetous impulse down. Ivy had killed several Sidhe, and for all I knew, she was even more powerful than Lady Whitefall.

"Hellhounds," said Ivy, shaking droplets of blood from her sword. "I haven't seen one of those for a while."

"My magic didn't work on it," I said. "Don't suppose you know why?"

"They're powerful Unseelie beasts, so they're immune to a lot of Winter magic," said Ivy.

"That explains it." I turned to Cedar. "Did you make it to half-blood territory?"

"I did," Cedar said. "There have been a couple of other Vale attacks there, but nobody saw your father. I didn't see the Sidhe, either."

"Neither did I," said Ivy. "I should probably let Vance—the Mage Lord—know about the hellhounds. But I was on my way to update you. The tracking spell did take me to half-blood territory—to the forest. I spoke to the Hemlock witch coven. They know more about Faerie than most other supernaturals in this realm."

"If they live in the forest, they must know the Little Person of Hemlock Way," said Cedar.

"You know the witches?" Ivy raised an eyebrow at him.

"No, but I'm told they don't like the Sidhe," said Cedar.

"The Sidhe tried to burn their forest down... several times." Ivy turned to face me. "The witches claim to know about your father. People who've fallen victim to the Sidhe have sometimes taken shelter in their forest, so I reckon they're telling the truth. The Mage Lords can vouch for them, as can the other witch covens, for what it's worth."

Damn, Dad. What have you got mixed up in?

"And Lady Whitefall?" asked Cedar. "Have you heard anything more of her?"

"I asked in a few of the half-blood communities, but nobody was talking." Ivy smiled wryly. "I'm not the most trusted individual amongst the fae-kind. But it doesn't look like any Sidhe have been in this realm recently."

"Not the Summer messengers?" I asked. "Are you sure?"

Ivy shook her head. "Did you throw them off your tail?"

"Oh," said Cedar suddenly. "I think they might have thought we fled to the Grey Vale. They didn't see *where* we disappeared to when we left Faerie. They might think we've joined the exiles."

I couldn't help feeling insulted. "As if. They must really hate me. If they leave us alone in this realm, though, it'll help. They should be focused on protecting their own Court instead, seeing as Lady Whitefall will probably target it at some point."

I imagined she'd go for Winter first, but who knew how her mind worked. Maybe she'd go back to the palace. I hoped not, because it was Viola's home, and she was bound to our entire family. But the palace was Lady Whitefall's too, technically, because her magic kept it standing even if the keys had passed onto me. Hopefully Viola would have found somewhere else to go. She'd stick with Rose, who at least wasn't chained to the Hornbeam Family now its leader was dead. Unless Aspen had taken over. He hadn't seemed too interested in conquering the borderlands the last time I'd seen him, but I wished I had one ally I could trust enough to make sure my friends were safe.

Right. We're going to see the witches, and then we'll get the Little Person of Hemlock Way to get us back into Faerie.

"I wish I could help," Ivy said. "I'm supposed to be an ambassador between here and Faerie, but I can't walk into their realm without an invitation *and* an extremely good reason. I'd say the end of the world was a good reason, but they take bloody forever coming to an agreement on anything."

"I figured," I said. "Are you absolutely sure the witches can help?"

"They don't invite just anyone into the forest. Their territory might be close to the half-bloods, but their hatred for the exiled Sidhe knows no bounds. They won't harm you, though. Their forest's magic's pretty good at picking up on threats."

"They're human?" I asked.

"If you stretch the definition a little," said Ivy. "The forest is pretty straightforward, if you've been there before, but it has a tendency to throw you off the path and trick you. Kind of like Faerie, I guess."

Great. Like the real thing wasn't bad enough.

"Their territory must overlap with my—with the Hornbeam family's," said Cedar. "The Little Person uses a small liminal space to travel to Faerie from there. He's helped me escape danger a few times when Lady Hornbeam sent me to the mortal realm on quests."

"And saved me when I got attacked by a hellhound," I added, glancing at the dead bodies of the fallen hellhounds in the road. "We should get rid of these."

"Not a problem." Ivy smiled. It was singularly the most disturbingly devious smile I'd ever seen on a human. "Let's say the local mercenaries and I have an understanding of sorts. It'll be gone in half an hour."

Cedar and I exchanged perplexed looks, but Ivy didn't offer an explanation. I hoped we could trust her word about the Hemlock witches. Allies were in short supply, and I suspected that when the Sidhe came searching for me, even the witches' forest wouldn't be safe from their wrath.

3

———

"Nice." I looked ahead at the path to the witches' forest, which wound away into shadows, then back at Cedar. "Are you *sure* this place belongs to the witches? Because it looks like they took decorating tips from the Unseelie Court."

Last time I'd been here, Cedar and I had fled a half-blood gathering into the woods in search of passage back to Faerie. Its creeping expanse was made up of dark paths, tangled undergrowth, and sinister noises belonging to wild fae from both Courts. The shrill voices of piskies mingled with the growls of wild hobgoblins and the rustle of dryads' tree branches.

"Ivy did mention the forest contains a high concentration of magic," Cedar said in answer. "Makes sense, considering its proximity to half-blood territory."

"Yeah, it's got to be on the spirit paths." I dug my hands in my pockets, feeling the comforting shape of the knife I'd grabbed before coming here. "I doubt I can find the way back out if the forest changes like Faerie, though. Don't suppose you have any breadcrumbs?"

"I can mark the path." Cedar's hands glowed bright green, and a bramble unfurled itself, sprouting bright neon green flowers and wrapping around the nearest tree. He stepped forwards, and the bramble moved, too, following our path.

"Nice trick," I said.

Hardly a noise disturbed the silence, but Cedar and I remained on our guard. The path was barely visible, criss-crossed by thick tree roots and other obstacles. Not much in the way of fae beasts—just a handful of stray will o'the wisps trying to lure us off the path, a nest of hobgoblins, and a few nixies swimming in a pond who waved at us to join them. The trees were ancient and gnarled, forming cage-like barriers around us and forcing us to follow their path. Cedar tried to use magic once, but shook his head when the tree didn't move to follow his lead. A soft, menacing power hummed through the boughs and the whispering silence. Not faerie magic, but just as ancient.

Light-coloured threads began to appear and stretch between the tree branches, which converged into an arch-like shape overhead. They looked a lot like—

I stopped walking. "Spider webs. You have *got* to be kidding me."

Cedar stopped to examine the threads of light. "I don't think they're spider webs."

Green light shone from the thin interweaving patterns. I bloody hoped they *didn't* come from a giant luminous arachnid, but it'd just be my luck if they did.

"I think it's writing," said Cedar, drawing back. "Not faerie magic, but some sort of spell."

"Huh." I scanned the webs, keeping at a distance. The lines did look like squashed symbols of text, but spider webs were intricate enough in themselves. They were too bloody smart. That's why I didn't trust the buggers.

We resumed walking. The webbed patterns continued for

a while, then stopped. So did I. I hadn't noticed they were the only source of light until the faint green glow disappeared, leaving nothing but thick trees blocking out the sun.

"Damn," I said quietly. "Does this mean the witches are nearby?"

"I don't know," Cedar said. "I sense magic, but not like ours."

I didn't know a huge amount about how the mortal realm's own magic worked, but I *did* know this forest hadn't existed in its current form before the faeries had come. Our magic warped nature and caused it to grow wild. But it wasn't our magic that ruled this place.

"This better not be a trap," I muttered.

"Might Ivy have tried to trick us?" asked Cedar.

"She'd have no reason to." I knew his trust issues, like mine, stemmed from being screwed over by too many people, though I was trying to give Ivy the benefit of the doubt. I was more inclined to think the witches, or some kind of fae, were the ones messing with us. "Besides, if she wanted to bump us off, she'd have skewered either of us with that talisman of hers. She's on a level with a Sidhe. Easily."

A growl came from behind us. I spun around, magic springing to my palms, as true darkness folded over me like a curtain.

"Cedar?" I called into the dark.

Silence answered. I held up my glowing hands, but magic didn't illuminate the gloom. Like a force had sucked all life out of the world. A chill danced down my spine. Either Cedar had vanished, or the forest's magic had tricked both of us. Even the way back was masked in shadows. I stepped carefully over a tree root, feeling my way along the non-existent path. All my light-footed thief instincts had disappeared. My other senses weren't terrible—most half-bloods' sense of smell and hearing were sharper than humans'—but the witches' magic had masked all sound and scent, too. There might have been a chimera sitting in front of me and I wouldn't know it.

It's an illusion.

No shit, Raine. Didn't mean I knew how to switch it off. My Sight didn't work on non-faerie magic, unless I found the person responsible for the spell.

I found an opening beside the nearest tree and climbed through, around tangled branches and tree roots protruding from the earth. Cedar *must* be here somewhere, but I couldn't sense my own magic, let alone his. Minutes ticked by in frustrated silence as I scrambled and climbed, occasionally hitting my head or arm on a low-hanging branch. Eventually, water washed over my shoes, indicating I'd reached a pond or river. I stopped walking, using my right foot to edge around the water. The odds of something nasty lurking inside were too high to risk wading into it.

A splash cut through the silence, and the darkness peeled away. For a moment, the forest reappeared. Then it vanished. And so did I.

———

I sat alone on a chair, looking down at a polished floor stained in blood. Not a chair—a throne, engraved in gold. Bodies lay in puddles of crimson, both human and half-blood, goblin and troll, fae-kind of all species. A thousand pairs of empty eyes reflecting the high ceiling of the hall back at me. A river of crimson reached the skirts of the long dress I wore.

Where am I?

The polished floor, slick with blood, looked familiar. *The court room at the ice palace.* Was this a memory? Wait—the dress, too. I'd seen it, in a memory. A dress I'd coveted as a child.

Her. I'm her. Lady Whitefall.

I held the sceptre in one hand, and a dagger in the other. And an entire Court lay slaughtered at my feet.

I recoiled, and the scene changed.

Laughing Sidhe surrounded me, pointing at me, cruel mouths twisted in smirks. Somehow I was on my knees in full human guise, covered in dirt. They kicked and spat at me, calling me names. Anger churned inside me, and a voice whispered in my ear—*Kill them. Kill them all.*

The voice wasn't mine. It came from the object in my hand. The sceptre glowed, and the floor rippled as spikes shot up, impaling everyone they touched. The laughing Sidhe had nowhere to run. Screams replaced laughter, and blood splattered the polished floor.

I laughed, high and cold as her. But the voice that came out of my mouth was mine, not my mother's. It was my magic, and my talisman.

A hand grabbed my ankle. Cedar crouched at my feet, bleeding from deep wounds. He'd been caught in the spear-sharp trap, too. His eyes, wide with desperation, met mine.

"Raine," he whispered. "You can't… you're not her."

I didn't move. His blood was on my hands, trickling from a corner of his mouth.

"You're right," I said softly. "I'm worse than she ever was."

I pointed the sceptre at him.

No. I'm not here. This isn't me. I was in the forest… Cedar was with me…

I jerked back, and the spell shattered like glass.

I lay submerged in water, its bitter taste choking my lungs. I turned my head to the side and spat out a mouthful, coughing uncontrollably. If I'd been stuck under the spell for much longer, I'd probably have drowned. My clothes were weighted down with the water they'd absorbed. Shivering, I reached for my magic, and blue light shone around me. My soaking wet clothes transformed into fresh ones. I heaved out a breath, coughing again, unable to rid my skin of the sticky feeling of Cedar's blood.

There was no sign of him, but the darkness had gone. The pool of water nestled in a small clearing, surrounded by tall, thick trees, their branches forming a thick canopy which blocked out the sun.

"Cedar?" I whispered, then called his name, louder. The woods caught my voice and threw it back to me, but nobody responded. I was far off the path, wherever it was. Cedar might be back there, or he might have wandered into a trap of his own. And our trail had long since gone.

I edged around the pool where I'd been feeling my way in the dark. Tangled undergrowth snagged at my clothes. Losing patience, I blasted them with magic, but nothing happened.

An anguished shout ripped through the darkness.

My body went rigid. "Cedar?" I yelled, running for a gap in the trees. I stumbled over roots and undergrowth, cursing the blasted forest and all its inhabitants. A second shout drove me forward, in the direction of the noise.

I kept running, and ran smack into Cedar. His gaze was wild, unfocused, and a trickle of blood ran from a cut on his forehead. He held his knife in a white-knuckled grip.

"Whoa!" I was fairly sure—well, almost—that he wasn't an illusion. He looked and felt solid, without the blurredness that'd accompanied the vision.

Cedar's lip curled in a snarl, green light flashed in his eyes, and he swung the knife at me. *Okay, perhaps he thinks I'm not real.*

I dodged and caught his knife arm. "Cedar! It's me."

Breathing heavily, he lowered the weapon. "I've been

chased all over the woods by versions of you. I'd hate to have to kill you again."

"So would I, considering it's really me."

He closed his eyes and opened them again. "Good. I don't know what magic is at work in here, but it's as strong as any faerie enchantment I've ever encountered." He dabbed his bleeding forehead. Already, the wound was half-sealed over. His healing ability worked the same here as it did in the faerie realm. "Why are you all wet?"

"I nearly drowned in a pond after seeing a vision of myself murdering everyone."

"Ah." He stepped back, looking around us. "I think it's designed to test us, somehow. I'm assuming that means we're close to the witches."

"Right you are," growled a quiet voice.

I spun around, looking for the speaker. At my feet stood a small figure covered in fur. "I take it you're here to see the Hemlock coven. Ivy Lane warned us of your coming."

I sagged with relief, then stifled a yelp as the tree roots beneath my feet moved, revealing a door between two thick-trunked trees. Marked with a symbol, it exuded ancient power that momentarily stole my breath. Behind the door lay a cramped-looking cave, decorated in luminescent webbing. I scowled. Just bloody perfect.

Cedar rested a hand on my arm and shook his head, indicating the nearest web. *Oh.* Now the darkness had cleared, it was obvious they weren't webs. Lines of text wove together like some ancient incomprehensible spell, not in any language I knew.

The furred person beckoned us into the cave with a clawed hand. She was definitely some kind of shapeshifter faerie. Odd—I'd thought the witches hated the faeries.

"It's been a while since another of the fae came here," she said. "Come in. Don't be shy."

Bracing myself, I stepped into the cave. In the centre lay a huge tree, its roots sprawling on the floor. Except it wasn't alive, more like a giant rock sculpture shaped like a tree than a living thing. And a *face* stared from its centre, ancient and craggy, with pit-like eyes. Other faces were etched into the stone walls. Their eyes were open, their foreheads wrinkled, and they were… alive. A raw kind of power, unfamiliar and terrifying, bound them to this cave.

The ancient witch in the trunk-like sculpture leaned forward, her gaze landing on the crescent moon mark on my neck.

"You're the one," croaked the old witch.

I swallowed, my throat dry. She was older than any person without faerie blood had the right to be, yet intelligence shone in her gaze. "I'm Raine Whitefall, yes."

"And you?" She turned to Cedar.

"Cedar Hornbeam."

"Two heirs. I don't believe we've ever met two of you at once." She looked from Cedar to me. "I am Cordelia of the Hemlock coven. I take it Ivy Lane told you to come here."

I nodded. "She said you knew where my dad went."

"Your father," she said. "You might want to sit down."

My heart lurched. "Is he okay? Tell me."

"He's alive."

"Good." I closed my eyes, some of the tension unknotting inside me. "But—how do you know, and why did I have to come here to find out?"

"It's easier to show you. But first, I must grant you some context. You know a year ago that this realm almost fell to rogue Sidhe again." She paused for a moment. "There was once an outcast and impostor who called himself the Huntsman, carrier of the dead and leader of the Wild Hunt. He intended to use the magic that enabled the Sidhe to be reborn after death to create his own army. Ivy Lane put a stop to him, destroying the source of all immortality in the process."

Ivy destroyed it? So Ivy—all along, *she* was the reason the Sidhe were no longer immortal? If I hadn't seen the talisman she carried, I'd never have believed it possible.

"Ivy?" said Cedar, sounding just as stunned as me.

"The very same," said Cordelia. "Her magic is from a talisman infused with the power of a god—one of the most powerful types of magic there is. And one of yours is, too."

"The sceptre?" I gaped at her. "The power of a god? But—it's from Winter. It belonged to my family."

"Yes, it did," said the old witch. "However, the gods' magic was similar to the Sidhe's. Similar enough that very few people suspect it may reside inside some of their talismans… though yours is a special case."

My body froze. *How can they know?*

Because the forest saw everything. It'd been responsible for the vision I'd seen, and the witches knew more about the Sidhe than any human I'd met. Maybe even Ivy.

"You're saying my talisman's magic—isn't from Winter at all?"

"I think that's the least of your concerns, Raine," said the witch. "It's risky taking the power into yourself, as you did. It can still be torn out of you."

I stared at her, unable to find words. She *couldn't* know that. Even I hadn't, when I'd claimed the talisman. I couldn't bring myself to look at Cedar, either.

"I am not your enemy, Raine," said Cordelia. "Would it shock you to know we fought and killed the Sidhe who attacked this realm? We know your magic. It nearly destroyed us. Now we have such defences set up that it can never be used against us again. But we bear you no ill will. Your ancestors' crimes are not your own."

I licked my dry lips. "So why… are you like that?"

"A curse, young half-blood. Our blood is cursed, our spirits bound to this forest as long as we exist, longer than our natural lifespans." She gave me a grim smile. "As to the source of our knowledge, the forest is infused with magic, warped by the curse. It reads the experiences and memories of everyone who comes nearby."

"I met a faerie with similar magic once," I admitted. "But—what does this have to do with my father? He's human."

"He's not human."

My heart missed a beat. "No. He is. I'm half-blood. You *called* me that."

"Half-blood or three quarters, it's all the same to the Sidhe," said Cordelia. "You might be mortal still, but your father carries the blood of a powerful line of faeries, from the Summer Court."

I took a step back. "No. You're mistaken."

"The forest doesn't lie," said Cordelia. "Your father believed he was human when he came to this realm, but he wasn't always. We saw memories he'd forgotten… memories of the Sidhe."

Dad was half-Sidhe. Which meant…

My mother doctored his memories to turn him into the person he is now. He never was totally human.

"You're wrong," I said. "If he had faerie blood, she wouldn't have damaged him. She wouldn't have taken his memories—"

"Invocations can work as well on faeries as humans. As can your magic. You should know."

"No." Could I believe my mother had cursed my father into thinking he was human? She was certainly capable of it. But I'd known him my whole life—I'd spent twenty years with him as a human.

I'd know.

But I hadn't known I had magic, though I'd lived with it

as long as I'd lived with Dad. And if even *he* hadn't been able to remember...

"*Where* is he?" I demanded, my voice echoing off the cave walls.

"He already crossed over to the Summer Court, Raine."

"No." I looked at the other witches, desperately searching for a sign she was lying. "That—no. If it's true, they'll kill him. They want me dead."

"They don't kill their own," said Cordelia. "I highly doubt they know you're related. His memories awakened when he came here, though he didn't know what force drove him. With your mother's return, it was impossible to keep his past concealed forever."

It's a lie. My mind whirled, my head throbbing as though under the weight of the new revelation. I couldn't stay in this cave a moment longer.

"So to find him—" Cedar broke off. "The Seelie Court? Are you absolutely sure?"

"The forest never lies," said Cordelia. "It tells the truth, however painful it might be."

I stepped back, then again, all but sprinting through the cave door. If Dad was in Faerie—the thought alone was absurd. But if it was true—if she'd really stolen him from Summer—then she'd screwed over *both* Courts. And the Sidhe had never retaliated. She'd been able to get away with what she had because the Sidhe cared so little about us half-faeries, she could murder us in droves and they'd neither know nor care.

Dad had walked into Faerie—to the one part of Faerie I couldn't follow him to—and I was utterly powerless.

Icy magic wrapped around my hands, strengthening my resolve. If I survived this, the Sidhe would face a reckoning for their crimes.

4

Apparently the witches had wanted to help me get out, because the path changed to a more straightforward one leading out of the forest. I walked apart from Cedar, in cold silence, pursued by memories.

I vividly remembered the moment I'd realised Dad couldn't take care of himself anymore. I'd come back from school—back when I'd made an occasional effort to go—to find him huddled alone in the flat, surrounded by pieces of broken glass from shattered mirrors. While I'd been cleaning up the mess, the truth had struck me: this wasn't the first time I'd had to be the adult. The sinking feeling in my chest had nothing to do with the actual responsibility and everything to do with the fact that I'd taken over as the grown-up without even noticing. I'd just carried on as normal, to keep both of us alive.

Similarly, no matter how many times the Sidhe had screwed me over, part of me had believed deep down that they were at least in control of what happened in Faerie. My mother had been an anomaly. Except from what I'd heard today, she wasn't the first. Not by a long shot. It was pretty damn clear the Sidhe weren't drunk at the wheel—nobody was steering at all. Nobody was coming to save us. And I didn't have a clue how to keep us all alive this time.

"Raine," Cedar said, breaking the silence. "The Little Person's house is on our right, if you do want to go back."

I stopped walking, looking around at the trees. "If we go to Summer to find my father, I'll be sentenced to death," I said quietly. "If the witches are lying, now would be a great time for someone to tell me."

"I don't think they were lying, Raine," said Cedar. "The forest—it knew things I've never told anyone. Lady Whitefall—"

"Stole my dad's magic," I said. "It'd have given him away otherwise. But I didn't inherit anything from him. I got hers instead." I gave a bitter laugh. "Even if he did remember being part of Summer, why go back there? If he's really half-blood, he knows what they think of us. And he never told me. That doesn't suggest he had a choice in the matter."

Unless, of course, I'd been abandoned by both parents. But Dad's personality wouldn't have changed, right? A cold knot of dread formed in my chest. I'd felt alone for so long—for years—but I never had been. Not as long as we had each other. If the Sidhe truly had taken that away… suddenly the image of their mangled bodies impaled on my magic didn't seem unreachable after all.

"Did he know how to defend himself?" asked Cedar.

"He *didn't*," I said. "But he was also fully human and didn't have magic. Sidhe's blood, has anyone in my life *ever* told the truth?"

A rustling noise came from the trees in front. I raised a hand, conjuring up magic in warning. Bright blue light illuminated the path—and a pair of hooves attached to a person trying unsuccessfully to hide in a bush.

"Denzel?" I narrowed my eyes. "What are you doing here?"

"I… I was looking for you," he mumbled. "There are rumours you're back on half-blood territory. If you have anywhere to hide—you have to go. They're coming. The Sidhe."

I lowered my hand. "What? Why are you telling me this?"

"Why? You might think you're too good for us mere mortals, Raine, but you were my friend. I don't want them to kill you."

I extinguished my magical attack. "You finally get it, do you? This isn't a game. It never was. The Sidhe are ruthless bastards, Denzel, and my dad's missing. Did he look any different when you saw him? Like—magical?"

"Now you mention it…" He frowned. "Yeah, he sort of did. He had the look. I know a Summer half-blood when I see one. But he's human, right?"

A sharp knife twisted underneath my ribs. I blinked, hard. "Sure. Last time I saw him."

Denzel blinked at me. "Wait a second. Why are you soaking wet? You look like you've taken a bath in a lake."

"The forest," I said. "I wouldn't go any further inside. Who told you the Sidhe were coming?"

"Rumours. You don't trust me, do you?"

"No," I said, figuring honesty was best. "Honestly, though—just keep out of the Sidhe's way. Oh, and if you see my mother, or hear anyone playing the pan pipes, run like hell."

"Pan pipes?" His brow furrowed. "Why those?"

"Just be careful," I said. "There are some nasty individuals going around putting half-bloods under hypnosis. If anyone's acting oddly, they might be under the spell."

He looked at me like he thought I'd definitely lost my mind. "Right, right. No more fake talismans."

"Definitely not," I said sharply. "Nor real ones. Just so we're clear on that."

The trees behind me rustled. Denzel stumbled sideways into a tree, while I spun around, conjuring magic to my hands.

Ivy Lane peered between the trees, her talisman glowing bright.

"Faerie killer!" yelped Denzel.

Ivy frowned at him. "Do I know you?"

"Nope." Denzel backed away, and disappeared from sight, clip-clopping down the path.

I swivelled to Ivy. "What was that about?"

"No idea." She lowered her sword. "It's possible he's seen me threaten someone before."

"If you've ever taken anyone to task for selling fake goods, he might have been caught up in it."

"Ah." She nodded. "The market. Knew I'd seen him some-where. The Mage Lords busted a fake amulet shop the other week."

"Sounds like him," I said. "We talked to the witches. There's trouble—"

"In the Summer Court," said Ivy. "That's what I came to tell you. They were attacked."

"Shit. Was it Lady Whitefall?" *Wouldn't she target Winter first?*

"Whoever it was, they apparently stole something impor-tant," said Ivy. "They haven't sent messengers here yet, but there are whispers."

"What did she steal?" asked Cedar. "Another talisman?"

Ivy shook her head. "That's what I wanted to find out, but nobody's talking."

"I actually know the talismans of the Summer Court," Cedar said. "If I had more clues, I'd be able to figure out which one she took."

"Does it matter?" I asked. "She already has it. But it makes no sense for her to target Summer first. You know, this would be easier if we could get both Courts to support us in fighting against her."

"It's inefficient," said Ivy. "I'm not saying that because I agree with them, by the way. I think they're lazy sods far too used to resting on their laurels. They think it's not worthwhile to send troops into the Vale. The rules for crossing realms mean they have to send their best soldiers, and if an enemy doesn't want to be found, they won't be."

"I thought not," said Cedar.

"Me, too," I said. I might not know all Ivy Lane's secrets, but her words carried the voice of experience. It was surprisingly bolstering to know that she, like me, had good reason to expect the Sidhe to be completely unhelpful in times of crisis. "If the Sidhe are coming here, we need to go back into Faerie. Now, ideally."

Ivy nodded. "If nobody saw you, I shouldn't need to set a false trail. But be careful."

"Will do." I turned to Cedar. "Best leave before anyone can spot us." Provided Moss Beard the Little Person didn't ask for a huge favour this time. He'd already saved our lives once.

As Ivy disappeared into the trees, Cedar said, "Yes, I think you're right. I don't like the idea of using the rift at a time like this, but the Sidhe probably won't expect to find us on the Hornbeams' territory."

"Let's hope not."

We left the path and made our way to Moss Beard's place. As before, the little cottage nestled in a small clearing in the forest, just far enough away from the back of half-blood territory for a swathe of trees to block their view. The front door opened, though we'd approached without a sound, and the moss-bearded Little Person came out.

"You shouldn't be here," he said. "I helped you escape for a reason."

"And did you help my dad get back into the Court?"

He paused, long enough for my suspicions to rise—and the last thread of hope that this was some horrible mistake melted away. "You did, didn't you? Are you all *trying* to get my family killed?"

"I would never harm one of your kin," he said, with the slightest tinge of hurt in his voice. "Your father requested passage, and I provided it. But I would advise you not to follow him to Summer."

"They're coming here," I said. "We have to get away."

And find Dad—but how, with his Court searching for me? Unless I found a way to wriggle out of the death sentence hanging over me, I'd never see him again.

Moss Beard sighed. "I'll regret this."

He beckoned us to follow him into the trees. Mist spread between the thick boughs, signs of the places where this realm overlapped with Faerie.

A flash of light engulfed Cedar and me, and the forest changed. Though it didn't look too different to the witches' lair—unlike the heart of the Summer Court, the borderland forests were dark and tangled—my magic responded to the change in realms even on Seelie territory. Soft beams of light filtering through the canopy above only made the darkness of the shadowed areas between the trees more pronounced.

"Hope Viola left the palace," I whispered. "The Summer Court shouldn't arrest her instead of me, but I don't know how desperate they are."

"More than before, if they've just been robbed," Cedar murmured.

"Great." I stopped, hearing a snapping noise. "There's someone up ahead."

The trees rustled, and a troll barged through, meaty fists

swinging. *Grey Vale beast.* Apparently a few stragglers had remained behind after the battle.

The troll turned on us with a loud bellow. I ducked underneath its arm and sliced a shallow cut across its ribs. Its skin was too tough to be affected by most weapons, including iron. I tapped into my magic instead, hitting the showering leaves and turning them into deadly sharp instruments.

The troll bellowed again as the leaves sliced its skin, but even that wasn't enough to bring it down. Before I could leap in and put it out of its misery, Cedar's hands lit up green and the undergrowth rose around the troll, squeezing its neck and locking its arms behind its back. Swiftly, Cedar whipped out a dagger and cut the beast's throat. Damn, he moved quickly.

"Are we near the palace?" I listened out, but didn't hear anything else move.

"We aren't far. I think it's likely where Viola is, Raine, if the Whitefall territory is still at risk from your mother. The Hornbeams won't have appointed a new heir already."

"Maybe they did." My heart sank. What if Aspen came back and claimed this territory as his own? He was eligible, and had already claimed two talismans. But the soldiers here had risked their lives to fight against the exiles—on *my* side. Of course, they hadn't known at the time that the Summer Court had put a death warrant out for me.

"They didn't," Cedar said. "There is no talisman left to claim."

"Because she stole his magic?" I frowned. "But—Lady Hornbeam had a whole collection of talismans."

"Lord Hornbeam handed them over to the Summer Court after he failed to claim them." He smiled grimly. "Probably for the best, considering what happened to him."

My mouth dropped open. "Seriously? Didn't he name an

heir? Surely he knew he wouldn't last long as leader without a talisman."

Cedar's jaw tightened. "I wasn't allowed into his inner circle, so I don't know what his decision was. I was removed from the running as heir, like the other eligible children of Lady Hornbeam."

"What a complete prick."

The branches parted again, and Cedar hissed a warning, raising his weapon. Several soldiers approached us, dressed in the iron armour unique to the Hornbeam family.

I remained still, ready to lash out with magic if they attacked. Cedar's former family were an unknown element. I'd helped save them from Lady Whitefall, but would owing me their lives outweigh loyalty to their Court?

"What are you doing here?" asked one of the armoured soldiers, a half-fae male with silver hair and deeply tanned skin.

"Who is your current leader?" Cedar asked. "I want to speak with them."

"There isn't one," said the second guard, who carried a crossbow across his broad body. His ebony skin gleamed with sweat, like he'd been standing out in the forest for hours. "Seeing as Aspen's gone to the Vale."

So they didn't appoint anyone. Maybe without any talismans, nobody would be able to claim the spot of leader.

"She killed Lady Hornbeam," said the first guard, eying me.

"Lady Hornbeam deserved it, though," his companion responded. "She sent us to war against the Blackcrows. Nearly killed half of us taking out their forces. And she locked Lady Whitefall in jail, didn't she?"

It took me a second to realise he meant me—and he'd called me by my title.

"Yeah," I said. "Lady Hornbeam locked me up, and then

forced me to fight to the death. She died because she didn't care how much damage she did." It'd been a combination of my magic and hers which had torn her territory apart and killed her in the process. Unfortunately, there'd been no direct witnesses to tell the Summer Court that.

"Aren't you heir?" the first speaker asked Cedar. "No—you were the thief, right?"

"I was," Cedar said carefully. "If you remember, Raine helped save you from Lady Whitefall. We all owe her a debt, and we wish to go to the palace. Neither of us wish harm upon you or any member of the Hornbeam family."

"All right," said the first speaker, but he kept one hand on his iron knife as he moved aside.

The two of them flanked us while we walked to the palace. I couldn't let myself relax, but just being given a chance to explain myself loosened the tight feeling in my chest. And when I saw a familiar half-blood female with long curly black hair amongst the other soldiers, I couldn't stop the grin that spread across my face. Above her head floated a bright blue sprite.

"Viola." I walked away from the guards, towards her. "What are you doing here?"

"Waiting for you," she said. "I figured you'd be back soon, but the Whitefall palace is likely to be a target. So I came here."

"And they're okay with you staying here?" I glanced at Cedar, who shrugged, apparently unsurprised at this development.

"I'm an ex-soldier." She grinned knowingly. "I know all sorts of things that they wouldn't want getting out. It's not like I can report on them to the enemy, besides."

"Meaning me?" I said. "Honestly, I'm just glad you're safe. I was worried she'd target you next."

"People are staring," she said. "Let's go somewhere quiet."

Viola led the way in through a side entrance to the palace. The other soldiers milling around stepped aside, though some gave her suspicious looks. She opened a few doors, and when she found a room filled with weaponry, she beckoned Cedar and me inside.

"Nobody will come in here until shift change," she said. "I forgot how *crowded* this place is, especially without Lady Hornbeam swooping around terrorising everyone. Anyway, I'm guessing it's been longer for you than it's been for me. I only left a few hours ago. Packed up my stuff from the palace and came here. I'd agreed to meet Rose, but the others let me onto their territory anyway."

"It's only been a few hours here?" I asked. "But—someone stole from Summer. I wasn't sure if you knew."

"Some of the soldiers went to report Lord Hornbeam's death and found the Court's centre on lockdown," Viola explained. "They're not letting anyone in or out. Not everyone actually knows what happened, though. I didn't want to panic the soldiers, not after the day they've had."

"Damn. So there's no way to find out what Lady Whitefall stole?"

"I think we can all guess what she stole," said Viola. "But you look like you've had a hell of a day."

Drawing in a breath, I began to speak. Viola's eyes widened while I recounted my story. She was no stranger to family drama—she'd told me about her half-blood parents being disappointed in her for not being a son, not to mention breaking her vows to the Hornbeam family's army after falling in love with Rose. But I couldn't trust that any of my memories of my own childhood were even accurate anymore. Dad had told me my extended family had died in the invasion. Maybe they'd never even existed. And that was the *least* fucked-up part of the last twenty-four hours.

"So my mother must have gone to Summer right after she

ran back into the Vale," I said. "I'm guessing she took one of Lady Hornbeam's talismans, though I might be wrong. She'll go to the Winter Court to take back the one they confiscated, for sure. And the sword in the palace, too."

"She doesn't know we found the sword," said Viola. "But she must know it's impossible for her to steal from the centre of the Unseelie Court."

"I wouldn't discount anything as impossible," said Cedar, who'd listened to my explanation with a pensive expression, as though thinking hard.

"Not where she's concerned," I muttered. "Damn. How are we supposed to predict her next move? If it's talismans she's after—well, she's probably figured out the sceptre's worthless on its own, but we can't remove every talisman before she gets there."

"Maybe we can," said Cedar.

I frowned at him for a second. Then I got it. "You mean, replace them with fakes? That's..."

"Dangerous? I think we're past that now."

He was right... but I'd take the Court's wrath over my mother using the talismans to obliterate everyone in both realms.

"You sure you can outdo her?" I asked. "I don't think I've ever actually seen you steal anything."

He smirked. "That's the point. You don't see."

"You cocky little shit." I couldn't help smiling back. From the way he'd sleight-of-handed Lady Whitefall, of all people, I didn't doubt his ability to steal from the Sidhe. He'd robbed the Erlking himself... as a child. But playing with Lady Whitefall with the Courts breathing down our necks went far beyond normal danger. "You can't be saying you have a room full of fake talismans waiting to be used... right?"

"Almost," he said, beckoning me towards the door. "I'll show you."

5

I'd never seen most of the inside of the Hornbeams' palace before. While mine was decorated in white and honey-coloured tones, the corridors here were painted in grey and green, like a muted version of a landscape painting. As we climbed to the next floor, the decor changed. Tapestries adorned every wall, depicting bright sunny groves flanked with ancient trees. Faeries ranging from imps to piskies surrounded the beautiful armoured Sidhe. Even faerie hands couldn't capture their majesty in paint, however they tried. Then we came to the war tapestries, where Winter's faeries were depicted as gruesome hideous monsters fleeing from Summer's armies.

Cedar stopped abruptly and turned to the right. "That way leads to Lord Hornbeam's old quarters. He tore Lady Hornbeam's down."

On the left was another tapestry showing Lady Hornbeam herself sat on a golden throne. The tapestry was shredded as though hacked at by a blunt sword.

"Lord Hornbeam really hated her, didn't he?" I said.

"I think it was Aspen who destroyed it, actually," Cedar

said. "The royals have the whole west wing of the palace." He led me down the corridor to a staircase, spiralling up into what I assumed must be one of the towers. "I wasn't considered royalty, but they didn't want me living near the soldiers."

"Speaking of Aspen," I said. "What if he comes back?"

"He's been gone too long. Lord Hornbeam will have fixed the palace's defences to act against him." Cedar halted at the top of the stairs. "I wasn't able to say much before my vow broke. If there's anything else you'd like to know about the Hornbeams, I can probably tell you."

He produced a key from his pocket and opened a carved oak door.

"So this is your room." I peered over his shoulder at a compact room with bare wooden walls and floor and plain furniture. The austereness of the décor betrayed no hints of personality, but he probably kept it that way deliberately. An unmarked mahogany cupboard sat in the room's corner, which he unlocked with another key. Inside were fake talismans. Dozens of them. Swords and daggers, sceptres and bows, staffs and a scimitar. Carved with precision. If I hadn't seen the real deal, I might have been fooled.

"How'd you make them?" The shimmering glow around the cabinet drew my eyes, the thief inside me longing to lay her hands on them.

"Using a combination of glamour and ordinary objects. It isn't hard, provided the original object isn't made of iron or any similar metal."

I reached and picked up a knife. Its blade was hard enough to open the skin on my finger when I touched the tip. They were real weapons, enchanted to look like talismans. In fact, they even had the trademark green or blue glow of their Court's magic.

"Are they all modelled after real talismans?" I turned the

weapon over in my hand. Had it been the real thing, I'd have been able to sense its power.

"Yes." He took the dagger carefully from me, turning it over to reveal a faded insignia on the back. "They were all talismans Lady Hornbeam desired, but she didn't steal all of them. I don't have a copy of the one we gave to the Unseelie Court."

"The one you faked," I said. "You must have seen the real thing first. How'd you even do that?"

"I saw Lady Whitefall's talisman when she was threatening prisoners in her castle," Cedar explained. "So I memorised the design and glamoured another weapon to look like it. She already knows it's fake."

"You glamoured it. On the spot. In the Grey Vale?" I'd been too relieved at my narrow escape from death to question at the time, but now I thought about it... the fake must have been pretty damn good. "I've never heard of glamour fooling a Sidhe before."

"She wasn't paying attention," he said. "That's how I got away with it. She realised it was fake pretty quickly. You can't mimic magic."

"I should hope *not*," I said. "How many talismans did Lady Hornbeam steal?"

"At least five. She had others from before my time. But as I said, Lord Hornbeam handed all of them over to the Seelie Court."

"I keep forgetting she was over a thousand years old." I paused. "I know it's a long shot, but is it possible to prove any of her talismans were stolen from other Summer Sidhe? Some of them must have been." It was my last desperate hope —that if the Summer Court worked out she'd planned to overthrow them, then maybe they'd spare my life.

"There's no proof, unfortunately," Cedar said. "The main Court doesn't have any interest in the borderlands."

"Except when a half-blood kills a Sidhe. Never mind the madwoman looking to invade their Court." I sighed.

"Even if there *was* proof, they're too set in their ways to reduce the punishment." His mouth turned down at the corners. "Lady Hornbeam told me so herself. If I'd got caught stealing, the punishment would fall on my head, not hers."

"Evil woman," I said. "You know, I'm not sure it's worth the risk of replacing any talisman unless we know for sure she's going to try to take it. If we get caught, it's game over. And Summer is bound to be on guard."

"I was going to suggest going to your palace first, because you have the key," Cedar said. "I see no harm in replacing the sword."

"I can't touch it," I said. "The magic inside it is still loyal to her, and it wouldn't surprise me if she'd already found it."

Cedar reached inside the cupboard for one of the swords. "This one is close enough in appearance. I need to add the symbol..."

Green light shone around the blade, rippling along its surface. The shape of a lightning bolt formed on the hilt, uncannily similar to the real thing.

"Damn," I said. "And I thought my transforming magic was badass enough."

"This is a simple cosmetic spell, hardly more than glamour." He tossed the sword from one hand to the other. "I'll get rid of the light..." The green tint died down, and the sword looked for all the world like it didn't belong to a Court at all. The only thing missing was the sensation I got whenever I was in the same room as it, like something invisible and malevolent was watching me.

"Nice party trick," I murmured. "Seriously, Denzel's fake amulets have got nothing on you. It's amazing how often half-bloods fall for those, and most witch spells don't even work for us."

"Well, if we ever end up stranded in the mortal realm..." He trailed off suggestively.

A smile stirred. "Yeah, now we've actually met the head of the Mage Lords, I'm not so sure I want to piss him off. There are more than enough fake artefacts floating around as it is."

"Hmm." He laid the sword down on top of the cabinet and turned back to me. "Speaking of transforming magic, you can change your appearance. A Sidhe would be able to see through glamour, but not your magic. Have you ever tried?"

"No. I probably *can* do it, but it's hard to get right, and you have to actually *want* to make the change. I don't fancy turning myself into a troll and then not being able to turn back. Learning from scratch isn't the same as intuitively knowing how to use magic my whole life."

"I know," Cedar said, "but assuming we have to go into one of the Courts—we need a way in that doesn't involve too much glamour."

"Hmm. Okay. Got a mirror?"

He opened the wardrobe door in answer, revealing a mirror. I picked up a limp lock of hair. "Viola used magic to curl my hair once. Let's see what I can do with this."

I kept an eye on my reflection as I directed magic into my hand. My hair darkened, and grew longer, thickening into curls like Viola's.

"That's better than glamour." He trailed a hand through my hair, and my skin prickled in response. "Can you change it back?"

A flick of magic and my hair was straight and bone-white once again, almost silver in the glow left by my magic. Cedar stood behind me, his hand inches from my shoulder before it dropped to his side.

"Want a go?" I asked, half teasing. Even when he'd had glamour on, I'd seen his real face underneath—angular like most half-bloods', framed by dark curtains of hair which made his hazel eyes look deep brown until you looked closer. But it wasn't his looks that made my body respond to his closeness, my heart swooping low as his hand brushed my shoulder.

"I think I'll stick with glamour." He ran a hand over his face, catching the edge of his scar. It felt intrusive to ask why he'd never removed, transformed or glamoured it, when that sort of magic was so commonplace here, but I'd always wondered.

He arched a brow, having seen me looking. "It's her mark," he said. "She wanted to mark me as her thief. So no matter what disguise I wore, she would know me as that. It can't be removed."

"I'm sorry."

I found myself instinctively touching the crescent moon shape on my neck. My mother's mark. We were both bound to the Sidhe, in blood if not by vows. Magic lit up my palm once again, and I willed it to disappear... but when I looked back at my reflection, the mark remained.

"Guess I'm the same." I swallowed, dropping my hand. Cedar caught it, covering the inches between us.

His lips pressed against mine, giving me the chance to back away. I didn't. My mouth parted at his prompting, and his hand cupped the back of my head, tangling in my hair. The buzz of his magic wrapped around me, sizzling between my skin and his like an electric current. Winter and Summer, coldness and warmth, complementing and challenging one another. His free hand circled my waist and pulled me tight against him. He murmured against my lips and released me. Both of us were breathing hard, flushed with tension. I'd expected a Summer faerie to feel warm, but not that my own body would react so intensely to a simple touch. Magic blossomed up and down my torso, bringing my skin out in white-hot tingles. Too intense, too much. If I touched him again, I'd ignite.

I stepped back, out of range, my body aching in protest. Never mind that him touching me was nothing compared to the emotional barriers he'd knocked down already—I was on enemy territory as long as I remained in this realm, and we'd been played against one another more than once already. We'd won time, but not enough to waste.

"We should go," I whispered. "Before she reaches the palace. We need to get that sword away before she takes it back."

His throat bobbed, as though he'd swallowed down the words he meant to say, and he nodded.

———

Cedar and I crept through the woods, crossing the invisible boundary between Hornbeam territory and mine, assuming my mother hadn't claimed it. I'd glamoured our clothes to hide our Court allegiances, however little it mattered now. I also carried the fake sword strapped to my waist.

Sharp icy spikes formed a gate in front of the Whitefall palace, and an expanse of snow covered the vast gardens. The palace itself was a magnificent ice sculpture, but the inside looked more like a modern hotel from the mortal realm. I took the key from my pocket, which unlocked every door and window, inside or outside.

"Better try the back way, in case she's planned an ambush." When Cedar had been captive here, he'd used magic to bend a tree to allow himself to escape through the back window, and it remained where he'd left it, drooping against the palace's sheer, smooth side.

"I don't think you should go in alone," he whispered.

"She might have put up the security again. The palace's

magic works for her as well as me." It wouldn't attack me for that reason, but that didn't mean it'd spare him. "Give me a shout if anything happens."

I considered the sheer wall. Her magic kept the palace standing, so I couldn't transform the features of the building itself to make it easier to get in. Including the statues in the hall, which were actually living beings who'd presumably insulted her at some time or other. Thinking about it, maybe the reason I couldn't undo the spell on them was because she was still alive. Which meant if she died, the palace would truly become mine.

I reached for the tree branch and pulled myself up, the sword strapped to my waist. Cedar remained on guard, holding his crossbow. I reached the window and shoved the key into the lock, then hauled myself inside. Swiftly, I ran through the guest room out into the corridor. *Time to find that damned sword and get the hell out of here.*

Conjuring magic to my hands, I opened a door into the entrance hall.

On the other side of the door stood a female faerie. Not my mother.

"Raine," my sister said. "Give me the real talisman."

6

J une, my only surviving sibling, wore an expression as icy as the palace's exterior. Her eyes were dark hazel but looked black next to the paleness of the palace décor, and the sheets of dark hair framing her angled cheekbones. "Surprised to see me again?"

"Guess I should have known better than to expect her to show up in person," I said. "The door's that way. Get out."

"I think you'll find this palace is mine." She pulled out a sword. Its lightning bolt carved hilt shone in the palace's bright light, which came from all around, including the crystal chandeliers above the polished floors.

Of fucking course.

I said, "She *let* you claim it? Or did you steal the sword yourself?"

"I was gifted it. Unlike you."

"I followed the laws of succession according to the Courts. The sceptre chose me. I claimed it fair and square. Still bitter about it?"

"You're nothing more than an ignorant human girl."

"Keep telling yourself that." Goading someone who

wielded a weapon that had nearly killed me once already probably wasn't a good move, but I *had* beaten her out over the sceptre. So why would the sword—which had rejected me—pick her? I'd already claimed one talisman, but perhaps there was more to claiming magic than I'd thought. Maybe it was only tangentially to do with strength or power, and more to do with personality. It figured that the sword which had nearly killed me when I'd touched it would choose to align with someone like her.

Her eyes narrowed and her hand twitched on the sword hilt. Apparently my flippancy annoyed her. If she was working with my mother, maybe she really would kill me, unlike my brother. He'd been playing double agent for the sake of self-preservation. As far as I knew, she just wanted the power.

"You're welcome to the sword," I told her. "But the palace is mine. I claimed it."

She pointed the blade at me. "It's hers, and mine by extension. Leave."

"Oh, no." I rested my hand on one of the sharp knives I'd grabbed from Cedar's collection. "If you think I'll let you use *my* palace as the gateway for her Grey Vale army to get into the borderlands, think again."

The door slammed shut behind me. "I think you'll find this palace answers to me alone."

"Not if I have anything to do with it."

June swung the sword in a wild, untrained arc, which I easily dodged. Too bad she hadn't practised waving a sword before trying to kill me with one. My own weapon was much shorter than hers, but it was sharp as hell, and she hadn't thought to wear armoured clothes.

I sidestepped her clumsy strike smoothly and retaliated. My own blade drew blood first, slicing open her wrist, but as it wasn't iron, it didn't have the effect it might have. She swung the blade again and a horrible coldness brushed against me, chilling my bones. I did my best to ignore it, moving swiftly, dodging her strikes. Blood sprayed from small cuts to her thighs and arms as I caught her, repeatedly, backing her into a corner.

Her sword cut the air with a menacing whistling noise, and coldness wrapped around me like an icy cloak, slowing my movements. *I shouldn't be able to feel the cold.* A keening sound like a high voice laughing or screaming cut the air along with the blade. I stumbled back, my fast speed slowing as the icy feeling spread through my limbs. What the hell was her talisman doing—freezing the blood inside my veins?

You traitorous piece of shit.

I stepped back out of range, my hands numbing on the knife hilt. I had her beaten skill-wise, but as long as the talisman's freezing effect was in place, my speed advantage was gone. But though the palace might be immune to my magic, the air wasn't.

I raised my free hand and blasted the air with magic, which froze into dagger-like shapes. She danced out of the way, lip curled in hatred. Icy shards brushed past her on either side, but she didn't drop the sword. The blade sheared the air, and I barely blocked it with my dagger's side. *She didn't move that fast before.*

Ice burned my hands, and the two pieces of the broken knife slid from my grip. I stepped back, grabbing for my backup weapon. My movements were sluggish, too clumsy. *It's the sword's magic.* It wanted her to win, and me to die.

Blue light surged up my arms, and ice shot from my fingertips, wrapping itself around her ankles. The sword made a hissing noise, cutting through the air and narrowly missing my chest. June shrieked in fury as my icy spell bound her legs together. Quickly, I used the same spell on her arm. When the air froze, she remained stuck in position, her hand frozen mid-motion, the sword hanging from her fingertips.

Her eyes narrowed in fury. "You cheated."

"Speak for yourself." My gaze flicked down her body. Only her head was free of the spell. "Get out of the palace. It's mine."

"I won't," she said, her voice echoing off the high ceiling. "It's more than my life's worth to leave here."

"Should have thought of that before you sided with *her.*"

"I didn't pick the losing team. You're going to die, you foolish little mortal."

"Ouch." I put a hand over my heart. "I don't know how I'll ever fight back now you've wounded me so deeply."

In another life, I might have seen us arguing with one another like normal siblings. But Faerie didn't allow that life, and had taken it away before I'd ever known it might be a possibility.

I darted forwards and hit her over the back of the head with my dagger's hilt. Her legs gave way, and from the panic in her gaze, she didn't have healing magic. I'd cut her dozens of times with my icy magic while dodging her hits, and blood soaked through her trousers. Not mortal wounds, but painful enough to hobble her progress. It'd be easy to finish her off, but doubtless my mother had wanted us to fight to the death. Just like my brother and I had. He'd given his life to ensure my freedom.

You get one chance, sister.

I looked down at her. "Have you ever seen the dungeons? Allow me to introduce you."

The trapdoor sprang open at my command, directly underneath her. She fell down the stone steps, her body still bound in ice.

A shout came from outside. *Cedar.* Closing the trapdoor on her, I ran to the front doors, pushing them open. A decapitated troll lay sprawled in the snow. Skirting around it, I followed the sound of a wounded shriek several feet away. Viciously sharp plants with blade-like leaves protruded from the ground, while the nearest trees had been literally uprooted, goblins impaled on their roots.

Cedar was locked in battle with a long-limbed tree faerie and three redcaps. While the tree faerie attempted to gouge his eyes out with deep stabs, he dodged smoothly. I ran up to help, and the ground cracked open, underneath the tree's feet. The tree-beast shrieked as its own hands wrapped around its neck. A second later, the tree went limp. It'd strangled itself thanks to Cedar's Summer magic. I ran up and killed one redcap, and the other two disappeared shrieking into the bushes.

"Whoa." I looked at the dead tree faerie. "Did you dig up my entire garden?"

"My apologies. I can clear it."

He waved a hand, and green light flared from his hands to the ground. The sharp roots and the creatures impaled on them were drawn into the earth. Not so much as a bloodstain remained.

"They disarmed me," he explained. "I had to work with what I had left. What happened in there?"

"My sister." I grimaced. "She won the sword and seemed to think the palace was hers. That talisman is a piece of shit. Luckily, nobody taught her how to fight with a sword."

"Is she dead?"

"Nope. Injured. She's under a vow to capture me, so it's not like I'm in a position to reason with her. But I can question her for details of my mother's plans."

"Leaving her here might not be wise," Cedar said.

"Not like we have much choice." I scanned the grounds, making sure no new enemies watched us, and walked back into the entrance hall.

With Cedar behind me, I opened the trapdoor again. June lay sprawled halfway downstairs. Her grip on the sword had slackened, and I kicked it away from her before lifting her limp form over my shoulder. The light of a hundred small faeries lit the way into the unappealing dark rooms where my mother had kept people—humans—locked in misery and despair. The dungeon brought goosebumps out on my skin, like the wind blowing from nowhere carried the echo of the prisoners' screams, and the damp floor smelled of old blood and misery.

"She was chosen by the sword?" asked Cedar in a whisper.

"Yeah. I have a feeling my mother must have had a hand in it. That's why I kept her alive and didn't try to claim it."

However little I cared for the Courts, I knew what wielding that sword would do to me—assuming it didn't kill me first. If I followed my murderous instincts, gave into the whispering temptation to claim every talisman and kill the ones who wielded them, I'd end up next to my mother, doomed to die in the Vale.

I put June down inside one of the cells. Her legs continued to bleed, but the wounds wouldn't be fatal. The cell door swung shut behind her, and my trusty key locked her inside. She curled up and moaned, cringing away from the iron bars of the door.

Cedar's gaze went to the sword, which lay gleaming on the damp stone floor.

"I wouldn't pick it up," I said quietly. "It's plain evil. I'm guessing my mother brought it from the Vale, like the sceptre."

"Are you sure about leaving her here?" he responded.

"Absolutely. She and Horace the spider can be friends."

Cedar walked up next to me, as June began to stir again. Her eyelids flickered, and her gaze focused on the ice encasing her feet. The spell wasn't permanent, but the iron bars would be enough of a deterrent if she decided to make a run for it.

"This was supposed to be your prison," she croaked.

"Too bad. Our brother's dead—did you know? Where have you been all this time?"

She staggered to her feet. "You can't beat her. The Courts will never help you."

"Like I ever thought they would." I watched her, but she didn't move closer to the iron. "Tell me why you're here. You need the palace. To bring in a legion of Grey Vale beasts, right?" The other, secret, dungeon had only one entrance—a narrow tunnel in the back of Lady Whitefall's old wardrobe. I'd need to triple-check it was sealed, but if my mother could bring whatever monsters she liked along for the ride when she crossed realms, we might be screwed either way.

Or maybe she can't. Maybe there is a limit to how many people she can bring. Her allies were outcast for a reason.

"You know her plan," said my sister. "She told you."

"I think I wrecked her last one when I got half her army killed, freed her prisoners and gave her best soldier a public thrashing." I'd left so much chaos behind, I hadn't realised how many of Lord Hornbeam's former soldiers had managed to escape back to their own territory. She had fewer allies than I'd initially thought. But if she'd been walking around handing out talismans to the likes of my sister, I could only assume she'd changed her plans.

June scowled. "She held back on you. She didn't wish to harm her own flesh and blood."

"Yeah, she did call me her favourite."

I was rewarded by a blank look of shock. "You're lying."

"Nope," I said, my grin widening. "She preferred me to all her other children. Did you know I actually lived here in the palace when I was a kid?"

She launched to her feet, tripped over the ice binding her

ankles together, and hit the cage bars. A shriek of pain escaped as the iron connected with her bare skin.

Cedar stepped forwards. "June, tell us what you know and we might show you mercy."

"I—can't." She choked on the words. *Damn. Her vow must be strong.* I needed to be more specific. It didn't matter if I told her my guess, because Lady Whitefall hadn't exactly been subtle with her latest scheme.

"I know she's after talismans," I said. "The usual. Steal talismans, amass power, and screw everyone over."

"The Sidhe deserve it," she said. "You know they do."

"Yeah, but the humans and half-bloods don't. I'll bet she won't think of the collateral damage. What did she steal from Summer?"

"Only what was rightfully hers."

"Rightfully hers?" Wait. "You mean Lady Hornbeam—she stole from *Lady Whitefall*? Seriously?"

She laughed bitterly. "You walked into the middle of an ancient feud, you foolish girl. You should have stayed in the mortal realm."

"I don't know, ridding both realms of Lady Hornbeam did everyone a favour."

"You'll fail," she said. "You're mortal. This realm was made to be ruled by true immortals, but they're dying out. Our mother is one of the last of them."

"She's no immortal," I said. "The Sidhe aren't, none of them. You can call me weak all you like, but you're the same. They all are. And she doesn't give a shit about you."

"You're lying," she spat. "You're a liar."

"No, she is," I said, my voice dropping. "Her promises are lies. Her favours are illusions. Every word she says is calculated to ensure obedience. She doesn't need you. She needs soldiers who will obey her without question. So I guess my question to you is… would you continue to serve her of your own will, not under hypnosis but out of choice, because you can't think of anything better to do with your life?"

"I'd serve her till my death, as I vowed." She looked at me defiantly.

"Then there's nothing I can do to help you." I stepped away from the cage. "I might come back later. I might not."

She lunged forwards, but stopped short of the iron bars. I gave her a smile and turned to Cedar. He'd stepped back into the dark, holding the sword with gloved hands. *He picked it up.* An unexpected current of jealousy slithered through my chest, but I clamped it down.

I led the way upstairs into the entrance hall. The trapdoor disappeared at a wave of my hand, and I conjured up the door to my mother's suite. It remained locked, suggesting my sister hadn't been inside—but it'd been less than a day since the Grey Vale army had attacked, and my mother had apparently been busy raiding Summer instead of gathering her forces.

The door to Lady Whitefall's room opened when I touched it. The wardrobe was sealed, too, the way Viola and I had left it. I couldn't hear anything moving behind the doors. Hopefully it didn't mean there was a wraith hiding underneath the palace. I didn't plan to actually stay here, but the secret entrance to the Vale was just one more strike against me in the eyes of the Courts.

Cedar gave me an unreadable look. "Are you sure she has more information?"

"No," I said. "I can't tell how much of what she says is brainwashing rather than ambition, and if I found a way to turn her in, the Courts would follow the trail right back to me. She's half-blood. No chance of a trial."

Cedar fell silent, lips pressed together as though thinking. "I'd suggest transferring her to the prison on my own territory, perhaps, but that wouldn't take care of the sword."

"No. I wish I'd left it with the Little People," I said. "What do you want to do with it?"

Cedar turned the sword over in his hands. "Leave the fake one here, as we planned."

"Watch out," I warned. "It nearly killed me for picking it up. I know it's hers now, but its magic isn't like the others'."

"I don't think we should take it to the Hornbeams' territory," Cedar said. "But here's about as safe a place to leave it as you can get. It can't damage the palace. Is there an ideal room to leave it in?"

"I'll find one."

Once we'd left my mother's room, I locked it behind us and opened another door, into a small cloakroom filled with dust and not much else.

"Leave it in here," I said. "If she comes back, she'll search every room anyway, but it's as far from the dungeon as possible."

Cedar threw the sword into the room. "I don't think this is a permanent solution."

"It isn't, but I don't want you to get hurt carrying it."

There was a pause. Then it hit me what I'd said, and how he might have read it. But hadn't I all but admitted I cared for him already?

I closed the cupboard door, waved a hand, and it vanished. "Done." I drew the fake sword from where I'd sheathed it at my side, opened a door into the weapons room, and left it in a prominent place amongst the other weapons. The lightning bolt on the hilt gleamed just like the real thing.

"So," I said. "You can make killer plants appear on an enemy's territory, glamour random objects to look like genuine faerie talismans that can fool even the Sidhe, and move whole trees around. I don't know if I should be impressed or worried about what else you're keeping quiet."

He gave me a smile. "Probably less than you'd think. Would you prefer to stay here? Because leaving the palace unattended might invite your mother to come back."

"She's coming back anyway. I don't know what she was thinking leaving my sister in charge." I closed the weapons room door and made that one vanish, too. "I didn't tell Viola I was coming here. She'll be waiting to nag me back on the Hornbeams' territory. I think that works as a better safe house. This place still belongs to her, after all."

Outside the palace, the evidence from Cedar's fight was gone, but I still felt like I was being watched. I locked the palace doors and walked to the gates, my weapons out. When the gate closed behind us, Cedar drew his crossbow, eyes trained on a nearby tree.

Tentatively, a person came out from behind it, hands held up in surrender. Robin.

7

Robin looked like he'd been sleeping rough under a troll's bridge for a week. His cornflour-coloured hair was matted and grimy, and dirt streaked his angular features. Mostly, exhaustion was etched into every line of his face, like the end of a performance week minus the high. Of course, that might be because for most of the time I'd known him, he'd been feeding off the energy of my magic.

"Robin," I said coldly. "If you've come to collect your little friend, you're too late."

His throat bobbed as he swallowed. "I—I can't stay long. I'm not here for her."

"Not for Lady Whitefall?"

He shook his head miserably. "You know how powerful she is. But I had to find you."

I took in a deep breath, fighting to find calm underneath the torrent of emotions he'd stirred up. After we'd broken up three years ago, I'd hoped he'd at least have the decency to stay the hell out of my life. Instead, he'd played messenger boy for the Hornbeam family, and *then* I'd found out he'd been stealing my magic throughout our entire relationship.

And thanks to him, I'd bet Lady Whitefall knew all my weaknesses.

"Robin," I said. "You have ten seconds to give me a reason not to kill you and bury you beneath the snow like the last collection of rogues your boss sent after me."

He took a step back, his face ashen. "I—"

"Better hurry up." I called magic to my hands, the air freezing underneath my touch.

"I can tell you her plans, Raine, I swear."

"Way ahead of you." But I lowered my hands. "You're vow-sworn to her, right? That means you can't answer all my questions." I wasn't as clueless about vows as I'd been when I first came into this realm. I knew, at least, that you could tell more from what a person didn't say than what they actually said.

"I can still tell you—important things."

I considered his words. "She has everyone else under her control? Not just vows?"

He gave a hesitant nod. *Gotcha. She's still hypnotising them.*

"You're immune," I told him. "Aren't you."

The word was barely a whisper. "Yes."

"So," I went on, "it might be possible you overheard something while you were close to her. She's looking for talismans. You knew?" If I told him what he already knew, it should be able to get through the vow. That'd happened for Viola, anyway.

He gave a short nod, but didn't speak.

"You can't say which." Obviously. If Lady Hornbeam had robbed my mother in the first place, maybe petty vengeance was first on her list... but it didn't mean Lady Whitefall didn't have her eye on more difficult targets.

"Has she any interest in taking back the talisman she intended to use to kill me? Is that one next on her list?"

He shook his head jerkily. *Okay, that's weird.* Why target Summer first? She should know her own Court better, right?

"Then…" I stopped. "Is it her former Court?"

"No."

"But definitely a Court."

He dipped his head.

"Okay, that means it's Summer by default." Maybe she was after another talisman that either originally belonged to her, or belonged to someone who'd wronged her.

Robin said hesitantly. "You know her *other goal.*"

"Conquer the Courts?" Cedar suggested.

Robin nodded frantically.

"Wait, she's making an open bid for power? Now?" My heart sank.

"No." Robin looked down. "She once said to me… it wouldn't be a war or an invasion. She'd just walk in."

"So whatever she's after will allow her to do exactly that," I said. "She's planning to steal something from Summer which will give her direct access to the Court?"

There was a sharp intake of breath from Cedar. Then Robin jumped. "There's—*ah.*" He stumbled to the left, moving jerkily as though yanked on an invisible string. *The vow.*

"Don't tell her you spoke to us," I said unnecessarily. He'd die if he did, and it wasn't like he'd told us anything useful anyway.

Cedar, however, started to walk away.

"Wait." I hurried after him. "What do you think her plan is? She's not going to kill the Erlking, is she?"

"She can't," Cedar said. "But if she's planning to steal a talisman to allow herself into the Courts—that limits the possible talismans it might be. She's already attacked Summer in the last twenty-four hours, so for her to attack again means she must have set up a trap."

I stared at him. "Damn. That doesn't make it safe for *us* to go in there, right?"

"No," he said, picking up speed, "which is why we need a plan."

Damn right we do. But Cedar gave no more clues as to his potential theory before we reached the Hornbeams' gates.

I found Viola in the grounds with Rose, practising throwing knives. While Viola looked entirely like a Winter princess even when she didn't use magic, Rose had leaves and flowers braided into her curly dark hair, and her sun-kissed skin gleamed underneath the shadowy tree branches. The other soldiers milled around, none standing too close to them. Possibly because Viola was a ridiculously good shot.

Viola threw her knife, which embedded itself in the centre of the target, and whirled to face me. "I can't believe you went back to the palace. I'm assuming she wasn't there."

"Not her. June, my sister."

Her eyes widened. "Shit. Are you okay? You were with Cedar, right?"

"Yep. He's gone." I waved a hand vaguely. "But I've heard from a reliable source that Lady Whitefall's going to target Summer next."

"Again?" Rose put her knife back in its sheath. "Better not talk about it here. There are enough rumours going around as it is."

Viola retrieved her knife from the target. "Yeah, the others wouldn't be pleased to hear about the attack. Some of them suspect we were involved in the last one, though we've been here the whole time."

"That's a bit unfair."

With Volt the sprite hovering over her head, Viola led the way to the palace's side entrance, Rose just behind her. They dropped their knives off in the weapons room, where a few soldiers stared at me. Not hostile, more curious. I held my head high, knowing I couldn't expect them to trust me right away. Not least because I didn't trust *them*. We might have fought alongside one another against the Vale faeries, but one battle didn't make us allies. I doubted they'd made an alliance with a Winter family before. Those who openly supported Lady Whitefall would probably have stayed with her—unless there were spies.

Viola beckoned us to follow her through a door into a cafeteria, where she pointed out a table in the corner, too far away to be overheard.

"Is this really a good place to talk strategies?" I whispered, sitting opposite her.

"I wanted to show them we're allies," said Viola. "Besides, I'm starving."

So was I. Thanks to Faerie's time-skipping, I didn't know what day it was, here or in the mortal realm. I loaded my plate with a selection of food—skipping the weird-looking spiny plants—and returned to the corner with Viola and Rose.

"They don't mind that you're here?" I asked, jerking my head towards the other soldiers.

"They're more bothered by you," she said in an undertone. "You're a Sidhe, in their eyes."

"I'm not…" I trailed off, glancing around. Several soldiers made unsuccessful attempts to pretend not to look at me. I tensed, expecting accusations to fly, or them to blame me for Lord Hornbeam's death as well as his wife's. But nobody made a move to talk to me.

Can they actually be afraid of me?

Oh shit. They might have been half-awake for their capture, but they remembered I'd hypnotised them. They knew if they attacked, I could stop the whole room in its tracks. Yes, they were absolutely shit-scared of me. A hundred trained soldiers were too frightened to look me in the eyes. I couldn't wrap my head around it.

I looked back to see Viola raise an eyebrow at me across the table. "Well?"

"I think they're a little unsettled," I said.

"That's the thing." She shovelled food into her mouth. "We don't want our allies to be frightened of us. And there's no way we can take her army down without their help."

I had to admit she had a point. Unless I tapped into the most dangerous side of my magic and potentially got killed in the process, we needed an army, one that wasn't dependent on the whims of the Sidhe.

"They don't have a leader," I whispered.

"Sure they do," said Viola. "Lord Hornbeam wasn't their commander. Half their commanding officers died or defected, but there are a few high-ranking soldiers left. And me."

"You?"

"I nearly made high rank," she admitted. "That's why they were so reluctant to let me go. I haven't outright asked to return to my former position, but when I left, I was in charge of a whole unit. Some of the kid recruits still call me by my former title. It's weird."

"She was known as Soldier V," said Rose, with a wink. "It's catchy."

"It's annoying," said Viola, but she smiled. "Apparently they haven't forgotten respect. All they need is to know they have a Sidhe at their head, and they'll follow you."

I shook my head. "Not me. I'm from another family."

"So am I."

"And I can't lead an army for shit," added Rose. "You're more qualified than I am."

"I didn't live here," I said. "I've never belonged to their Court. If Lord Hornbeam's supporters blame me—"

"No, they don't," said Rose. "You'd be surprised how many of them are grateful for your helping them escape the Vale. Didn't you see how they declared themselves on your side against Lady Whitefall?"

"I guess they did," I relented. "But what about the part where I'm wanted by their Court for murder?"

"Most of Lady Hornbeam's most vocal supporters left," said Viola, "and most of the remaining ones serve whichever leader takes charge. Talk to them. They'll come around."

Talk to them. I wasn't what you'd call an expert diplomat, for a half-blood who'd worked with dodgy thieves and other minor criminals in the mortal realm and had only tangentially experienced the Courts until I'd been dragged here. Then again, it wasn't so different. You just had to outdo their underhanded tactics. The problem was, I didn't know a thing about winning loyalty, especially of soldiers trained to obey someone I'd hated.

I looked around and spotted a teenage soldier not ten feet away. He was the kid I'd given my knife to when Aspen and his army had attacked the Hornbeams' palace. He'd survived after all, though presumably he'd been taken captive to the Vale. His eyes shone with awe and fear as I approached.

"Hi," I said. Apparently I still hadn't got the hang of 'friendly', because he paled and nearly slipped off his chair. "Don't worry. I'm not here to hurt anyone."

"Are you here to take Lord Hornbeam's place?" he asked, his voice quiet.

"Me? No. I'm interested in getting Lady Whitefall out of the way."

He hesitantly said, "I heard you… I thought you left. Because the Summer Court wants you dead."

"I don't always make wise decisions."

Several others had moved to listen in, not very subtly. *Okay. How to use this situation to my advantage?* Their fear kept them from attacking, but any of them might snap and turn on me if they did think I was out to steal their palace from them. And if word got out to the Court... it wasn't like I could use my hypnosis indefinitely to hold them to their word.

There was only one way to be sure: put everyone under a vow. Considering how the last one turned out, I knew better than to expect that method to work. And after what they'd been through with their last two leaders, it wouldn't surprise me if they never agreed to submit to being controlled again. I couldn't blame them for that, at least.

The kid gave me another awed look. "You fought Lady Whitefall."

"I did."

"You nearly beat her," added another solider, who looked hardly older than twelve. Was there even an age limit for soldiers? "She's worse than either of them, right?"

I nodded. "You know Aspen, right? He's her right-hand-faerie."

"He has Lord Hornbeam's talisman." He swallowed nervously. "With him, she has more magic than our entire Family."

I didn't expect low-ranking soldiers to know which talisman she'd stolen. What mattered was figuring out what she planned to steal next, but I was fairly sure asking everyone *where are the security talismans for the entire Seelie Court* wouldn't endear me to them. Especially as they probably didn't know. But Cedar, who'd once robbed the Erlking himself, definitely would.

"That magic you used," one of the soldiers said slowly. "Are you using it now?"

"I'm not using any magic on you," I said. "I used it in the prison to stop *her* from controlling you."

"You set us free," added the kid next to me. "I remember."

"I can't promise she won't try the same thing again," I warned. "You need to be prepared. Talk to me if you have any suspicions about what she's planning. As far as I know, I'm the only family leader working against her."

Silence followed me as I walked back to the others, as though everyone held their breath. A faint whistling noise caught my ear, and I couldn't say I hadn't seen it coming.

I stepped to the left, and the arrow struck less than an inch from my foot. I followed its path with my eyes, conjured an arrow of ice, and threw it at the archer. He fell, gasping, but nobody ran to help. The ice had punctured a hole in his chest. His legs twitched, and he fell silent.

Cedar chose that moment to enter, which to be honest, was more startling than the arrow. Had he been listening to me talk to the soldiers?

"Now that's taken care of," I said. "Anyone else want to take a shot at me?"

8

Cedar scowled at the dead soldier. "One of you can clean up the mess," he said, his voice echoing through the room. "If you're thinking about trying the same, I'm as much your enemy as she is."

Whispers broke out. Cedar ignored them, turning his back to leave. I paused, then ran after him before he disappeared.

"Did you expect that?" I asked in a low whisper.

"No, I thought they'd have more sense." He slowed his pace to let me catch up. "The majority of them look up to you. I heard."

"You mean they're terrified I'll put them under hypnosis. Viola said I needed to convince them to support me in case I need an army at some point."

"She's right," said Cedar. "We need all the support we can get."

"And have you worked out whatever it is you went off to figure out? The talisman?"

He nodded. "It's risky, but I believe she plans to steal a security talisman. I'm intending to go to the Court tonight. A major family's holding a revel, open to the public. Meaning anyone in Summer. It's the perfect moment for me to replace the other talismans."

"You're not serious." I stared at him. "Glamoured or not, if they catch you—are you *sure* it's not a setup?"

"The Sidhe are known for having skewed priorities. They're confident in their security, and would not cancel an event unless war threatened."

"At this rate, it probably will." I stopped walking. "Wait. Is there a chance they might have been compromised? Look at Lady Whitefall, and Aspen—they both have the ability to trick people. If their abilities work on the Sidhe... maybe they've already used their powers to persuade them to open the doors."

Cedar's eyes met mine. "I did wonder. There's no chance they can actually get into the Erlking's palace—the event is at the home of a lesser noble. But there's a talisman with the capacity to unlock Summer's top security, and it's likely to be present at the event. The guards never leave their posts without it."

"Shit. So you think she's already sent someone in to steal it, and they'll be at this event?"

"The talisman requires a code to unlock it, but it frequently changes hands between the guards at Gatherings. So it's possible she's planning something tonight. Either way, there's no better opportunity for us to replace it with a fake, and hide the real one somewhere she can't find it. If we manage it, the Summer Court will be closed to her."

"You're actually being serious."

"Yes, I am," said Cedar. "It was my job to know how to enter the Court. Lady Hornbeam was one of those entrusted with the code to unlock the talisman, as were all higher Sidhe. It's possible she told Aspen."

"Shit," I said. "Okay. I'm going with you."

Cedar looked at me. "Don't hit me for this, but the top secure part of the Seelie Court is totally sealed against anyone who doesn't have Summer magic. And *strong* Summer magic, at that. I don't plan to breach it, but if it comes to it, I'll have to go alone."

"Not to this event," I said. "You know I'm immune to her power. If she's there in person..."

"The guards don't wait to ask questions before attacking intruders. The price on your head only worsens the threat. And..." He paused. "It wouldn't surprise me if she knew we were working together. I don't believe for a second that she's forgotten what you can do."

Maybe he was right. Going along would risk falling into a dangerous trap designed precisely to repel Winter faeries like me. But Cedar risked being arrested, too. They'd punish him if they caught him. And...

"My dad's in the Summer Court," I said. "What if she's found him? Or if he's there?"

"He might be," Cedar said. "Half-bloods are allowed into the event. I wouldn't consider going otherwise. I have an alias I use in the Court, but I haven't been there in over a year."

"You've been there that recently?"

"Lady Hornbeam sent me to learn the layout of their most secure areas, in case she needed the knowledge," Cedar explained. "It was the only time she permitted me to wear glamour."

I suppressed a shudder of revulsion. She couldn't be dead enough in my book.

"But you've definitely seen the security talisman," I said. "It's still risky as hell."

But the thought of seeing Dad again—even if I had to glamour myself and sneak into a Summer event—it tempted me more than it should have.

"They still think the thief is a child," he said. "It's not the first time I've sneaked in."

"How did you survive to adulthood without getting beheaded?"

"I've often wondered that myself. Are you sure you want to look for your father?"

"Positive." There was no other option.

"Even if he doesn't want to be found?"

A sharp nail dug into my chest. Dad was hardly lucid the last time I saw him. Nothing about him as half-Sidhe made a jot of sense. Much less why he hadn't at least tried to get a message to me before disappearing. If he'd reached the Summer Court, surely he knew they wanted me dead or arrested. So why not try to come back to me?

Had his human disguise been the one who loved me? Was his real self as ruthless as his wife?

My eyes stung unexpectedly. Maybe the insults he'd thrown at me in a temper had held more truth than either of us had admitted. But I had to know what was real. Whether the witches told the truth, and whether he was a tool of the Sidhe.

I looked away. "My hypnosis doesn't last long. If you want me to hit the guard carrying the talisman with it, you'll need to say when."

His mouth tightened. "If anyone picked up on the Winter magic…"

"Then they'd assume it was her. I'll be careful." The last time, the hypnosis had lasted less than fifteen minutes. Not a lot of time at all. "It's the best we've got. Unless you have some other secret ability…"

"No, I don't. And there aren't any hidden entrances—not that we can easily access from the outside."

"So how'd you get in when you were a kid?" I asked.

"I glamoured myself to look like a hobgoblin. It's considerably easier to do that when you're ten years old. Lady Hornbeam had it set up as a test."

"So you had to pass a test by stealing from the Erlking? And if you'd failed?"

He shrugged. "I'd have been demoted to an inferior position, I imagine."

"That's…" I'd been going to say 'messed up', but considering all the other shit Lady Hornbeam had done, making Cedar rob the Summer Court was nothing. "So we just… walk in the front door? I guess now's the time to see if my transforming magic can actually turn me into someone else."

"That won't be necessary," said Cedar. "You can stop listening, Viola."

Viola stepped out of the shadows, shrugging guiltily. "I figured you wouldn't say if you were sneaking off again."

"I would," I said. "She's going to attack Summer next, and if we don't at least try to remove the talisman she's targeting, she'll mow the Court down. Apparently they're hosting a revel tonight, despite the robbery. Either they're too over-confident for their own good, or they're already compromised."

"You're not seriously thinking of walking in there?" Viola's eyes widened.

"I'm dead if they suspect I'm in Faerie anyway," I said. "If she gets past their security, she can bring any of her fellow outcasts in. And then it'll be a massacre. Or she'll turn them against Winter. I've no idea what her plan is."

"Right." Viola chewed on her lip. "What you need is a way to get in without anyone knowing you're from Winter."

"There's not a reversal of my talisman, is there?" I looked at Cedar.

"Not that I know of," he said. "I have an alternative plan which involves less trial and error."

"You have got to be joking," said Viola.

I frowned. "What?"

"There's one person who might help you," said Viola. "A powerful fae who specialises in shapeshifting... on other people. But she also overcharges, likes to ensnare you in bargains, and disappears when you need her. I hired her once and ended up not being able to speak to anyone for a week."

"Damn." I looked at Cedar. "Who?"

"We don't have much choice," he said. "She owes me, besides. I helped her once, years ago."

"You'd better be right," Viola said. "Are you absolutely certain about this?"

"Nope. But my dad's somewhere in there. I need to get him far away from her."

She nodded. "All right. But be careful."

———

After transforming my clothes into a convincing Summer outfit—deep green, with leaf-like patterns—I walked with Cedar, covered in a light glamour he'd cast to turn the naturally blue glow of my magic pale green. My skin prickled like anyone I passed could see right through me. Glamour might fool the magic-less fae-kind. It certainly wouldn't fool the trained soldiers guarding the Summer Court.

As we walked, the fog in the forest cleared, and the sun brightened despite it being early evening in Faerie. Then heat surged through the air and brushed against my skin—not from the sun but from the life magic present in the very air itself.

We passed through a leafy clearing adorned with impossibly bright flowers unlike any I'd seen in the mortal realm, and certainly not in Winter. Huge ancient trees flanked us on either side. No clouds obscured the sky here. I knew Summer was as ruthless as the dark heart of Winter, but it sure as hell didn't look that way. The warm air caressed my skin, bringing the scent of apple blossom and crushed leaves, earthy smells complementing the soft, lovely music coming from all around. I listened out for familiar eerie notes, my body tensing, but it wasn't Aspen's pan pipes.

"Is Summer how you expected it?" Cedar spoke in a low voice, as though to reassure me. "I forget you've never been into the heart of our Court. I have to say the borderlands aren't a good example of it."

No kidding. The borderland forests were grim and more Winter-like than these cheerful open spaces bursting with life. Birdsong mingled with the sound of softly flowing water, and all the trees were heaving with bright green leaves. The perfume scent of the flowers stung my eyes. Cedar's warm aroma of scented candles and woodsmoke seemed subdued by comparison.

"The Sidhe don't do subtle well, do they?" I murmured.

"Don't let it fool you," he said lightly. "This is royal territory, mostly for show."

"Hmm."

Part of me belonged to Summer, too, apparently, but my magic didn't stir in response to the thrumming life inherent in the atmosphere. We passed between hedges bordering fields which ran up to large houses and estates which presumably belonged to Sidhe families closer to the central Court than the borderlands. Though they doubtless had their own disputes, there was no warfare and talisman theft happening here—at least, not in plain view. The two of us were evidence enough that one could walk openly on their territory without provoking conflict. Past the estates were clusters of smaller buildings. A village. Nobody stared, to my surprise—apparently my glamour was good enough, or maybe they just didn't care. As for Cedar, despite the tension in the air, he looked almost relaxed, for one of the few times since I'd met him.

We walked through the village, into another patch of woodland. I'd long since lost track of the way back, and hoped Cedar knew a shortcut to the path in case we needed to make a run for it. Just as I was about to ask, Cedar stopped beside a large, ancient tree grown into the shape of a house. Gnarled branches formed the outline of a small cottage.

As Cedar knocked, I whispered, "You know your way around the whole territory?"

"I was required to know," he said in an undertone. "I have my suspicions about the event's location, but we'll have to enter as guests. Luckily, I can glamour a forgery of an invitation."

"Er." I tapped my face. "Bright blue eyes. White hair. See either of those things in Summer?"

"Actually, yes, but only on nixies."

"So you want me to strip naked and dye my skin blue."

He smirked. "I doubt nixies would be allowed into such an event. I do have a plan, but you won't like it."

He knocked again. The door opened, and an ancient faerie with bark-like skin peered out.

"Hornbeam," she said, with a sniff. "Your timing might be better."

"It's been a while, Gladys," said Cedar. "I've come to call in my favour."

"For yourself? Or her?" She jerked her head towards me. "That's a pretty glamour, but you should know better than to try to trick me with illusions."

"Merely a precaution to reach you unharmed," responded Cedar. "As a matter of fact, we came in search of something better."

"She's powerful," remarked the old faerie. "And Unseelie. I can't transform her nature, and her magic is out of control. There's no covering it. May I ask the occasion? There are some disturbing reports coming out of the Court."

"We're looking into it," said Cedar. "There's a revel tonight which I suspect might be connected to the attackers. Unfortunately, our names aren't on the guest list."

A slow smile appeared on her face. "I see how it is. Lord Niall is the host, and he has been quite vocal about the punishments to await trespassers. Instant execution, I believe. His guards aren't patient."

"Precisely why I need your help," he said.

"I owe you one favour," she said. "To whom may it apply —you or her?"

"Her. I've made my own arrangements."

"Very well." She strode closer to me, her hand outstretched. I instinctively stepped back into the rough wall. Earthy fingers trailed over my skin, and my magic reacted, lighting my hands up blue.

"We can't have that happening, can we?" she muttered. "Right."

The crone pointed at me. My back arched and a horrible rippling sensation passed over my body like my skin was stretching. I fell to my knees, biting back a yelp of discomfort. Needles prickled up and down my arms and spine. When I looked down, my hands were blunt and scaled, dark red in colour. I pushed to my feet, looking up—way up— because I'd shrunk. A lot.

The crone, barely concealing a grin, held up a mirror.

A hunched scaly creature stared back. She'd turned me into a hobgoblin.

"What the actual fuck?" I croaked.

"You're welcome," said the crone. "Your magic is entirely hidden. It's a good job, if I do say so myself."

"For *how* long?"

"Three hours. Don't look at me like that. As a lesser fae, they'll look right past you. They'll think you're a servant."

"And Cedar gets to stay in human form?" I shot him a glare.

"He's accomplished in imitating nobles," said Gladys. "You… I don't know *what* you do."

"I'm a thief," I croaked. "A thief and a Sidhe-killer. If this doesn't wear off, I'll turn you into a lawn ornament."

I turned my back, shouldering the door open, and damn near tripped over the threshold with my clumsy goblin feet.

"Raine," Cedar hissed, closing the door behind us. "It's okay. It won't be permanent."

"I can't even see properly from this height," I growled. "Let alone sneak around. You know who this Lord Niall is, right?"

"Yes. It's as I suspected. We can get into the event's location through the front doors, but once our task is complete, we'll have to sneak out through the back. There's a tunnel behind the tree at the back of the hall. I've never used it, but I'm told it comes out somewhere in the forest." He spoke in a low voice. "Before then, we need to pinpoint which guard is holding the talisman. It's in the form of a key with a stag carved into it, and the guard usually wears it around their neck."

"Gotcha," I said, recalling the details of our plan. "So we figure out who carries it, create a diversion, and steal it. I'll do the hypnotising part, and you…"

"I'll take it," Cedar said. "The royal I'm disguising myself as would have an alibi for holding the talisman, if it came to it."

"But I have to play this… thing." I looked down at myself in disgust.

"Your magic is distinctive," he said. "They'd never guess it came from a hobgoblin."

"I feel so honoured." I scowled. "Why would they carry something so important around at an event like this?"

"It's deliberate." Cedar exhaled in a sigh. "They're too confident that nobody will ever act against them. So few actually know the code to use the talisman on the gates to the centre of the Court. I hope Lady Whitefall doesn't, but considering she's worked out this much…"

"What if she's there?"

"That," said Cedar, "depends on whether she wants a Court left to rule over."

"I honestly don't know if she does." My voice shrank to a whisper, and the rasping overtones of my nasally hobgoblin voice didn't help at all. "Winter's more open to her. Coming here—it feels like we're missing a crucial piece of her strategy."

"She could want any one of a hundred things," said Cedar. "To weaken Summer's defences. To spike a war with Winter. To draw out the Sidhe. Anything. In any case, we're unlikely to get a better chance to strike than this evening, and if there are any signs of her there, stopping her is more important than not exposing ourselves."

Though it might mean death sentences for both of us, even for trying to protect the Seelie Court.

"When this is done," I said, "I'm never working with the Courts again. I'm retiring."

"Let's hope we get that option," he said.

9

Experiencing the forest as a hobgoblin made the vast areas of Summer seem even more tangled than usual. My legs were shorter than I was used to and kept getting caught on the undergrowth, though my feet were twice as long with sharp nails. At least I could give someone a good kick if necessary. Not being able to sense my magic, however, was like having a vital sense cut off.

"How am I supposed to dance like this?" I growled. "I'll be lucky not to trip over these clown feet."

Cedar tried and failed to hide a smile.

I flipped him off. "You'll see who's laughing. Where's your disguise, anyway?"

The air shimmered green. Cedar's face subtly altered, his hair turned silvery blond instead of black, curling to his neck and masking the scar on his face. He looked like a pretty Court faerie, but a stranger to me. Then again, I was hideousness personified. At least I didn't smell like a wild hobgoblin. But I'd lost my speed and gracefulness in the transformation. I couldn't captivate the crowd under a spell even as a last resort.

80

Please don't let this be a mistake.

Cedar led the way, moving easily down the path out of the woods. My clumsy feet seemed painfully slow, and the winding paths didn't help. Would my magic work while I was stuck in the form of a non-magical creature? Really, the lesser fae didn't have an easy time of it. Their roles were set, like ours. Hobs were either servants to Court families, or scavengers. In Winter, they tended to be more brutal and bloodthirsty. My nails were long enough to gouge out someone's eyes. But I kept my head down, meekly playing my part.

A river swirled past, bringing the scent of earthy freshness with it. Not ice-cold and frozen, but alive and thriving. Other faeries began to appear throughout the shining green fields as we passed by yet more Sidhe estates. Horses bore riders dressed in finery, some with elaborate coats made of feathers or grass, thorns and flowers woven into their long hair. Most were lesser royals, probably, since the Summer Court had a single king whom few people ever saw. Between the royals ran goblins and elves and brownies, helping to get the horses ready and to wait on the higher Sidhe hand and foot. There were half-bloods, too, I saw to my surprise. Must be heirs to the royals. I'd bet they'd had a nicer welcome to Faerie than I did.

Piskies flew around emitting humming noises, while fireflies of all colours flitted up and down, basking the lawns in a patchwork of light. A group of nixies and merfolk lazed around a pond where the river halted, apparently not in a hurry to leave for the event. The horses all headed towards a grand old house behind a gate made out of living, creeping thorns. Long-leafed plants flanked the entrance, swaying in the faint breeze. I'd bet some of them were poisonous like the ones by Lord Hornbeam's palace.

The guards hardly looked at me, though I scanned for any

tell-tale signs of hypnosis. Anyone would pick up on it immediately in this haven of Summer magic. Cedar kept close behind me, nodded politely to the guards, and we were in.

Walking through the doors was more like entering an indoor garden than a palace. Cobbled paths wound between fountains and marble statues and beautifully arranged flower displays. Gold and white flowers bloomed along the walls, while thorny stems snaked outside the windows, promising a painful landing if we tried to climb out. The ceiling was a network of blooming red flowers, the occasional petal falling to the ground like a droplet of blood. The perfumed aroma that seemed to linger everywhere didn't seem so over-whelming as a hobgoblin. Now I understood why she'd chosen this form for me. My senses were blunted, and even my sensitivity to magic had been dialled down. Based on the intense green glow of vital Summer magic, I might have fallen under any one of a dozen spells upon entering the room. My mortal blood wasn't made to withstand this level of Seelie magic, and being Unseelie didn't help.

My shorter stature made it difficult to see over people's heads and work out where the exits were. Cedar feigned casualness as he walked, and I could only assume he'd left his iron weapons behind or hidden them well. Some carried weapons here—swords sheathed at waists, conspicuous daggers, often with a sheen which drew the eye. *Talismans. Holy shit. They all have talismans.* Each and every one of the royals had an unknown power—and my mother might be hiding amongst them.

Someone handed me a platter of drinks, thinking I was a servant. I took it and continued to walk slowly, head down, nobody looking twice at me. Why would they? I was just a hobgoblin, honoured to be serving the Court at such a pres-tigious event. My mind whirled. Any of those talismans might turn into a murder weapon if my mother's hypnosis entered the mix—and I'd never know, because my senses were dulled to the presence of magic.

My spine prickled at a shriek from the corner. A couple of trolls yanked the wings off piskies and threw them at one another. My stomach turned over. Maybe it wasn't safe here even by Faerie's standards. The Sidhe hardly seemed to notice, and if any of them worried about an attack, they hid it under smiles and laughter.

When I circled the fountain, pretending to serve drinks, I spotted Cedar conversing with two other royals. I let the crowd's momentum carry me until I reached a large tree at the back of the room, so huge it'd fused into the wall. Its trunk formed a large section of the back wall, and its branches must stretch much higher. An ancient tree... a source of power, but alive, moving slightly. This must be the tree Cedar had mentioned as our back door exit later tonight.

My path carried me past the royals again, and I looked closer this time. A sharply-dressed male royal wore a key around his neck where it gleamed under the lights dancing around the large fountain. It matched Cedar's description exactly, to the pair of stag's horns etched on its face. *There's my target.*

I caught Cedar's eye. He'd manoeuvred his way to a group of court fae not ten metres from the guard in a way that looked totally natural. The guard was heading in his direction, entirely oblivious.

Despite my clumsy feet, I stole silently after him. Once I passed within the guard's sight, he'd get the first taste of my magic. His path carried him behind the fountain. The crowd moved, unseeing, pretty faces and magic and life swirling around, unaware of the monsters in their midst. *Here we go.*

A familiar tugging sensation caught my chest and yanked

me to the side, nearly sending me falling into an elven knight.

Shit. What *was* that? Had someone used magic on me? I looked around but saw no traces of a threat. When nothing happened, I continued to make my casual way forward. For the magic to work, the guard had to be looking at me, but not realising what I was doing. My feet moved as though guided by someone else, my heart thundering so loud I feared someone would hear me. *That won't work. You need to believe you can do it. Like on the stage...*

The knot in my chest loosened as I drew closer, feeling the familiar hum of magic inside my chest. Just a few more inches and he'd fall under my spell.

Raucous laughter came from the crowd, and a drunken faun stumbled in front of me. I sidestepped it, and the weird tugging sensation caught me again, spinning me around on the spot. It was like a thread connecting me with—someone in the crowd.

Oh hell.

I'd felt it before. I knew what it meant: a vow. Aside from Cedar, there was only one person I'd ever sworn a vow to. Not my mother.

But where was he?

Focus, Raine. I swiftly walked forward, crossing in front of the guard. Magic flowed to my feet and into the air, catching his gaze. For a heart-stopping moment, I thought it hadn't worked, and I was about to be exposed. The guards here were pure Sidhe, after all—but for all that, they were also minor royals, and not immune to my mother's magic.

The guard stopped, the faintest trace of blue reflected in his eyes. I slipped up to him, holding out the plate of glasses on the pretext of offering him a drink. "You're going to take off the key around your neck and put it in your pocket, and keep walking past that group of nobles," I murmured. "You won't say a word about me. Take a drink."

He did exactly that, not breaking stride. No trace of my magic remained as a hint of the spell I'd put him under, though I cursed my stumbling goblin feet for costing me seconds in getting the hell away from him, behind the fountain, swept up in the crowd again. I didn't dare get closer to Cedar, but hoped he could pull off the theft before anyone suspected what I'd done. I'd pickpocketed people in broad daylight before. I sure as hell hadn't blasted someone with Winter magic within a Summer-only Gathering in public before. At least the guard wouldn't be able to give me away.

But the tugging sensation in my chest didn't abate. *Aspen's here. Somewhere. And the vow's still active.*

He had a Sidhe's magic. Lady Hornbeam's. Powerful enough to get through security. Worse, he was *from* Summer, so his magic would blend in—including those blasted pipes.

A faerie with familiar features slipped away from the crowd, heading for the back of the room in a smoothly casual manner. *Thanks, Cedar.* Relieved, I altered my steps to follow him.

Once we'd reached the tree, he turned to smile at me. *Wait. We're not supposed to make eye contact.*

Something was wrong. Not just because of the disguise he wore… but because he wasn't Cedar. Oh hell.

The false Cedar's glamour melted away, revealing Aspen's face. "Surprise," he said softly.

10

The vow clenched around my chest and yanked me forward against my will, as Aspen spoke. Too quiet for me to hear the words, but I'd sworn to obey him, and as long as we both lived, the vow still held. In this form, I couldn't summon the magic to resist. He must have been watching carefully to know it was me underneath the disguise.

As I drew closer to him, magic rippled up my hands, too subtle to detect—I hoped. The air froze around him, forming an icy dagger inches from his throat.

He raised a hand and the ice melted the instant it touched him, evaporating into thin air. My magic had failed.

"You swore to serve me," he whispered, too quiet for anyone to hear but me.

"The vow has gone," I hissed through clenched teeth. "I left you behind. I won the battle."

"The vow can't die if you don't set conditions on it, you foolish girl. If you'd said, *I will serve you until I defeat you in combat* or *until I leave this realm*, you'd be free."

He was right. Damn the bastard, he was right. "You'd never have let me."

"True." He smirked. "I order you not to speak a word to anyone until I say so."

My throat closed up, my mouth sealing itself shut. Panic shot through my nerves and I lunged at him, intending to knock him off his feet.

"Stop."

My body screeched to a halt. If his will was more powerful than mine, I'd stay still until he next commanded me. But he hadn't said *stop forever.*

I pushed against the thread pulling at my chest, hard. It was worse than the mind control, because I was fully aware of everything I was doing, yet as powerless to stop it as if someone else used my body. Which in effect, they did. Worse was the painful ache inside me, promising pain if I veered from the path he'd set me on. My brother had been directly ordered to kill me. By disobeying, he'd started bleeding, and killed himself to stop the pain. Vows weren't connected to talismans. They might even be more powerful. The guard I'd hypnotised would snap out of it within a few minutes. Cedar and I were supposed to have gone.

What have you done with him?

Aspen smiled. "I want you to dance, but not using magic," he said. "On the table. There. Draw a crowd. Don't use any magic."

So he does want a diversion. I fought every step, but the vow reached inside me and dragged me up onto a chair, then the table.

Someone giggled and pointed at the dancing goblin. I cursed Aspen to oblivion, fighting with every step. I couldn't use blatant hypnosis on an entire room of Summer faeries. They'd shoot me dead on the spot. But I could still move, as long as I obeyed. I kicked plates off the table, knocked glasses over, and moved in the same direction as Aspen, drawing as many eyes that way as possible. But he'd hidden too well. I kicked another plate over, and my foot caught on a wine vat. Desperate, I lunged and picked it up, faked drinking from it, and I collapsed onto my back.

The vow stopped tugging, as though I'd surprised him. I writhed, pretending to choke. My throat was closed up from the vow, and my hobgoblin voice made the sound convincing. The nobles' laughs turned to outraged shouts, and a scream came from an overhead piskie. Then another buzzed past in a panic, picking up on my message. They thought someone had poisoned the wine. And I'd landed right in front of Aspen, who was backed into a corner. *Good luck making a quick getaway.*

The vow half-heartedly tugged at me, but I carried on writhing as chaos ignited. *Aspen's distracted. I can push back while he isn't paying attention.*

I pulled *hard,* and fell off the table. My knees cracked off the hard floor, and my body was swallowed up in the crowd. I stumbled to my feet, then ducked into the melee and ran as hard as I could. He'd been hiding, and now the crowd knew there was an intruder, his attention would be on hiding himself, not drawing me back to him.

Then a guard shouted, "Thief!"

Shit. Shit. Had Cedar managed to replace the talisman? Or had Aspen got there first? I risked a look over my shoulder, but I was too short in this form to see over the crowd. I was positive I'd caught a glimpse of the guard I'd hypnotised, and he'd been carrying a sword.

Either Cedar had succeeded… or Aspen had got the same idea.

I pelted to the tree at the back of the room, slipping around the back into an alcove in the wall. Ducking out of view, I scanned the crowd from above for Cedar. Flittering piskies spun around the ceiling, shrieking out warnings. Sidhe nobles callously tossed lesser fae out of the way— goblins, brownies, fauns—as they sought to find the intruder. The overturned table I'd danced on was surrounded by shouting nobles, all of whom looked suitably agitated as to not be under mind control—but that was the point, wasn't it? To do a convincing job, you had to order people to act like normal, pretend they weren't obeying you. But it was nigh on impossible to know whether Aspen had used his pan pipes or Lady Whitefall had been here. I held myself out of sight, desperately scanning for a familiar face, and the tree moved as someone climbed up the side. I tensed, preparing to strike—but the real Cedar gave me a grim nod. He was covered in blood, half of his face swollen with bruising, but still in his disguise. Except the scar, which I recognised underneath his glamour.

Cedar gestured and the tree's roots parted, letting us through into a narrow tunnel. We fell several feet down a slope into a small cave. Tree roots covered the walls and floor, and there was a constant hum of magic in the air. The tree itself pulsed with magic, like a beating heart.

"This is under the palace?" I croaked. *Damn the Sidhe.* The vow must have let go, because I could speak again.

He nodded. "We need to run before security locks this place down."

"Shit." I scrambled after him. "I hope they catch Aspen and turn him into a deer. He copied your glamour. He must have seen us before we got into the palace."

"I was afraid something like that would happen," he said. "Aspen's magic gives him a free pass to the Summer Court."

"Bloody typical," I growled. "You know, if I wasn't stuck like this, Aspen would be dead."

Cedar shook his head. "They'd have caught you. I've seen Winter fey-kind who look identical to Summer ones get caught trespassing by someone who picked up on their weak magic. The very air we breathe can detect any hint of the Unseelie."

"I got this close to cutting his throat." I measured the distance between my fingers. "I should have guessed she'd use him. He's nobility *and* he has two talismans. He could rule over Summer and she'd have Winter."

"She's still using him," Cedar said. "She doesn't want a puppet in control, she wants to rule in person. He's there while it's convenient, that's all."

We stopped, reaching a wall of tree roots. Cedar cursed quietly. "The way out is sealed. I'll have to give it a nudge."

"What?" I whispered. "They'll know we're in here."

Green light lit up his palm. The roots began to twitch. I could almost see him coaxing the plant to move out of the way, reassuring it that we weren't here to cause harm. As the roots opened, a slope leading aboveground beckoned. Underneath more roots, we emerged into the forest. But the sunlight had fled, and darkness filled the gaps, swarming with sharp-toothed creatures. Every wild fae around had apparently decided to come to get a closer look at the party. Cedar's magic brushed against me, and I turned to see he'd disappeared.

Cedar's hand rested on my back. "I'm glamoured. So are you."

"Guess the spell will wear off soon."

My legs moved more easily with every step, and magic tingled up and down my arms. If Aspen had hypnotised just one person in Court, he'd be able to get in again. It'd taken more than a day for the effect of his pan pipes to wear off, and that was with me *knowing* he'd put a spell on me. What if he'd hit someone before he'd found me? I'd been locked into his vow, but I should have done more to stop him from coming back.

"Cedar," I whispered, when we'd reached a deserted path where we were unlikely to be overheard. "Did you get it?"

"I did. Your hypnosis drew the guard right to me."

I exhaled in relief. "Thank the Sidhe. I thought Aspen and his vow wrecked everything."

Cedar's hand squeezed mine in the dark. "Don't worry."

I didn't answer. It was too easy to let my guard down around him. Too easy to forget it was someone from his very family who'd wormed his way through my defences and humiliated me. His magic buzzed against mine, and I hit my head on a lower branch.

"Crap. The spell wore off."

"I'd have thought you'd be glad not to have to spend forever as a hobgoblin."

"Very funny. What did you plan to do with it? What if she comes looking?"

Silence followed. My heart sank. We might have stolen their security talisman, but it'd be for nothing if she figured out we had it. Yet if we hadn't taken it, Aspen would have.

"We'll hide it," said Cedar. "They know there was an intruder. With luck, they'll think it was her."

"Doubt we'll get that lucky. If Aspen hypnotised the others—I can't detect whenever he's done it. Anyone there might have been under his influence. He probably knows the Court as well as you do."

"Yes, Lady Hornbeam frequently chose him to accompany her into the Court," Cedar said quietly. "However, the Summer Court… its armies aren't what they used to be. Certainly not as disciplined as the Hornbeams' army in the borderlands, anyway."

"They *have* an army, right?" I asked.

"Several," said Cedar. "But… Raine, there's a reason nobody's seen the Erlking in years. He's been ill for decades —dying, even. It's why he never leaves his home. Some know… some in Winter, even. It's not a well-kept secret. But if Aspen gets into the Court, he'll leave the way right open for a coup."

My mouth fell open. "He's sick? The Erlking?"

"Yes," Cedar said. "I don't know who the heir is, but they're more vulnerable than most people know. We temporarily stole her means of accessing the Court itself, but if Aspen hides amongst the royals long enough—if he knows half the methods of spying that I do—he'll find a way in."

"I think you're giving him too much credit, and yourself too little," I said. "You're the master thief. He's probably never stolen anything in his life, because it was handed to him. The Sidhe are experts at seeing through deception. He dropped my vow in a second when I drew attention onto him."

"I hope you're right," he murmured.

Silence followed our path, far quieter than before. A voice in my ear whispered that it didn't matter to me if Summer fell. But it did. If she took one Court, the other would either follow or declare war. And all the consequences would reach both the mortal realm and the borderlands. Besides, too many people I cared about belonged to this world. Even my father.

I'd seen no signs of him amongst the other half-bloods. Part of me was relieved I hadn't, but it was a reminder that he hadn't even tried to find me. He'd come into Faerie for one reason: for her. Not me. I *knew* it was down to her magic, that it wasn't his fault, but the wounds inflicted by people you cared about the most took the longest to heal. I should know.

As we reached the path leading to Winter territory and the borderlands, a horrible scream came from the woods. I tensed but didn't stop. Creepy noises in the forest were par for the cause—but the awful ragged cry that followed made the hairs rise on the back of my neck.

Cedar cursed in the faerie tongue. "Someone used evil magic here," he said softly.

Ahead, a commotion brewed. Wild fae ran in all directions, some collapsing with horrible injuries, and my eyes watered as the smell of burning drifted on the breeze.

Burning... from Winter territory.

11

I kept walking. Blood darkened the snow and more bodies lay around us. Goblins, and a troll lying sprawled over the path. Brutal blackened marks like burns covered its skin. It was one of the territory's security trolls I'd run into before. I readied myself to attack, but there was no target. Fire on Winter territory was pretty much unheard of.

"Cedar, if you walk any further, you're trespassing." Not to mention he carried one of Summer's security talismans.

"That's not my biggest concern." Cedar pointed to a tree, which was burnt to a crisp, its once snow-clad branches brittle and sooty. "Summer magic did this."

My heart lurched. "Oh, shit."

I ran past burnt debris, skidding to a halt in the mud. A nearby house blazed with bright flames, which had melted the supposedly eternal snow into a river tinged pink with blood. Two bodies were impaled on the fence posts. Their wide-open eyes shone bright blue.

Winter nobles.

I looked at Cedar in disbelief. "How? Aspen can't have come here."

"She must have sent someone else." Cedar drew his weapon. The area surrounding the house was eerily silent. The occupants would be dead, permanently so. Normal fire had no effect against Winter magic. The attacker had used magical fire, powerful enough to bring down a house sustained with magic itself. I'd never heard of such a thing.

Wait. "*What* other Summer talismans did she take?"

"I don't know," he said quietly. "Nothing else could have broken the defences on a place like this."

"She didn't send someone. She came in person."

And we'd taken her bait and let her get away with it. She'd purposefully engineered two attacks at once.

Cedar strode around the front of the manor, the air shimmering as he disappeared under a fresh glamour. It wouldn't fool Sidhe, but the only two I'd spotted near the house were dead.

I skirted the river of blood and followed Cedar through the gates. The windows had been blown out, and the house gutted, everything inside reduced to cinders. Magic lay thick and heavy over the place. Dead magic. The person whose magic had held the house upright must have died, but the attacker had burned through the remains anyway.

After scanning for the glint of a talisman, I backed out of the gates, and nearly tripped over the body of a giant wolf lying in a bloody heap covered in more awful wounds.

"Whatever talisman did this, it was brutal," said Cedar quietly. "They burned through the foundations of the magic keeping this house alive."

"That's what I thought." I swallowed hard. "I can't see any weapons. Can you?"

"No. The only magic here is dying."

A groan came from close by. "Stay where you are," whispered a voice.

I whirled around. Lord Lyle lay in the bushes. He'd turned from wolf to human again—and was still alive, despite the wounds lacerating his chest.

"Shit," I whispered. "Can—is there anywhere we can take you to help?"

"Help?" He coughed. "You're not here to finish me off?"

"No, we're not with—whoever attacked you. Please tell me you saw them."

"The messengers sent out a distress signal," coughed Lord Lyle. "I picked up on it. When I came here the house was dead. The aftermath hit me before I could run."

"But what did it?" I whispered. "Faerie magic can't burn anyone. Why did someone attack this place? To steal something, right? Did she steal back her talisman?"

"You shouldn't know these things, half-blood." Blood bubbled up from his throat, darkening the corners of his mouth. He choked, his body shuddering, and green light shone over him.

"Cedar. What are you doing?"

He muttered under his breath in the faerie tongue and the light grew brighter. Lord Lyle's wounds began to disappear. The damaged skin healed, and he gasped and shuddered.

I gaped at Cedar. "He's from your enemy Court!" I didn't care if he heard. He'd already seen us together, and I didn't have the energy left to care. Not after what my mother had done.

"I don't *have* a Court," Cedar said. "And he's a viable source of information."

Lord Lyle's eyes opened, focusing on me… and Cedar.

"You." He stood, easily, despite the bright red blood soaking his clothes. I'd never seen a Sidhe look anything other than immaculate. "What did you do?"

"I healed you." Cedar stepped towards him. "As I saved your life, you owe me."

"That only applies to Sidhe." Lord Lyle's mouth twisted.

"I *am* one. And so is she. We're the stand-in heads of our respective families, and that means we're equal to Sidhe as far as the requirement for owing a favour is concerned. As I saved your life, you will grant me one favour of my choosing. The favour I ask is this: you're to take Raine under your protection against anyone who threatens us—including the Seelie Court."

What? Of all the favours to ask for—was stopping me from being arrested higher in priority to Cedar than finding Lady Whitefall or even Aspen?

Lord Lyle's face reddened. "You—you have the audacity to ask me to set myself against the Seelie Court and the will of my own Queen?"

"Does your Queen support Raine's arrest or exile?" Cedar enquired.

"It's not her concern. Summer is in charge of enacting whatever punishment they see fit. I'm not permitted to go onto their territory, so if you decide to go anywhere near the Seelie Court, no favour will prevent them from slaughtering you."

"Well, then." Cedar looked him in the eyes. "It is done. According to the rule, you will aid us if we're attacked again at any point here on Unseelie territory, including the borderlands."

"It is done," said Lord Lyle stiffly. "You half-bloods will meet a brutal end someday."

"Was that a threat?" I asked. "Because let me tell you, we're doing our best to stop Lady Whitefall from attacking the Courts, and it'd be a hell of a lot easier if you cooperated with us. What exactly caused the explosion?"

Lord Lyle's eyes narrowed. "I don't know. I didn't see the attacker."

"Was it a talisman?" I threw caution to the winds. "She— that's why she came here, right? Did she take back the confiscated talisman you took from her?" I had to know the truth.

"She did," said Lord Lyle. "I'm sure I don't need to remind you of the consequences of repeating that information outside of this territory. I found it missing shortly before the distress signal went out. Before I caught up with the thief, the house caught fire. At a guess, the magic she used exploded when it came into contact with something inside the house."

"Can it happen? Magic can overload, like… I don't know. A car engine exploding?" That didn't sound right. "An electrical device? I don't know what you have here that's equivalent."

"I think you're right," Cedar said. "But it'd take something incredibly volatile, and we should have felt the impact over in… on our own territory."

I'd guessed he was about to say *in Summer.* Lord Lyle didn't need to know about our excursion, even if he was supposed to protect us now.

"I must report to my Queen," said Lord Lyle. "It's entirely possible she will order me not to help you, in which case, the favour is null and void."

"So you aren't going to tell on us?" I called after him as he turned his back and began to walk away. He didn't answer, quickening his pace, treading blood into the melted snow.

"No," said Cedar quietly. "I doubt he'd survive the humiliation of admitting he was saved by a Summer half-blood."

"I didn't know you could snatch a favour from a pure Sidhe so easily."

"It's not commonly used," he admitted. "Mostly because

the Sidhe rarely end up in near-death conditions. I wasn't sure it'd work, but I needed to force his hand."

"Isn't saving his life a good thing?"

"Not here," said Cedar. "He nearly died, which isn't an experience most Sidhe have had, much less owing a debt to a member of the enemy Court. It's lucky I have no intention of leveraging our bond for all it's worth. I've had enough of vows for a lifetime."

"Same here. I didn't know…" I stopped. Talking about my own issues with Aspen's vow seemed selfish compared to the hell Cedar had experienced from his own family.

"Didn't know what?"

"Aspen. He didn't use the vow when I was hypnotised. I guess he didn't need to, but I forgot it was active until tonight."

Specifically, I'd been shocked at the physical pain it'd caused me before he spoke a word. Was it that way for Cedar all the time? No wonder he'd taken issue with all my attempts to act against the Hornbeams. They'd been reminding him they could take his life with every heartbeat.

"It didn't look as though he planned for us to be there," said Cedar. "He knew, but he didn't anticipate our actions."

"But he and Lady Whitefall have this new weapon, whatever it is."

The trees rustled and snow fell as a cloud of birds took flight nearby. With one last look at the wrecked house, I turned away. I doubted the Unseelie Queen would show up in person, but appearing at a murder scene wouldn't help my case. At least Lord Lyle would hopefully stand beside us against Lady Whitefall if it came to it… assuming she hadn't attacked the Unseelie Court, too.

"She's too much," I muttered, as we walked. "Robin's either a liar or he didn't know she had two plans on the go at once. Now she has at least one talisman from Winter, maybe more. And whatever she stole from Summer. And she'll know we have the security one."

"I'll hide it," Cedar said.

"Good. That makes *two* renegade talismans in our hands now," I said. "At this rate, people will think we're hoarding them."

I'd attempted to lighten the tone, but Cedar shook his head. "If I tried to take a talisman, it'd destroy the trust I've built with the other soldiers. They're only loyal to me as long as I don't treat them like their last two leaders."

I looked at him curiously. Not for the first time, I wondered why it hadn't immediately occurred to me that Cedar might choose to step in as leader. He had powerful magic—more powerful than he let on, and he was Lady Hornbeam's son.

"They respect you," I said. "I think you should take the position."

"I virtually exiled myself by siding with you," Cedar said. "That alone means I don't qualify as leader. The only reason I got away with telling Lord Lyle I did was because the Summer Court hasn't released an official statement banning me from the Court. I'm banned by default, but not in so many words."

"More word games." I sighed. "All right. So Lord Lyle has us under his protection. That's sort of like a vow, right?"

"In theory," said Cedar. "But if the Unseelie Court orders him to oppose us, he will."

"But *she* doesn't know," I said. "Look what happened last time she thought she'd bound people to her, but they were actually loyal to me. We can use that against her."

Cedar looked at me, his face unreadable. "How, exactly?"

"Let my sister out of jail, and force her to swear a vow to serve me or rot down there in the dark."

12

Cedar didn't say a word while we walked through the darkening forest, treading through Winter territory to approach my palace from the back.

"You can tell me it's a bad idea," I said to him. "I won't hold it against you."

"I don't. I think it's risky, and Lady Whitefall is likely to anticipate that your sister isn't doing her bidding."

"You don't think she's been busy enough tonight?" I arched a brow. "A vow can't be seen through. She'd know if I used hypnosis—but I'm pretty sure my sister's immune anyway. That's why my mother had to recruit her or kill her. She's such a model parent."

"No doubt," Cedar said darkly, "but her attention won't be scattered forever. She has enough people under her thrall that any discrepancies would be noticed immediately."

"Like in the Summer Court? She's even less attentive than they are. There's only one of her, for a start. She might have talismans, but she can't watch everyone at once."

I circled the palace from the side, using the front gate this time. The bright and cold entrance hall with its glittering icicles and chandeliers stood in stark contrast to the carnage we'd just witnessed. Once the front door was closed behind us, I opened the way into the dungeon.

Icy cold lashed me like a whip the second the trapdoor lifted. I stumbled back, magic springing to my hands and freezing the air. My clothes turned to armour, even my gloves. I waited, but no attacker appeared. After a second, I jumped downstairs into the dungeon, ignoring Cedar's hissed warning.

My sister remained behind the cage bars. The sword lay a few feet away.

"How the hell did you get down there?"

A hissing came from the talisman, a noise that definitely shouldn't be possible for an inanimate object to make.

"Come back already?" asked June. "Is your conscience bothering you?"

"Not in the slightest." I moved closer to the bars, one eye on the sword. "What if I offer you a way out?"

"You're lying."

"Nope. I wouldn't have come back here if I didn't need something from you."

She didn't look so tough slumped against the wall. I kicked the sword away from her into the dark. Creepy thing. I needed a way to permanently be rid of it, but I'd never actually asked Cedar how to go about destroying a talisman. Let alone one that could apparently travel through walls.

June scrambled upright, eyes darting to the sword. "What are you doing?"

"Making sure you can't fight back."

She swallowed. *Still think I'm too soft for Winter?* Genuine fear shone in her eyes. But she made no move to strike first, as my brother had. Her hands remained fisted at her sides.

"You're going to swear to tell me the truth and not deceive me in any way," I said. "Under a vow. Or I'll kill you, and it won't be a pleasant and quick death. Do we have an understanding?"

"I swear to tell you the truth," she ground out.

"Good enough. Now, swear to do what I say."

"I can't," she said.

"Does her vow prevent another person from putting one on you?"

"I—no." She shook her head.

"Then you'll swear to me, or you'll die. I killed our brother. Don't think I won't finish you off, too."

"I swear to do as you say."

The vow snapped into place like a piece of elastic connecting us through the bars. This time, I hardly felt it. It must be stronger for the person affected. *Not my problem.*

"Firstly, tell me if you were aware of her plans tonight. All of them."

She jerked her head to the right. "I—I can't."

"You can if I already know. And I do. She attacked Summer using Aspen to sneak into an event. What was the purpose?"

Her eyes bulged. "How do you—?"

"You're the one telling me secrets. And you're not allowed to tell anyone you spoke a word to me, or give any hint that we have been in contact at all. And if they guess we have, you're not to speak a word of what we said to each other. Is that clear?"

She swallowed and nodded. "Summer wasn't my job."

"Aspen's. He was already there, after the robbery. To sneak into the Court?"

Another nod. So we'd swiped the talisman tonight just in time. But the first robbery…

"Do you know what she stole from Summer prior to the attack? Which talisman?"

She pressed her hands together. "I'm not—I wasn't told."

Damn. "Does she have another Sidhe working with her? Someone who can cross realms?

Her head jerked sideways.

So she came herself? Shit. Was she still here, waiting to strike? Or had her people come through the dungeon? Most likely—yes. Maybe one of her people had had moved the sword. It seemed more likely than the talisman moving by itself. Nobody had let June out of her cage, but Lady Whitefall's people were probably no nicer to one another than they were to their enemies.

"All right," I said. "You're going to come with me, out of your cage. You're only going to walk where I tell you to, when I tell you, and you're not to attack me or Cedar or anyone else unless I order you to. Is that understood?"

"It is understood."

I unlocked the cage. She stepped forwards, fists curled at her sides, and walked alongside me upstairs to the open trap-door. Cedar kept looking at me, but I ignored him, not wanting to allow her to overhear anything that might get back to Lady Whitefall.

"Now you're going to wait here." I indicated a spot in the entrance hall. Then I opened a door in the opposite wall, into the weapons room. Inside, the fake sword lay where I'd left it, its glamour faded. The lightning bolt symbol had gone. "Damn," I muttered.

"I told you it wasn't permanent," said Cedar, the door closing behind him. "That was a rushed job. I can't transform things, only glamour them. It's not even the right size."

He was right—the fake sword was too short. I studied it. "I can transform things." I lifted the sword, turning it over in my hands, and blue light flared around its edges. The sword extended, green light mingling with the blue, and a lightning bolt appeared on the hilt. A blue glow sprang up as though it really did contain Winter's power. "Huh. That's weird."

The sword dipped in my hands, suddenly heavier. Like the real thing. All that was absent was the cold, creepy sense of being watched by an inanimate object.

"I'll give her this one," I said. "We'll take the real thing back with us."

I opened the door into the entrance hall again, where my sister remained where I'd left her.

"You're going to take this," I told June, holding out the fake talisman. "You're not to tell her I gave it to you, and you're not to so much as hint that I or my friends had anything to do with it. You're going to go back to wherever she told you to meet her, and when she announces another attack on Summer, Winter, or both, you're not going to join the army. You'll find me instead."

A strangled noise escaped her, and her hands clenched around the sword's hilt. "I won't be able to tell you her plan. She'll slaughter me first."

"I don't need you to. I think I've worked it out."

The problem was, I was counting on Lady Whitefall not being here in person. Her magic would set any alarm in Summer blaring and unlike me, I doubted she'd consent to being turned into a non-magical being. She wanted to get into Summer, but only after bringing it down from the inside. And whatever had caused the explosion... if it caused half as much damage in Summer, she might not have any need for security talismans.

"Also," I added, "if you run into Aspen and are able to speak to him alone, tell him I want to meet him in confidence... and tell him we're amassing a collection of talismans of our own."

"Are you?"

"You'll have to work that one out for yourself, sister." I flashed her a smile. "She's a fool if she thinks I'll engage her on half-blood rules. I'm her equal, and I'm intending to snatch that little kingdom of hers right out from underneath her. I know she has pacts with other Sidhe outcasts. I won't meet her as anything less."

The light went out of her eyes as my words sank in. She believed me. Let her think what she liked. If the Courts thought I was a talisman-stealing thief who wanted a kingdom, like her, maybe I wanted them to.

"She'll never meet you on your own terms," June said. "Never."

"I think she'll be interested in what I have to offer."

Which wasn't a lot, to be honest. Aspen needed to be taken off the table, and if he thought we had our own collection of talismans, I doubted he'd be able to resist the bait. Even if not, I'd stolen another of Lady Whitefall's puppets out from under her nose.

"One last thing," I added. "You aren't to let any word of what I said slip to anyone you meet. Not to Aspen, not to her, not under duress. Also," I added. "You're not to use the real sword, or pick it up. At all."

"I swear," she croaked, lifting the fake sword. "It looks like the real thing."

"I know, right?" I smiled broadly, approaching the door outside. "Now, you're going to go and join her, and remember everything I told you."

She moved through the door, slowly, eyes downcast. I'd backed her into a corner, and hopefully she'd be too scared of incurring Lady Whitefall's wrath to risk letting anything slip.

Now for the real talisman.

Cedar's hand caught my sleeve the moment the door closed behind my sister. "You want to convince her *we're* amassing talismans?"

"She doesn't know me. For all she knows, we *could* be. Anyway, I want Aspen gone first. Once I'm away from his vow, they won't be able to pry another one out of me."

"I wouldn't underestimate any of them," said Cedar. "Aspen, though—I doubt he's as important to her as he thinks. She won't let him take the Court for himself. She's the one we should be worrying about, in the end. She can always replace her servants. It's not worth chaining yourself to them."

"I think it's the other way around." His stare was a little too penetrating. Maybe he understood a little of what I felt— or maybe he hated what I'd done. My mind was a whirlwind of anger and betrayal, starting with Aspen's vow and ending with June's claiming a talisman that should have been mine. For once in my life, I'd wanted to be the one in control of my own future before the Sidhe snatched it away from me. "We need to remove that sword."

"I have it." He held it up in gloved hands, and a jolt went through my chest. *Stop it.* Rationally, I knew I didn't want or even need the weapon, except to keep it out of Lady Whitefall's reach... but either my thief's nature or the weapon itself said otherwise.

"Then let's go." I opened the palace doors again. The snowy grounds remained undisturbed with no signs of my sister. Cedar sheathed the talisman at his waist, and I tried to avoid looking at him.

"Raine," he said, softly. "Don't take this the wrong way. I can't pretend to know what it was like having Lady Whitefall doctor your memories, but I *do* know how getting tangled in the Sidhe's mind games can turn you into something you're not. Being caught in a vow and unable to escape it—" He broke off. "Even the other way around, it binds you to the other person in a way that's impossible to escape. Your mother might even exploit your connection."

Bitter words rose on my tongue, and I bit the inside of my cheek to avoid speaking them. Of course he wouldn't want me using a vow on anyone. He'd been shackled to someone in the same way his whole life.

"You think I should have let her go free, or left her in the jail for my mother to let her out?" I asked. "Or killed her? It's their game. We play by their rules and exploit them for what they're worth, or they trample us flat. You said as much when I first came into Faerie. Lesson bloody well learned."

"That was *never* my intention," he said, walking closer to me. Too close. My fingers twitched as a spark like static zipped up my arm, alive and furious.

I stopped walking. "Cedar, can you feel the sword?"

"Feel it?" he asked.

"I think my magic's reacting to it." That was the only explanation I had for the raw emotion—avarice, tinged with bloodthirsty hunger for power. Even at my most pissed off, I'd never wanted power for power's sake alone. I'd wanted the Sidhe out of my hair. Forever. Not to turn into a half-blood clone of the mother who'd wrecked my life. "I'm pretty sure it's alive."

Cedar gave me a sceptical look. "Talismans aren't alive. They're powerful, but shaped by the will of the person who wields it. It's possible you still sense your sister's—"

"It was like that before. When I failed to win it over." I held up my hand, which bore the scars from where I'd held it the first time. "It's always felt different to the others. And how did it end up in the dungeon again when you moved it?"

"Good question, but it's not unusual for a faerie object to be bespelled in such a way. Perhaps that's it."

"If you say so." I took several steps away from him and continued to walk in silence for several moments.

"It's possible you picked up on something I didn't," Cedar said. "Your magic's from Winter, too, after all."

"Yeah, I couldn't sense the magic that destroyed the house

was Summer's," I said. "We must be more sensitive to similar magic to ours."

Cedar paused for a moment before saying, "What vow exactly did you swear to Aspen?"

Changing the subject wasn't like Cedar, but I said, "Obedience. As his prisoner, I was trapped in an iron cell. There was no way out other than swearing to obey him. I figured I'd say the words because I could run when I was out of the cage. I thought my will was stronger than his."

I stiffened as Cedar put an arm around my waist. "You are one of the most remarkably strong-willed people I know," he murmured. "Don't doubt it. You *can* beat her. But she's trying to push you to the brink, and she's been playing this game longer than both of us."

No kidding. As for Aspen, it was ridiculous that a vow, which didn't physically exist, was so much more powerful than both types of magic I possessed. It took a different kind of will to resist, the sort that urged me to snatch the sword from Cedar's hands and use it to take his life.

Maybe the only way to beat Lady Whitefall was to embrace the part of me who had come from her, after all.

13

"Wow," said Viola, staring at me across the table at breakfast. I hadn't omitted a single detail in my recount of last night's events—okay, aside from the part where I'd nearly attacked Cedar to take back the evil sword. Cedar himself had remained quiet while I'd told her, adding in the occasional comment. We'd arrived back late, and I'd spent a restless night in a guest room, tossed from one horrible dream to the next. Knowing the talisman sword was down the corridor from me, in Cedar's weapons cupboard, hadn't helped in the slightest.

"That about covers it." I picked at my food. "She blind-sided us. Attacked both Courts at once."

"So you have both June and Robin spying for you?" Viola didn't seem cowed about June *or* my rampant abuse of faerie vows. Of course, she'd been under commands herself, the whole time she'd been in Faerie. She wouldn't condemn the choices I'd made to keep her and the others safe.

"And Lord Lyle," I added. "But he's not so much spying as being a reluctant backup. Cedar saved his neck. He was nearly dead when we found him. They blew the house to pieces."

Her forehead pinched. "Blew it up?"

"With magic. Even Lord Lyle didn't know how." I paused. "She has her other talisman back, the one she nearly killed me with. But I still don't know what she stole from Summer, or if it caused the explosion. Cedar told me it was some kind of Summer magic."

"I can't think of any powerful enough to instantly kill multiple Sidhe," Cedar said. "Especially when they most likely had healing abilities."

"Shit, I didn't think of that."

"Damn." Viola winced. "You know you have a bunch of willing spies right here, don't you? I'll go into Winter to look for clues."

"No." I shook my head. "It's too risky."

"The soldiers already think we're going to war with the Vale."

"Shit, really?" I looked at Cedar.

"Yeah," she said. "Last night, a Vale ogre tried to breach the security. Some of the soldiers killed it, but they're worried. It's not the first time it's happened, but we're without a leader."

"I'll talk to them," Cedar said. "They need reassurance— I'm not surprised, considering."

He pushed to his feet and left the table. I looked at Viola and sighed. "I've really screwed this up. She wanted us to go to Summer so she could steal from Winter without being opposed."

"You couldn't have known," Viola said. "She's powerful and unpredictable, with the ability to turn anyone into an ally. But I'm trying to figure out her reasoning. I honestly think if she meant to kill us, she'd already have done so. If she can strike two Courts at once, she can strike here, too. She sent one ogre. That's hardly a battlefield."

"Don't speak too soon."

"No, I mean—think about it. She doesn't want to kill everyone, she wants to control us. Even when she had prisoners in the castle, she only killed Lord Hornbeam. She left everyone else alive, under her control."

"Ah." I nodded. "The hypnosis. It doesn't make sense for her to leave the remaining Hornbeam army alive, though. We turned on her. I *made* them turn on her."

"Yeah, I guess so," said Viola. "I'm not saying there won't be another attack, but we're not her priority. She wants the Courts. If she has Summer *or* Winter, she can stamp us out without lifting a finger."

"Not now we have Winter's security on our side."

"She doesn't know. Unless word's made it back to her overnight."

"Hmm." I considered the possibility. "I honestly don't know if she does have spies everywhere or if it's just a Sidhe thing. You know, where they give the impression they know absolutely everything about you, all the time. Of course, it might be because Aspen can dangle me like a puppet on strings."

"Not for long," said Viola. "Your will's stronger than his. He'll get his comeuppance."

"You bet he will."

Viola stood. "Right. I'm off to find Rose and see if I can persuade a couple of scouts to check out the latest in the Courts. They know to watch out for trouble, don't worry."

"And they don't have a price on their heads," I added. "All right. I'm going for a walk."

If the Hornbeam palace was to be my temporary home, I needed to figure out the directions. I walked around, memorising all the routes in and out, the gaps in the security—

everything that might be useful during an attack. I halted at the weapons room, which lay open on my right, and went to replenish my supplies.

One side of the room was given over to iron knives and arrows, but the rest of the room was filled with more standard faerie weapons, sharpened branches fashioned into swords. Like the one Cedar and I had transformed into a replica of the evil sword. Weird how convincing it'd been— almost like Cedar's glamour and my transforming ability had actually turned it into a proper talisman. Which was impossible. Talismans couldn't be made out of any old weapon. They were carved from the hearts of Faerie's most ancient trees, using spells the rest of us mere mortals could only guess at.

Right?

I selected a knife from the shelf, and blue light flared around it as I reshaped it to sword-length. I spun the new weapon in my hand. It was a pretty good replica, but definitely no talisman. Hmm.

"What are you doing in here?" called a male voice.

I turned to face the intruder. A silver-haired fae wearing armour and a crossbow strapped to his back like he'd just come off duty had entered the room.

"I'm having a look around." I tried to edge around him, but he moved to block my way.

"Were you at the Summer Court last night?"

Had Cedar told him? I erred on the side of caution. "That's between me and my confidants."

"You're not welcome here, whatever the others say." His hand tensed on his weapon.

"I don't have time for this," I said. "If you're betraying me, at least commit to it so I can jab an arrow through your eyeball."

"You can't—"

Ice sprang to my fingertips and formed a dagger against his throat. "Can't I?"

He paled, jerking back. "I'm not betraying you, but someone attacked the Summer Court. You were there."

"If you have spies following me, give it up. The most that'll happen is my mother's people will catch you and not me, and you'll die."

Behind him, someone shouted a warning. Screams drifted in from outside. My heart plummeted. *An attack?*

The soldier gave me one last glare. "You brought this on us, Whitefall."

I ran after him, still gripping my improvised weapon. Outside, soldiers ran in all directions, some shouting orders. I scanned the front yard, but saw no attackers inside the fences. The sounds of fighting came from the forest.

I sprinted out of the gates, calling magic to my hands. As a troll's club swung at a fae soldier, I aimed my attack at the tree behind him, which fell onto the troll, crushing it under its weight.

The Hornbeam soldiers had spread throughout the trees in a formation, crossbows out and knives in hand, firing on anyone who approached. An ogre tore at the gates, where a mass of plants blocked the way, sharp stinging nettles tearing chunks of flesh out of the creature's legs. *That's proper security for you.* Whoever thought Summer magic wasn't powerful hadn't seen a group of lethal plants take someone apart.

I conjured a handful of icy shards, which I threw at another troll's face. A tremor shook the earth, and the distant sound of howling wind engulfed the back of the palace. *They're attacking from behind.*

Cutting the troll's throat, I climbed over its body. I ran through the trees, circling the palace, and skidded to a halt. A whirlwind encased a section of the fence, surrounded by broken pieces of plant and other debris. Cedar was locked in battle with another faerie—half-blood or Sidhe, I couldn't tell from the back. The earth trembled again. *Damn. He has some kind of earth magic. He's going to break down the fence.* Parts of it lay in fragments, leaving the way into the palace wide open.

A scream came from my left, and an injured soldier crawled away from a long-limbed fae. As I ran forwards, it extended a branch-like arm and grabbed the soldier's neck. His mouth opened in a scream, his face—changing. Wrinkles spread across his face, shrivelling like a dead leaf, and he fell onto his front, dead.

The beast turned to me. Its long arms were like tree branches, deceptively brittle looking for appendages which had stolen life from someone with a single touch. It had a similar appearance to a skin-eating Vale fae, but appeared to be feeding on something else. Life force, maybe. Three more dead soldiers lay in its path.

"Get here," I growled. "Try picking a fight with me."

Magic surged from my hands, freezing the moisture in the air and earth, but the fae creature continued to advance on me, undeterred. Its feet must be made of blades to keep a grip on the ground, and icy shards didn't make a dent in its armoured bark-like coating. I aimed my magic at the dead plants instead, turning them into sharp weapons, but they bounced off its tough skin.

Long tendrils burst from its arms, surrounding me. Magic turned my clothes to armour, but it held on, tenaciously. If it touched my bare skin, I was dead. Struggling against its grip, I stepped back, falling into the set pattern almost unconsciously. Not that I needed it. I hadn't moved more than a step before magic blossomed from my hands, hitting the creature full in the face.

"Stop," I growled.

My hypnotic spell cast a glare over the fae's eyes. Its

branch-like arms fell to its sides. Swiftly, I stepped up and decapitated it. The creature collapsed into a heap of bark.

Cedar stumbled into my path, green light flaring around his arm, which was dripping blood. His attacker was bleeding, too. Green Summer magic shone from the male half-blood's eyes, and he wore armour the colour of bone.

"Hey, dickhead," I shouted, and threw a handful of icy shards in his face.

He didn't duck in time. The faerie yelled as the ice pierced his skin, shearing gaping holes in his face. Cedar lunged and tackled him to the ground. The earth shook beneath them, threatening to swallow them both up. I didn't dare throw my own magic into the mix. Thorny vines appeared and disappeared, forming a circle around the pair as they struggled against one another.

A flash of movement out of the corner of my eye drew my attention to a tree not ten metres away. Leaves rustled and the unmistakable buzz of someone using magic hummed through the air and the ground. Not from the attacker, but from behind the tree. Aha. That's why Cedar couldn't get a grip on the bastard. He had help from another faerie, hiding like a coward.

Swiftly, I raised my hands and used magic on the tree adjacent to the one I'd seen the movement behind. Branches creaked and fell. The attacker leaped aside as I fired magic at a root protruding from the ground. The root caught the female half-faerie in the face and she fell onto her back.

A yell from behind me told me Cedar had got the upper hand. I drew my knife and ran at the second one. She raised both hands, holding up a shield of shimmering green. Cloudy black hair surrounded her pale face, and her magic glowed green, shimmering in the air.

She brought her arms down in a sweeping motion and the shield dissolved into a current of air that sent me flying back a good five metres, narrowly missing colliding with the half-blood attacking Cedar. As I landed on my feet, the air attack hit the swirling magic surrounding the two of them. Cedar fell back, unable to keep upright as both air and earth shook with power. Too much power for one person.

I looked at the female half-blood, conjuring ice to my hands. "You're a tag team?"

Instead of answering, she sent a razor-sharp current of air at my neck. I ducked and rolled, throwing a wave of icy shards at her. My attack bounced off her armour. I struggled to stand, the earth shaking so hard my teeth rattled.

I rolled to the side, grabbing a tree for balance, calculating how best to help Cedar without putting us both in the line of fire. Every plant he conjured was immediately swallowed by the half-faerie's earth magic, while his partner circled from behind, her air magic tearing up the trees and pushing Cedar closer to his adversary. Trees tore up, and Cedar flew back, crashing into an oak trunk.

I threw more icy fragments at the earth faerie as he renewed his attack on the fence. Broken bits of dead plant surrounded him, and his partner's hands glowed green, conjuring a barrier of energy around the pair of them. Neither of our attacks could hit.

Cedar's palm slammed into the earth, and tree roots stabbed upwards out of the ground, only to smash into the air faerie's attack. The force sent me flying sideways, and Cedar disappeared from view. Sharp tree branches fell, aiming at my face.

I raised a hand and blasted them with blue energy, transforming the branches into spears aimed at the enemy instead. Green light mingled with blue as Cedar's magic hit mine—he must have used a spell at the same time.

Before my eyes, the branches fused together, the sharp edges blunting and turning into a living thing. *I didn't do that.*

Cedar's magic remained, and somehow—it'd connected with mine.

Like when we'd transformed the talisman.

A current of air, a miniature tornado, blocked the two half-bloods from view. Shards of dead plant rose in a frenzy, caught up in the whirlwind of her magic. As the earth faerie worked away at the gate, his partner had conjured a shield to stop us from attacking either of them.

The air faerie grinned wickedly, holding a shard of sharpened wood in her gloved hand, and hurled it at me. Air magic propelled the weapon, but I shot it with my own transformative power, and the shard exploded into fragments. She conjured another one, which I deflected. *Damn. I need to get them away from the palace.*

"Cedar!" I yelled. "Use magic when I say!"

He pushed to his feet, leaning on the nearest tree, bleeding heavily from one arm. "I can't—they're too strong. One of us will get hit."

"Trust me. Use magic when I say—now."

Blue light flared from my hands as green light shot from his, colliding with the sound of a thunderclap. The air faerie screamed as a deluge of plant fragments fell onto both her and her partner, burying them in a writhing tide, turning into a thorny net. I felt Cedar's magic guiding mine, and mine his, as the tornado died down, the earth stilled, and the net closed its grip around the two half-bloods.

I staggered forwards, the earth unsteady under my feet. "Who did that? Me or you?"

"Both of us." He stared at me a minute. "Did you know you could combine your magic with mine?"

"Not until I saw those two." I indicated the shards of plant spearing the two half-bloods. My magic had fused it together, but his magic had made it move like a living thing, crushing the two half-bloods between it.

"I'm fairly sure they're dead." I stopped. "And you're bleeding."

"It's healing," said Cedar. "How...?"

I slumped against the nearest tree, suddenly drained beyond belief. "I've no idea. I was just improvising. You know what we did to the sword, the one June took? I've never seen someone else be able to affect my magic before." Was it because our magic was compatible? Cedar and I had both used magic dozens of times, but never at precisely the same moment. As though in sync.

Cedar looked at me like the same thought had occurred to him. "It was good timing. Another minute and they'd have got into the palace grounds."

They'd already knocked down part of the fence. They could have killed half an army with that power.

"Who were they?" I murmured. "Was it them who blew up Winter?"

"I don't think so," Cedar said. "I'd know. The traces around the site of the attack weren't theirs."

"But they took the fence down without even using a talisman."

"Exactly." He grimaced. "If I had to guess, it's a new strategy of hers."

"And it worked." If she used two powerful half-bloods to blast her way into the Courts, maybe she didn't need a talisman after all.

But she doesn't know about us. What we can do.

Alone, my talisman's magic was powerful. With Cedar's, it was something else. A type I'd never seen before.

Maybe we'd held the key to beating her in our hands the whole time.

14

Lady Whitefall seemed to have had enough of attempted break-ins for now, and we spent most of the afternoon repairing the fence. The following day, I joined a patrol of the forest to look for threats, but found none. Nor the next day, either. Despite the lingering threat of another attack, my mother appeared to be suspiciously absent. And so did Cedar, most of the time. He claimed to be busy with security and spent a lot of time giving the other soldiers orders, but still apparently didn't want to commit to being their new leader. They certainly seemed to see him that way, though, hanging onto his every word. Two young teenage soldiers had also taken to following *me* around. It was weird, to say the least, after the army had spent so long trying to kill me on Lady Hornbeam's orders.

One morning, with nothing better to do, I decided to pay a visit to Cedar's private weapons room, where he'd put the talisman sword. I had no more clues on how we'd managed to conjure up our too-convincing replacement, much less the weird side effects of using our magic at the same time.

Unlike my own palace, the Hornbeam one seemed to contain no library with books on faerie history and weaponry, or anything else that might have given me some direction.

I pulled a thread from my jacket and transformed it into an improvised lock pick, and inserted it into Cedar's door. One twist, and it opened.

"You haven't lost your touch," Cedar remarked from the shadows. "Though I'll have to see if I can fix it. Most doors aren't immune to lock picks here."

"I figured," I said, turning to him. "How long have you been following me?"

"Since you left the barracks. Those two kids were tailing you, so I decided to make sure they didn't have ulterior motives."

"Nah, they don't want me dead. They just have crushes on me."

"It's unsurprising."

"Ha." I pushed the door open. "I saved their necks several times. I'd be worried if I didn't get a share of hero-worship." I stepped into the room, my gaze instantly going to the corner. Ice had spread in a circle around the cabinet Cedar had locked the sword in, as though it was making a valiant effort to get out.

"That's why you came here? You could have just asked me."

"I didn't know where you were, and I got bored." I shrugged. "The sword looks like it's about to break out."

"It can't. The magic of the palace keeps it contained. Though I have to say, it certainly doesn't behave like any other talisman I've encountered."

I looked at him. "Then you believe me?"

"I believe there's something different about it, but talismans can't be alive. Even Faerie has a limit, believe it or not."

"Okay, but you have a theory, right?" I tilted my head.

"I think it's possible talismans might absorb some of the personality of the person who carried it. Talisman owners take in the magic as part of themselves, so it makes more sense than the talisman itself being a separate consciousness."

"I guess so," I relented. "The sceptre sort of felt alive, when I first picked it up. I don't sense it now, but the magic's inside me, so I wouldn't."

A sudden chill settled around the base of my spine, and the vision from the witches' forest flashed before my eyes. And what about the times I'd used magic without consciously choosing what I planned to transform? No—it was instinct, like any other magic I used. Talismans weren't alive. Cedar's theory made more sense.

I took another step towards the sword, which lay dormant. My skin prickled all over. Its blade gleamed wickedly sharp, an invitation.

"Wish I could rip the magic straight out of it," I muttered. "Is it possible? I don't think we can get away with keeping it here forever."

"It's possible to destroy a talisman, but I suspect only the Sidhe could take apart that particular one."

I twisted my head to look at him. "You're serious. But—wait. You planned to destroy the sceptre, right? How, exactly?"

A silent moment passed. "Iron," he finally said. "A lot of it. If a talisman is surrounded by iron for long enough, its magic fades. I planned to bury it."

I couldn't believe it'd taken me this long to ask. In fairness, iron was the quickest way to destroy the magic inside a faerie, so it really ought to have been the logical conclusion. "I didn't know iron could destroy talismans. Destroy magic, yeah, but talismans are supposed to be indestructible."

"So are the Sidhe. Iron is their weakness. There's a reason Lady Hornbeam never actually touched any herself."

"What?" I stared at him. "You said she wanted to stamp out your weakness to it."

"And she did. But you were right, you know."

I blinked. "About what?"

"Being without iron. It's freeing. I've been able to use magic much more easily."

"Like what we did." I took in a breath. I hadn't only wanted to speak to him about the sword. "Cedar… how long have you been forced to carry iron?"

Confusion flashed across his features. "A while. Since I was old enough to hold a knife."

But of course. They induct their kids into the army at a young age.

"And how long have you been able to use magic?"

Still looking confused, he said, "Since I was a child. Why?"

"Cedar, you're half-Sidhe, for crying out loud—descended from one of the most powerful Sidhe in the border families. But until you threw the iron away, all you could do was move trees around. Since then, you've used glamour to fool Sidhe, sneaked us in and out of a noble's house without getting caught, and I don't want to know what else you can do with these killer plants. Wouldn't you have more ability, as Lady Hornbeam's son?"

"Not necessarily," he said. "Magic can be related to ancestry, but not always. Nothing I've done is exceptional for a Sidhe."

I poked him in the chest. "Cedar Hornbeam, you're so *dense* sometimes. You're the one who told *me* iron stops my magic working as effectively. Wouldn't the Hornbeams have reason to suppress the abilities of someone strong enough to depose them from their position of power?"

He shook his head. "I was never as powerful as Aspen, and *he* never managed to unseat her."

"You were a threat," I told him. "Your magic is off the

charts for a half-faerie. Face it, your mother never wanted you to think you were a contender. You were more useful to her as a thief. She felt threatened by your very existence. And so did Lord Hornbeam, in the end. And you know, from what I've seen, the others respect you. The soldiers. What if you offer them a better deal than the Grey Vale?"

"They will never accept me as heir," he said firmly. "I'm a thief, Sidhe or none."

I folded my arms. "Give them more credit. They rejected Aspen and Lady Whitefall. Risked their lives to do so. I reckon they'll follow us. This realm is in dire need of an overhaul, starting here. Half-bloods run to her because they have nowhere else to go. So we'll give them somewhere."

Cedar frowned. "That might work if we weren't wanted for murder."

"Just ask them. I guarantee nobody else will step forward. They're used to following orders."

"Maybe, but I never had any interest in becoming leader, and without a talisman, the family is vulnerable to being taken over by another. Or falling to her."

"Well, claim temporary leadership, then. Don't you want it? Your own talisman?"

"Do I want it?" He gave me a grim smile. "What I want is irrelevant. If I wanted to conquer and take Lady Hornbeam's place, I'd already have done it. I'd be in Aspen's place, prepared to usurp the Seelie throne."

"Cedar." I didn't like that tone coming from him. At all. "Claiming this house—your home, and your bloodline—isn't the same as world domination, for crying out loud."

"My bloodline?" He raised an eyebrow. "Half the others here might claim as much. Besides, there are no talismans. Lord Hornbeam saw to it. The closest I've been to a talisman is yours, and if I'd had ambitions to power, I'd have tried to claim it. As it is, Aspen holds two. That suggests he has more of a claim to leadership than I do."

"Not necessarily," I said. "I think it's more about compatibility. The sword rejected me and chose my sister. The sceptre picked me instead of the others. Because those particular talismans were right for us. I don't know. Don't forget Lord Hornbeam managed to get rejected by *all* of his wife's talismans, and he was pure Sidhe. You're more powerful than a talisman."

"I'm not sure if I should take it as a compliment that you're comparing me to an inanimate object." His gaze darted to the sword in the corner. "Have you heard from your sister yet?"

"Of course not. I'd have told you. She's supposed to give me a heads-up if Lady Whitefall launches another attack. I don't *think* I left a loophole in the vow, but..."

His jaw tightened. "I don't think Lady Whitefall is resting on her laurels."

"No, that'd be too much like a normal parent," I muttered. "Who raised you, anyway?"

He blinked. "Me? They have nurses to raise children. Any reason?"

"I haven't seen any children here, except those teenage soldiers," I said. "Seems weird."

"Neither Lord nor Lady Hornbeam had any children for a while," Cedar said. "Most are raised in the mortal realm. I can't say I know who's related to me or not... it's not seen as important. We're one family. All heirs, however, are potential rivals. They made that clear."

"Hmm." My gaze drifted to the talisman again. "I was wondering... is it uncommon for Sidhe from Winter to take a Summer faerie's talisman, or vice versa? Would it change your Court? It didn't for Lady Hornbeam."

"No, I don't think so," he said. "Perhaps it would for

someone with no magic at all. Otherwise the talisman's magic would add to your natural inherited magic as a separate kind."

I nodded. "Yeah, I thought so. Summer and Winter magic can be wielded by the same person. It's not like we're polar opposites. If it's possible to change Courts..."

And combine our magic into an impossible force...

"Any reason?"

"I think you know why." I took his hand, without warning, and a spark of magic jumped between us. "It has to do with why you've been avoiding me all week."

Behind us, the door creaked open. I dropped his hand, turning around.

"There you two are," said Viola. "I've been looking everywhere."

"Should have figured we'd find you cuddling somewhere," added Rose, a mischievous glint in her eyes.

"What's going on?" I looked from her to Viola, irrationally annoyed at the interruption, and conscious of the talisman sword behind me.

"We found out what Lady Whitefall stole from Winter," Viola said.

"What—the cause of the explosion?" I glanced at Cedar, who didn't catch my eye.

"A conduit," Rose said.

"What's that?" I asked.

"A specific type of talisman designed to hold magic to use later," explained Viola. "Not like a regular talisman, because the conduit works best when it doesn't have just one owner. Anyone's magic could be put inside it. Somehow volatile magic ended up inside it, and when it reacted—"

"It blew up the house?" Cedar finished.

"We're ninety percent sure," said Rose.

"Yeah," said Viola. "The conduit can store anyone's magic

—even if it belongs to someone else. It's like a giant storage device. She can use magic on someone without being near them at all."

"Shit," I said. Her hypnotic magic—or Aspen's—would be deadly in anyone's hands. "What if they put a Summer faerie's magic in there and used it to sneak into Summer's Court? Or the same for Winter?"

"Exactly," said Viola. "But Winter are furious. They're preparing for a potential war."

"It gets worse," said Rose. "Summer's Sidhe think Winter should take responsibility for their own outcast, and things are getting pretty heated out there."

There was a shout from downstairs. I jumped, as did Viola and Rose. "What was that?"

"No clue." Viola paled. "Shit, not another attack."

We left the weapons room behind, heading downstairs as swiftly as possible. Outside, a number of soldiers had gathered around the gate. Blue light flared in a circle, drawing my eye. My heart plummeted. Winter magic—I'd know that glow anywhere.

The crowd parted to let me through, to see the piece of parchment lying on the ground just inside the gate. In elaborate font were the following words: *I would very much like to speak to you, daughter. Come to the palace today, and nobody else will need to die.*

15

"What does it say?" Viola looked at me expectantly.

"She invited me to my own palace." I dropped the note, which disintegrated into glitter. "To talk to her."

Viola made a sceptical noise. "What, to negotiate? Or play head games?"

"Maybe she wants to win me over." It seemed more likely. "If it's a meeting she wants, maybe I can talk her out of going to war. Or lock *her* in the dungeon. The palace's magic is as much mine as hers. It won't act against me."

"But it might be a trap," said Viola.

"True," I acknowledged, "but don't forget Lord Lyle is compelled to help me on Winter territory. That includes the palace. If she brings her army through, she'll run right into an ambush. And there's no way she actually knows about our agreement."

"Then don't go alone," Cedar said. "Even on the off-chance that the Unseelie forces manage to corner her, she's too unpredictable."

"She's in my house," I said. "Besides, she has a thing for turning us against one another. I won't put you in danger—you neither, Viola."

"I never said I was coming inside," said Cedar. "But I'm not letting you face her alone."

I folded my arms. "She wants me on her side. She'd kill you without a second thought. I guarantee I'm part of her plans, and I'd rather be forewarned than blindsided again. And I'd definitely prefer to confront her on my territory rather than hers."

"I can turf her people out. I'm housekeeper," said Viola. "The palace can't act against me, either."

"All right, but you'll have to stay out of her sight. You know what her magic does, and you're not immune."

"No," said Viola. "But *she* thinks I am."

Cedar frowned at her. "You're not?"

"She gave me her transforming magic, not the hypnosis. Technicality."

"A technicality I hope she doesn't exploit," Cedar said. "She has more than enough allies, and I don't think she's ruled out taking the Hornbeam palace yet."

"Still doesn't mean she's strong enough to take the Court," I said. "I'd like to know what she's been doing for the last week. And Aspen. If *he's* there, I'll kill him, peaceful meeting or none. We shouldn't waste any time."

I looked down at my clothes. I didn't know if she expected me to dress for the occasion, but I turned them to armour, anyway. Viola already wore hers, as did Cedar.

Rose stepped forwards and briefly embraced Viola. "I'll be on guard," she said.

"Better be," said Viola. "We don't know if she's planning another attack. Have the army ready just in case. Wait for my signal."

Several other soldiers had begun to gather. As we made

for the gate, they followed behind me, remarkably quiet for people wearing heavily armoured clothes. I turned around, letting the others walk ahead. "Yes?"

I expected one of them to stop me, but they fell silent, watching me warily. Much like they'd watched me when I had them under hypnosis.

"I'm not hypnotising you," I clarified, in case there was any confusion on that front.

"You're leaving. To meet with *her.*" The silver-haired soldier who'd confronted me in the weapons room glared at me.

"To see if I can get her to stop attacking us without any more deaths," I said. "If not…"

"How do we know you won't join her and take over our palace?" asked another.

"Because I've no interest in ruling over your territory. Cedar has more of a claim to it than I do."

"But you want us to fight for you?" asked the crossbow-carrying guard who'd initially let Cedar and me into the palace.

"I want you to do what you did in the Grey Vale," I told them. "Defend your territory. Fight the Vale invaders. You've done it more than once already."

Most looked frightened, but they weren't cowards. The true cowards had betrayed their family for Lady Whitefall, and let her seduce them even knowing what she was like. These soldiers were a different story. They just needed an incentive.

"You want to do something useful?" I said. "Take off your iron weapons and replace them with non-iron ones. Then use the iron to make a defensive barrier around your territory. Even she won't be able to cross it."

"But we can't use it to fight," said a confused-looking teenage male.

"That's the idea. You might as well put it to use as a shield. Iron stops your own magic from working, so it'll stop hers. Did you see what she did to the fence, using her soldiers' magic?"

Several of the soldiers exchanged whispers, but nobody looked like they disagreed with me. They'd seen, all right.

"The iron won't drain your magic if you aren't touching it," I explained. "Lady Hornbeam wanted you to be weaker than she was. Not capable of challenging her."

"But iron kills," said the silver-haired soldier. "Wouldn't it work on Lady Whitefall?"

"As far as I know, yes," I said, "but how many people have died from iron poisoning since she started forcing you to carry it? Besides, don't forget she can hypnotise anyone who gets within range of her. No iron weapon would counter it. All it does is stop your own magic working. If you want to stay alive, then do what I say—or what Cedar or Viola says. Got it?"

Several murmurs of assent followed. *That's done, then.* Quickly, I left their territory to catch up with the others.

As we neared the palace, I motioned for Viola and Cedar to stay back. If Lady Whitefall knew I was accompanied, she might unleash her army. I walked calmly to the doors, which opened as though operated by an invisible hand. She wasn't waiting inside. Weird. Had she hidden somewhere and left a trap, or was she expecting me to play hide-and-seek in the palace? I was fairly sure I had foggy memories of doing so as a kid. Maybe the real reason she wanted to meet here was to use my past against me. I just hoped she was as clueless as me about where Dad really was.

I turned on the spot in the vast entrance hall. "Where are you?" I called, my voice echoing. "I think I'm a little old for hide-and-seek."

"In here, daughter," said a soft voice.

A door appeared in the wall beside me, and opened before I could touch it. On the other side was the absurdly over-sized living room. Lady Whitefall sat elegantly on the sofa, dressed in one of her usual sharp ice-white outfits—a mix of beauty and danger, a force of nature contained inside the semblance of a person. Her pointed ears, impossibly beautiful face, and above all, the magic pouring off every inch of her, were as far from human as possible. The bright blue eyes were mine. So was the white hair, an elegant sweeping curtain down to her waist. A silver and blue circlet glinted in the centre of her forehead, reminiscent of the sceptre's design. She looked every inch the queen she thought she was. The mortal part of me froze in terror. The faerie part wanted to strike her down.

I tensed when she finally looked at me. I'd turned half her army against her the last time we'd met, and she'd responded by having her soldier fatally stab me. I doubted she'd be in an amiable mood, yet she neither smiled at me nor frowned, her expression carefully neutral.

"I like what you've done with the place," said my mother. Her tone was just as measured as her expression. What reaction did she expect from me? Did she think we had a fresh start, or was this some new game?

I shrugged. "You left it to me. Which technically means you're trespassing, but we both know you don't give a shit about rules. What do you want with me, then?"

"I merely came to return this." She held out the sceptre.

I didn't take it. "I thought you worked out it's a prop."

My mother laid the sceptre on the table. "Perhaps, but it's a beautiful creation, whoever made it."

She really does think it's the fake one? She'd ripped the magic out of someone, but she didn't know it could be removed from a talisman? It made no sense. I'd be a fool not to press my advantage, and yet... her being here seemed wrong. She knew magic intimately in a way I, as a half-blood, never would. Or so I'd thought.

"Rather like the one your thief created," she added.

Oh hell. She knew Cedar had faked the other talisman, at least.

I kept my expression blank. "The thief isn't mine."

"You haven't used your magic on him? It's quite easy. You inherited more of the gift than I expected. You can make him do whatever you want him to."

"Is there any part of this where I'm not meant to think you're deranged? Or insulting me?"

"I thought you took pride in being partly human, and mortal," she said.

"Yeah," I said. "I do." Was she trying to goad me into bringing up Dad? He wasn't here. Surely she'd have paraded him in front of me if she'd had him captive. "Cut the charade. Where are your people hiding in here?"

"Nowhere," she said calmly. "I'm sure your thief isn't here. Though he could leave if he wanted to, since you failed to bind him."

"Why are you so interested in whether I've hypnotised people?"

She laughed. "So you're human still. No faerie queen would rule a Court with anything less than absolute obedience… unless you don't have a Court but merely a collection of outcasts."

"I'm pretty sure Summer and Winter don't hypnotise every single one of their subjects. They don't need to." I looked her pointedly in the eyes.

She got my meaning and her eyes narrowed a touch. "Well, daughter, I think you'll find ensuring loyalty is trickier than it seems. The Courts assume too much. That's how people slip through their fingers. The will of the Sidhe is not immutable."

"Speak for yourself." I lifted the sceptre from the table. "I'll take this back, if you tell me what you really want."

"To know how you removed its magic." Her hand reached out and brushed the sceptre. "It's the real thing, as beautiful as the day I found it. The talisman's power was locked inside the sceptre, and only I could remove it. Even if you managed to win the talisman over, taking the power *out* of the sceptre would only have been possible if you somehow found its opposite—that is, another talisman which syncs with yours."

"What?" I stared blankly. "I've no idea what you're talking about." The talisman's magic had joined me of its own accord...

Oh shit.

Cedar. He'd held the sceptre longer than I had. Our magic had connected—several times, including...when he'd pressed it into my hands in the arena to let me take the power.

Had the fact that we'd both handled it somehow unlocked the magic and allowed me to take it out of the talisman? Viola and I had the same magic, and I hadn't noticed anything unusual when we'd used magic in sync to break out of jail. No... Cedar and I were compatible—or rather, his own magic was in sync with the magic I'd pulled from the talisman.

I kept my face blank, but a tremor ran through my fingers. She *did* know magic better than I did. I'd made the mistake of assuming the sceptre worked like any other talisman... and even Cedar had. But it was something else entirely.

She smiled. "You truly didn't know? I confess it took a while for that small detail to reach me, but Aspen has been most helpful in aiding me in narrowing down my list of potential suspects whose magic enabled you to remove the talisman's magic."

My heart beat faster. *Cedar.*

"For one thing," she said, "there are only a limited number of witnesses to the stunt you pulled in the Hornbeams' territory when you took the magic from the talisman and used it to kill Lady Hornbeam. Right?"

"Not really," I said, with an attempt at a casual shrug. "Their entire family was present, plus people from other families who'd been forced to serve Lady Hornbeam. The thing about coercing people into serving you is that they're not loyal. You haven't won them over. And they left, after she died. Lord Hornbeam hardly had an army left. That's how you overcame him. Don't think overcoming the main Courts will be so easy."

"You aren't curious to know whose magic assisted you?"

"I think you're talking crap to divert my attention," I said. "Maybe you didn't know the sceptre as well as you thought. Or it decided to turn on you for abandoning it here when you faked your death."

"I think it's in your interests to cease this petty rebellion, child. I can guarantee you safety in my Court, as my ally."

"What you're talking about is a coup, an invasion, and a load of shit I don't want to be involved with," I said. "Though I don't get why you aren't making more of an effort to be there in person. I thought you thrived on attention, unless you're scared of getting your hands dirty."

"You think I merely want the Courts?" She laughed softly. "Dearest daughter, you of all people know there's more to Faerie than two insular gatherings of paranoid Sidhe."

My mouth parted. On what planet was taking over two Courts only a small step? What was bigger than that? I couldn't think straight. Not with the knowledge that what Cedar and I had done... if we could harness the power against her, we could win this fight. But if she guessed the truth first, she'd rip the magic from us while our hearts still beat.

"Whatever you're scheming, it won't work," she said. "I'm currently in possession of a rather dangerous artefact, one I won't hesitate to use against you."

"The conduit," I said. "Who has it, Aspen? I hope you'd have more sense than to let him carry a bomb around. He's a spoilt brat who'd dethrone you if he had half the chance."

"He has his uses. Scouting your weaknesses out is one of them. You freed your magic from the talisman using another's help, and I intend to find out who. I came here to ask you to pick a side. You have my magic. You'll wield it for me one way or another, but I'd prefer to give you the choice. You chose to step into this world, so the consequences are on you if you pick the wrong one."

"You're deluded if you think I'll come anywhere near your side if not to stab you in the back," I told her. "I'm staying here. This palace is mine, and so is the magic you thoughtlessly gave up."

"Very well." She rose to her feet. "I'd hoped that being in the place you spent your childhood would change your mind, but you're too set in your ways."

"I spent my childhood in the mortal realm. That's who I am."

"You don't look human," she said, tilting her head. "Humans are fragile, beautiful things. You have a heart of stone."

I laughed. "Says the person who created an ice palace. I don't suppose you'd like to free those people you imprisoned in the entrance hall?"

"I thought you'd gone beyond setting fragile mortals free," she said. "Then I'm sure you won't mind if I extend the same invitation to your father as I just offered to you."

Dad. "Tell me where he is," I said.

"The decision is yours, daughter," said Lady Whitefall. "If the Courts' peril, the precarious nature of your position and your father's safety aren't enough to convince you, then I look forward to seeing you on the battlefield again. I have my own Court to return to, but before I do, I must ask you once again to consider joining me. If not… the consequences will become clear very shortly."

"You know my answer."

"Then I will meet you as my equal, daughter, for what it's worth," Lady Whitefall said. "If you have a change of heart, seek me in the Grey Vale. The entrance in the dungeon will take you right to my palace."

I should have known she'd put a sting in the tail somewhere. Not that I had any intention of remaining at the palace knowing the door was there, but it was the ultimate temptation. Walk through the doors to her, and end the war, one way or another.

It'll never end. Not as long as she lives, and her hunger for power grows.

A scream came from outside the front door, which I'd left open. I tensed, my hand going to my weapon.

She smiled. "I do hope your friends are safe."

"Oh, we will be," I said in a low voice. "You picked the losing side, mother."

16

Once outside, I broke into a run. It wasn't long before I found the source of the screaming—a circle of dead hobgoblins, shot down by Cedar's arrows. Viola pulled a dagger from one of them. "Little bastards."

"I expected worse," I said, spinning around to face the palace again. The gates had shut. "Oh, for the Sidhe's sakes. She just wanted to lock me out."

"What's she doing in there?" Viola asked. "Did she give you any clues?"

"Well, we can't move back in," I said. "She told me the Grey Vale entrance leads right into wherever her lair is on the other side. I also have to go there and join forces, or face her across the battlefield."

"But she gave you the sceptre back?" asked Cedar.

"Almost compensates for her being my immortal enemy." I needed to tell him about our magic—and what we'd unknowingly done. But if she found out... she'd take him away and lock him into a vow or kill him. I'd never let that happen.

I turned my back on the palace, and we walked back through the forest. There didn't seem to be much point in sticking around. My mind was made up, as was Lady Whitefall's. She hadn't brought up June or Robin, so I assumed she was unaware I had spies on her side yet.

"So she didn't give you any new information?" Viola asked.

"Nope," I said. "Not really. She confirmed what we knew, about the conduit, but didn't give away who's actually carrying it. Then she suggested I'm better off joining her, because she'll run me down on the battlefield and swipe my magic from my corpse."

"So she doesn't want you as an ally, then?" asked Cedar.

"I doubt it matters to her. If I'm with her, she gets my magic. If I'm against her, she gets it anyway. I'm a stepping stone. She has other plans first. Like the Courts. And unless we get our own army, going into the Vale after her is suicide."

"Maybe," said Viola, "but we have an army. Her former army, actually. I reckon we have a shot."

"About that," I said. "She must have gathered new forces. Where'd she find those half-bloods who attacked last week?"

"She's raiding the mortal realm?" Cedar suggested.

"I've always found it suspicious that none of the other families have challenged us since the Hornbeams," said Viola. ""I think her half-blood army is mostly defectors from other families who were outcast or killed by Lady Hornbeam. Like the Blackwaters. I haven't heard a word from any of them since she died."

"There are others who haven't been heard of in a year or so," Cedar said. "We all thought Lady Whitefall died, so nobody would have guessed others would have gone to join her in the Vale. After all, there were no Gatherings for a year, and every family was focused on its own affairs. She duped us without even using magic."

"Her death was pretty damn convincing," said Viola. "With witnesses. And knowing what we do—she fled around the time the Courts had started investigating whether any Sidhe had ties to the rogues in the Grey Vale. Which she did. I can't help thinking it's partly my fault for not realising she was still alive. Her magic kept the palace standing. I thought it wasn't affected by her death because the talisman had all her magic in it."

"It wasn't your fault," I said. "She vanished for a year after faking her death. Besides, I wouldn't have come here if you hadn't." A tugging sensation grabbed at my chest, and I stopped. "Shit. I can sense..."

"The vow?"

Blue light shone from my hands. "Not Aspen's. My sister —she's back."

I picked up speed, walking through the trees, following the tugging sensation.

"What do you mean?" asked Viola.

"I told her to come and find me when my mother makes her next attack on the Courts," I said over my shoulder. "Of course she ordered them to do it while I was at the palace. Couldn't leave us alone, could she."

Sure enough, the moment we crossed into the Hornbeams' territory, my sister ran up to us, eyes wild.

"It's starting," she gasped. Her nose dripped red. "She ordered me to fight you. I can't disobey for long."

I punched her on the jaw. "Does that fulfil the vow's requirement, or do you have to hit me back? Was she specific about *who* to fight?"

She blinked, looking confused, then swung wildly at me and missed. "I guess it does."

"Word of advice: most vows have a way around them," I told her. "Hers included. And mine's the better deal, trust me. Can you tell me where she's attacking?"

"Her people are inside Lord Niall's house again. Aspen's leading the army."

"You gave him my message, right?"

"He said…" She doubled over, coughing. "He said he'll come to your doorstep with your father's head."

A ringing silence followed her words, reverberating in my chest. Magic sprang to my hands, igniting along my nerve endings. "If he does," I said, "tell him that his death will last a thousand days, and I'll make sure he's begging for mercy every second of them. And if you fight on his side against me, you'll meet the same end."

June stumbled back, her face paling. "I—I can't—"

Her body spun around as though pulled by invisible strings, and she ran into the trees, disappearing out of sight.

"Raine?" Viola said from behind me. "Don't yell at me, but I think it's a trap."

"Of course it is," I said. "But June's vow stops her lying to me. She's telling the truth. And we already knew he was probably in Summer."

"She'll be counting on you being desperate enough to fall into a trap," Cedar said. "I don't think it's wise to barge in there, even with security down."

"I planned to sneak in through the tunnels, actually," I said. "I remember where the entrance is. If you're planning a lecture, save it. This won't stand. I won't let it."

She'd done the one thing I couldn't ignore. Half-blood or not, my father wasn't strong enough to survive Faerie. She might have cared about him once, but she'd also cared about me. And Aspen wanted nothing more than to punish me.

"Raine," said Cedar. "If you're going to do this, we can't go alone. The two of us against an army, even on the side of Summer—the odds of us getting caught and arrested by our own side before we can deal a blow to the enemy are too great. And I wouldn't put it past Lady Whitefall and Aspen to play that up. Aspen—he was always cruel, even as a child. This is nothing more than a game to him."

Yeah, I know. He didn't just want me dead—that'd spoil the fun. He wanted to humiliate me first, to strip me of all dignity like he had the first time I'd fallen under his control.

"Then you want to bring the army?" I asked.

"Exactly." Cedar looked at Viola, who nodded slowly. "The Hornbeam family will fight for the Court, if I ask them to."

"I thought you had no interest in leading an army."

"I can't guarantee they'll all follow me," he said. "I refused to have them swear vows, so there's the risk that they might leave, but I never did figure out Lady Hornbeam's trick to keeping hold of a hundred soldiers' vows at once. Only a Sidhe can handle so many without letting them slip away. I suspect Lord Hornbeam lost control of so many of his soldiers because he struggled with that very issue. But you were right—they're the best shot we have at beating her."

I nodded. "They're loyal. And if not, it's okay. The world won't end if a couple of them run away. They're scared of me."

"They respect you," he corrected.

"I guess they do." I hadn't thought about how strange it was. I'd faced envy and anger and fear from other half-bloods before, and outright hostility, but respect... that was a new one.

Unlike my mother, who ruled through fear alone. Not loyalty. The moment she died, her people would scatter. But that didn't make her—or Aspen—any less dangerous.

When we reached the palace, Cedar strode ahead, where soldiers gathered near the gate. Looked like they'd actually taken my advice and built a wall of iron around the outside of the fence.

"Soldiers," he said loudly. "Come with me. I'm calling an

emergency meeting for everyone able to fight. Come to the front of the palace."

They came in groups—some archers, some sword-carrying warriors, even the servants. Though of course, everyone here could defend themselves. Their weapons were polished wooden bows and bone-coloured knives that resembled sharpened tree branches, but nevertheless looked deadly enough to put someone's eye out. The Hornbeams in warrior mode were a sight to behold, and without the iron, the presence of their magic was more obvious, too. A net of green light surrounded the lines of soldiers, and their skin glowed with it as though lit from beneath.

"We've received word that the heart of the Summer Court is under attack," said Cedar. "I believe it's our duty to defend them."

"When you say the heart of the Court, you mean the Erlking?" asked one of the soldiers.

"Perhaps," Cedar said. "The army of the Vale is trying to breach the security around the Summer Court's centre."

"Lady Whitefall?" called the silver-haired faerie who apparently didn't like me.

A dozen heads swivelled in my direction.

"Is she the one who told you?" asked another, with suspicion in his voice. "Because she's not part of our Court. She might be deceiving you, to make Summer turn against us. They don't like us, not after Lady Hornbeam angered so many of them."

"We know because I spied on them," said Rose loudly. "The Vale faeries stole some talismans from Winter and Summer and plan to use them to attack both Courts. We've never fought on Summer's side before, but there's a first time for everything."

I gave her a grateful look.

"That," said the first speaker, "is because every single time another family from the Summer Court requested our aid in the last Sidhe-knows-how-many-years, Lady Hornbeam declined. None of us have set foot in there, save for her select few nobles, and…" His gaze lingered on Cedar, probably because he'd guessed he'd been sent in there to steal things. So the Summer Court had requested assistance before, and the Hornbeam Family had ignored it? Or specifically—Lady Hornbeam had. She'd sat in this palace, building an iron army, hoarding all her magic for herself. No wonder the Court hated her.

The real question was whether they'd be willing to put those differences aside and accept help from her former soldiers.

"We haven't got any time to lose," I said. "We'll go first—Cedar and I. We know the way in. I don't think all you guys should come into the palace the same way. It's not technically legal."

"The route only opens to me," Cedar added. "The rest of you will have to approach from the front and sides."

He gave them all directions with the expertise of someone who'd done this before. Viola chipped in a few times, too, but it made sense for her to know how things worked, seeing as she'd been part of their army for years. The army divided into groups, ready to spread through the forest as they would during a battle on their own territory. As they organised themselves into lines, I edged closer to Cedar.

"Since when did you know how to direct an army?" I whispered.

"It's impossible to live in the Hornbeams' palace and not pick up some general directions. Besides, as I said, I know Summer's Court. The issue, of course, is that Aspen does, too. And he'll have received more in-depth instructions than I did. We're relying on him not knowing we had the audacity to bring an army."

"He won't expect it," I said. "He underestimates us both—you especially. I don't think he's said one word about you, not even as an heir. He has blind spots like anyone. I honestly think he forgot all about the Hornbeam family and his old duties the second she took him in. He didn't know anyone would try to escape."

"No, he expected to be able to lead them," Cedar said. "He even underestimated Lord Hornbeam's ability to keep control of his forces. More stayed than deserted, and it cost him in the end."

"True." I paused. "I guess he thought if a Sidhe couldn't claim a talisman, he wasn't worthy to serve."

"Aspen will change his mind when he finds out I'm commanding the army," he said. "I suspect it's a sore point, seeing as working for Lady Whitefall was supposedly meant to bring him control over that very army—on her orders. As it is, I think the only way to bring down Aspen is for him not to realise you're there. Hide amongst the other soldiers, and I'll have them distract him so he can't use the vow to lure you out."

"Are you sure?"

He bowed his head. "Of course."

He didn't say the words I read in his eyes—that he wanted to stop me from falling under Aspen's control again. Even with my clothes altered to look the same as the other soldiers', I stood out too much. Glamour did nothing. I'd walk into battle as Lady Whitefall, one way or another.

Cedar and I walked ahead of the rest of the army, with Viola and Rose not far behind. The former knew the army's workings as well as Cedar did and had helped with putting the various groups into order. The archers were trained to fight in the forest with stealth, so the plan was for them to fan out into the woods near the palace and find a good vantage point to fire on Aspen's forces.

I was so caught up in the rhythm of our beating footsteps on the forest floor, it took me completely by surprise when someone ran onto the path in front of us. Robin, dishevelled and gaunt, and entirely too late for a warning.

"Don't even think about it," I told him, glancing behind me. Cedar halted, but I ignored Robin and kept walking.

"Wait." Robin stumbled after me, reaching for my arm. "Don't go to Summer."

I yanked my arm away, twisting to face him. "I've made my mind up."

He shook his head urgently. "It's a setup."

"Obviously. I've been told the truth by someone who can't lie, and my dad's in danger from Faerie *again.* So stay out of this one."

"I didn't know about Winter, I swear," he said. "I didn't mean—"

"I didn't mean to steal your fucking magic, Raine, it was an accident." My words were acid, and the air froze as my magic ignited in my hands. It took everything I had to keep hold of it and not unleash my transforming power over the surrounding forest.

Robin went pale as a ghost. "Raine—"

"Robin," I said. "I'd go away. Now."

He did. Quickly. I breathed out, willing my magic to switch off. I didn't really want to punish Robin anymore. It looked like my mother had discarded him already, and all the vengeance in my heart was trained on Aspen.

I looked back at Cedar. "Cedar, c'mon. We need to move."

He shook his head. "This is—this is a hasty decision."

"Please don't tell me you believe him over me," I said through gritted teeth. "If my dad's not there—even if he isn't, she's trying to usurp a throne. We've been through the risks. I'll hide out with your army in the forest for long enough to get near Aspen without him using the vow. Then…" I mimed cutting someone's throat.

The vow was all that stood between me and getting the talismans away from him, away from her, before she destroyed the Courts.

Cedar's mouth tightened. "That would be the ideal scenario, but merely being forewarned isn't enough. There's doubtless more we don't know about the whole setup."

"Then stay. I'm getting my dad out one way or another, Cedar. I thought you wanted me to reject her and actually give a toss about other people."

A pained expression crossed his face. "There's no chance of going in there without exposing ourselves to Summer. If we win, you'll die or be exiled. If we lose—you'll die, or be hers for the remainder of your days. Then it won't matter if I survive. I'm next on her list."

My throat closed up. *You don't know how true that is.* I had no time to confide my suspicions, not when I didn't see any way our combined magic could outdo the spell Aspen had me under.

My voice was steely when I spoke. "Then we'll give them a battle they'll never forget. Summer will owe me a life debt if we win. I don't know if that'll outdo the price on my head, but dammit, Cedar, I'm not giving up before we've started. It's not me. If it was, I wouldn't be here."

The Sidhe thrived on forcing us into impossible choices. But I'd never regret standing up to Sidhe like my mother, in death or otherwise. She could call me a foolish mortal with a death wish all she liked, but words were meaningless now. Only action mattered. I might be on the losing team, but I'd rather die out there than spend a second on *her* side. And I'd tear the world down to rescue Dad.

Cedar met my eyes and nodded. "All right."

"I can say I'm leading the army," Viola put in. "I'm not

wanted by either Court. Summer doesn't know me. And I'm under no obligation to tell them the truth."

She didn't like to lie. That she'd do so for me… it meant more than words could say.

"Me neither," said Rose. "We can protect your identity. You know, on the off chance you get through the battle without using Winter magic."

"I wouldn't bet on it," I said. "But thank you. Come on. We need to move."

Our steps quickened. An odd silence lay heavy in the air. Not an absence of noise, exactly… more like something very loud had obliterated it. The smell of burning magic came from the Summer Court.

My heart sank. *We're too late. She used the conduit again.*

17

I carried on walking towards the smell of burning. If she'd hit the Court's centre, we'd be in real trouble, but from the sting of smoke in the air and the smell of burning magic making my eyes water, the explosion had taken place much closer. Before we'd reached the meadow at the end of the path, Cedar stopped dead.

A crater had opened in the meadow's centre, and bodies were sprawled on the exposed earth and the remaining grass surrounding it. Fae of all kinds—and a few Sidhe, with their horses, too—lay burned with awful wounds. Magic circled their bodies, a web of green light already unravelling. Death had been brutal but swift, and even the flowers had shrivelled and died.

"The conduit," said Cedar. "It has to be."

"I take it she changed her mind about using it to break into the Courts." I swallowed, hard. "This is—this is a meaningless attack. She wants us running scared."

And Aspen wasn't here. I didn't feel the pull of the vow at all. Unless he'd gone into Lord Niall's estate again. If so, he'd left a conspicuous trail behind him.

"June said the estate was the target, and she can't lie." I had to keep repeating that to myself. She couldn't have lied. Didn't mean there weren't more ambushes lying in wait, but Aspen's army had targeted the Sidhe first.

"This was a power play," Cedar said softly. "He targeted the place where the Summer Court overlaps with the mortal realm, too."

"Not subtle, is he?" I murmured. He couldn't have possibly said more clearly that he intended to destroy all semblance of peace in the Courts.

Not if I can help it.

The forest remained intact, untouched by the blast. Sunbeams through the canopy made striped patterns on our path. Under the decaying magic and horrible aftershock of its impact, life thrived, the web of magic which kept the forest alive. Summer might look shaken, but the power and strength of their magic remained in every living thing. They'd strike back—hard. I just had to hope they'd hit the right target. Not Winter—and not me.

"Looks like Viola's telling the other soldiers what happened," I whispered, hearing voices further back. "I hope they don't run away. The conduit's magic is beyond what they've faced before, even in the Vale."

"They won't flee," said Cedar. "If anything, they'll be more determined now."

"I hope you're right."

The lack of the Sidhe's presence suggested they must be fighting the enemy. In the central Courts, the families weren't rivals but allies. An attack on one of them was an attack on Summer itself. But my dad, caught in the middle of that—I had to get him out.

Cedar reached the huge tree first, using magic to part its roots and reveal the way into the tunnel we'd exited through last time. Behind, I heard Viola giving orders to the others to surround the palace and intercept any enemies who got out. The real danger was that the Hornbeam army might get mistaken for being with the enemy, too. After all, they hadn't come to aid Summer in years.

A small group of soldiers followed us into the hidden passageway, which was more cramped and uncomfortable than I remembered. If we hadn't used the passage before, we'd never have known the exit was here. I glanced around, my skin prickling. Summer's magic overwhelmed mine, making it difficult to tell if my instincts were right. Had Aspen been in here?

Cedar hissed out a breath. "Something's wrong with the magic in here."

"You sure?"

He nodded. I backed up. "Guys, we need to get out."

"Sidhe's blood," Cedar said in a low voice. "It's below the earth. Move. *Now.*"

The soldiers obeyed without a word, faster than I'd have expected considering the tight space. We backed out of the tree's shadow, and a whistling noise rang through the air.

Then a deafening blast went off. My ears rang as a torrent of earth rose up, trees torn from their foundations, crashing into one another. Cedar held out his hands, green light slowing down the crashing trees and preventing them from causing more damage. I sensed other Summer warriors doing the same. A current of green magic encased the forest, pushing the explosion back, away from the estate.

My stomach turned over. The palace's entire left side was *gone*, burned black and unrecognisable. That included the tree at the back concealing the way out, and the place Aspen had forced me to dance. Bile rose in my throat. It was the smell of burning faeries I could smell, under the decaying magic. Had we stayed in the tunnel, it'd have been us.

"Soldiers," Cedar said quietly. "The palace's defences are

down. You can take up position anywhere within easy reach of the surviving part of the entrance hall and grounds, but remember—if you sense anything like that magic, get out. Save your own lives first. Got it?"

An answering murmur went through the group. Amazing. He hadn't used a vow, hardly a command until now. The Hornbeams were the definition of loyalty—and I'd never thought I'd even think that of the family who'd been the first to teach me the brutality of this realm.

Cedar and I crept around the palace, making for the gate. As I predicted, nobody guarded it. The few Sidhe nearby lay in the mud, knocked flat with the force of the blast. By trying to kill us, Aspen had inadvertently given us a cue to enter without being stopped by the guards.

The doors to the palace lay bare, hanging from their hinges, revealing the chaos within. Bolts of green magical energy filled the air, and the floor was a mass of writhing plants. Hobgoblins held up fragile shields against falling bits of the collapsed ceiling, while arrows criss-crossed the air, striking down faeries on both sides. Sidhe knights fought with blade and spear, clad in golden armour from helmet to gauntlets. The fountains had turned red with blood from the fallen Sidhe, and bodies were strewn beside the wrecked tree that had once dominated the room. Half-bloods lay dead, too. Other fae-kind fought on both sides of the battle. Redcaps were in their element, biting and tearing into anything that came near.

I kept my head down and my knife out, cutting down any enemy who strayed into my path. I could only assume the vow hadn't activated yet because Aspen didn't realise I was so close to the estate, or he thought I'd died in the explosion. The blast had destroyed any high vantage points, but it'd also shattered the windows. Archers from the Hornbeam family took aim and fired at the enemy, following Cedar's instructions to circle the manor.

The conduit must be close, unless it could cause explosions from a distance. Smoke and decaying magic made my eyes sting and my lungs fill with the taste of ashes, but there were no signs of the source of the blast. Just burned bodies and magic that bristled against mine, raising goosebumps on my arms. Circling the fountain in the centre, its waters running red with blood, I spied an opening to a courtyard at the east of the estate. A wooden veranda stood at a crooked angle, and on top of the wreckage stood…

"Line up," Aspen said with barely restrained glee.

I stopped dead, out of sight. The Sidhe stood before him in rows, covered in blood, stripped of their weapons.

"Line up and swear loyalty to me, you pathetic excuses for sentries," he crowed.

"I will *never* yield to a half-blood," snarled a male voice. "Never. You'll die before your first command leaves your lips."

I stealthily moved forwards, out of Aspen's sight, but Cedar had other ideas. A *twang,* and an arrow left Cedar's bow in the time it took to blink, burying itself in the back of Aspen's neck—

Or, it *should* have. At the last second, the arrow veered slightly to the right, and exploded into a mass of wooden fragments.

"Iron," said Aspen. "It seems you haven't learned your lesson after all, brother." He turned around to face Cedar with a brutal smile on his face. "You didn't even bring a real army."

You haven't seen anything yet.

I kept very still. The slightest tug at my heart told me he knew I must be close. The blast had been designed to take me out… or bring me here. I'd need to get up close and personal to beat him, assuming I got past the vow—but how had he stopped Cedar's arrow? Another talisman?

My hand tightened on my knife, and the grass rippled as a current of magic flowed from Cedar's hands. Tree roots punctured the earth, aiming to strike Aspen down. Again, the attack bounced off an invisible shield, the roots shattering into pieces.

Aspen dusted himself off, looking bored. "Pitiful. I didn't think you had it in you to bind your people to serve you as leader. They deserve better."

"They deserve better than the likes of you," Cedar snarled. "You're an embarrassment to all of us. You know nothing about running a Court, much less inspiring loyalty."

"I can command an army," said Aspen. "It was my job, in fact. Did you think I wouldn't recognise the formations of my own soldiers?"

"You mean the ones you tried to coerce into betraying the Courts?" he said loudly. "Because you wanted power so badly that you went to the Grey Vale of all places to form your own joke of an army on the orders of an exile? *You're* pitiful. Lady Hornbeam would be ashamed of you."

"Treason," hissed a voice, and a murmur went through the crowd.

"I didn't want to resort to this," said Aspen, with a sigh. "Obedience is all well and good, but it's *boring* when everyone does what you tell them to, all the time. I think I'll give you some of your magic back."

He held his hand high, and the air rippled as green light illuminated what appeared to be a glass rod. *The conduit…* he'd put all *their* magic into it—taken it away. That's why they couldn't fight him. But the Sidhe retained their will, to some extent, if they could argue with him. Perhaps those pan pipes weren't as powerful when used on pure Sidhe.

Magic rose to my hands as I trod lightly around the fallen debris, giving myself a clear shot. Familiar steps coaxed out the hypnotic magic, which rippled over the crowd.

At the same time, the grass rose up, forming a barrier between the Sidhe messengers and him, breaking their eye contact with him. *Thanks, Cedar.* If I'd guessed right, Aspen was holding onto several vows at once, and it was a difficult feat, especially for a half-blood. Even with their power drained, the Sidhe's wills were stronger. I raised my hand for a second attack—and this time, Aspen's shield's glow lit up a second person, standing in front of the stage, visible from this angle.

Dad.

He didn't wear his ragged human clothes. He hardly looked like my dad at all. I'd have pegged him for his brother or cousin if I didn't know better. He was clean-shaven, his clothes were clean, too, and... faerie made. Plated armour, dark green to match the Summer Court.

The knife strapped to his side was what did it for me. My breath choked my lungs, and I didn't react in time to block when Aspen threw a handful of pure Summer magic at me, blasting me off my feet.

I hit the wall, hard. I dropped to my knees, too stunned to check if I'd broken anything. My head hummed with white noise and the shock of the impact. Dad walked towards me, wavering in my blurred vision.

"I can explain, Raine," he whispered.

My head throbbed, and my mouth tasted of ashes. "I don't *know* you," I spat. "Get away from me. Get out of my way."

"I can't do that, Raine. I'm sorry."

His voice was clear, familiar from his lucid days. He stood tall where he never had before... except when he'd been looking at *her.* But she wasn't here. I'd only seen him close to this way in the memory of our forgotten years, and even then he'd been entirely, utterly human. This man… was a stranger. A strange human in faerie clothing.

"Raine," he said. "It's really me."

"Get. Away." I held up my own hands in warning. "Don't think I won't use it on you, like her." The words were cruel, designed to bite deep, because despite the leaden sensation in my chest telling me it was really my dad, I didn't believe it was him. This Summer half-faerie was a stranger. My heart fractured with every second I looked at him. His expression crumpled, and he stepped back, green light connecting him… and Aspen.

It was his magic that protected Aspen.

"What did he do to you?" I croaked. "If it is you, prove you aren't working for Aspen."

"I can't do that," he whispered. "I swore a vow to her before you were ever born. I'm hers, and his by extension. When I got my magic back, it reawakened my vow. She took away my magic and erased all memory of my past. But I got it back, Raine. I found it in the witches' forest."

"You're lying," I said. "This is a sick joke. It's not funny. I've taken care of you all my life. You're one hundred percent human. And if you're not, you're not my father."

"This is touching," said Aspen, one eye on Cedar, the other on the crowd. The vow yanked me forward, all the sharper because he hadn't used it before. "I forbid you to—"

Magic arced through the air, and a dozen tree branches dissolved on contact with him. At the same time, I shot hypnotic magic from my palm, not aiming at Aspen but at the Sidhe spectators. "Get away from him!" I shouted— maybe they were too far gone to be hypnotised by someone else, but I had to try. "Warn your Court and bring backup!"

"You'll do *no such thing*," snarled Aspen, wheeling around to face me. "Any damage you inflict on me, your father will deflect. If it's too strong for him, I hope you're ready to face the consequences."

Darkness blanketed the garden, as suddenly as though someone had switched off the sun.

Aspen's yell of rage told me it wasn't him. "You—" he roared. *Who?* Not Cedar—one of the other Sidhe must have done it.

"You have a lot to learn about binding the Sidhe," hissed a voice that hardly sounded human. *Oh boy. He's done it this time.* Too bad Cedar, Dad and I were caught right in the middle of the Sidhe's revenge on Aspen for hypnotising them and stealing their magic.

"Stop them!" Aspen shouted.

I conjured blue light to my hands which showed me flashes of magic flying around, and Aspen in the centre, all attacks bouncing off him. Aspen stood alone, surrounded by enemies, yet didn't show a trace of fear. None of them could touch him—not without my father taking the blow.

All the magic in my hands couldn't stop him. The instant I moved, my father would throw himself between me and him, or he'd use the vow to bind me forever.

Aspen grinned wickedly. "Kill your father."

No.

He didn't need to use magic, let alone his new talisman. With one word I was powerless. With one word, my hands moved, magic rising, forming an arrow of ice, sharp enough to kill with a single strike.

"You're *not* my father!" I gasped. "He's not—he's not the man who I looked after all my life. He's a stranger." I spoke more to the vow than anyone else, fighting against the awful wrenching sensation in my chest.

"You ordered me not to use magic." I focused all my will on the ice, willing it to melt.

"I did not," said Aspen. "I thought it'd be more interesting this way."

"No, you did," I gasped. "You said so, last time. You didn't say *when* I could use magic again."

His mouth twisted. "You were a hobgoblin."

"I was still me. You ordered me, and I'm *under a vow.*"

The ice shattered, falling harmlessly to the floor. Dad wasn't looking at me. He stood rigidly, held captive by a vow, just like me.

"Fine," snarled Aspen. "You have other weapons. Kill him."

My hand jerked towards my knife. As I fought, pain exploded behind my eyes. I stumbled back, teeth gritted, fighting the burning sensation spreading from my chest to my arms and my fingertips. Hot blood trickled from my nostrils, and my eyes stung like someone had shoved needles into the corners. My hand locked around my dagger's hilt, and the pain lessened enough to breathe again. If I didn't obey, I'd die.

Dad looked at me, resignation in his stare.

"Run!" I shouted. "For the Sidhe's sakes, run—"

A heavy object struck me in the back, then a sharp tree branch locked around my arm, yanking me to the side like a living creature, and immobilising my weapon hand. *Cedar.* His intervention wouldn't stop the vow from acting on me— not even as an arrow struck my upper arm, bouncing off my armour. But it won me time. And the arrow was iron.

My legs moved without my telling them, all my instincts screaming at me to act and make the pain stop, but I grabbed the arrow and stabbed myself in the hand.

The pain disappeared in a flash, as did the unbearable impulse to kill. I knew it wouldn't last—for Cedar, it'd been only a few seconds—but I could breathe again. I called hypnotic magic to my free hand, and threw everything I had at my father. "Go," I told him, hating myself with every word. "Run for sanctuary! Run!"

The earth tilted under my feet, and I dropped the arrow, my hand stinging with pain. At the same time, another arrow tore through the air, embedding itself in my arm. My vision blurred. *Iron... no.* I dropped to my knees, and Aspen's cold laughter echoed in my ears as the world faded to blackness.

18

I came to, seconds later, breathing in the scent of Cedar's healing magic. He slumped beside me against the ruin of the collapsed veranda where Aspen had stood.

"Cedar!" I gasped, jerking upright. "Where—"

"Gone. The Sidhe drove him out, but I don't think they killed him." He struggled upright, pain flecking his face. An arrow protruded from his arm.

"Shit, Cedar."

"One of my own soldiers turned on me. The iron—my healing ability's not enough..." His breath rattled, and a chill formed deep inside me. The wound had healed with the arrow still inside. I might be too late.

"Let me get it out." I leaned over him, grasping the arrow. A hiss of pain escaped him. "I have to. Sorry, Cedar. This is going to hurt."

He yelled in pain as I wrenched the arrow free, and blood sprayed over my palms.

"Raine, we need to move!" Viola stumbled over to me,

bleeding from a scratch on her cheek. "The Sidhe—they're looking for you."

"Dammit." I'd let Dad go already. I wouldn't do the same to Cedar. The wound remained seeping blood. His healing ability must be in overdrive, but the iron... damn. I lifted his arm over my shoulder, and Viola moved into help us.

A huge shape with demonic red eyes reared up behind me. I stopped dead, but Viola moved in first. Her blades flashed, and the giant horse staggered back, hissing. I'd seen one of those creatures under Aspen's control when he'd attacked the Hornbeams' territory.

"Wait." Carefully laying Cedar down, I hit the beast in the face with hypnotic magic. "Cedar will die if we don't get back, and it's too slow to walk. I've ridden one of these beasts before."

"Are you certain?" Viola asked dubiously.

"No, but he'll die if we don't get him out of here."

Viola helped me pull Cedar onto the beast's back, and the horse took off almost before I'd swung my leg behind its ear. The ground tore away, and the trees seemed to move aside as though sensing my urgency. Cedar's grip on my back was barely existent, let alone my control over the horse. Where Aspen had got hold of them, I had no idea, but once I was riding, the faerie horse moved smoother and faster than smoke on a breeze, its steps gliding like a ship across the sea.

In seconds, we were on the path leading into the border-lands. I didn't stop riding, not until we veered closer to the plants guarding the palace...

And the figure waiting outside the iron barrier.

I felt the sword before I saw her face—its dark presence penetrated my skin. The cold laughter of June's talisman rippled up my spine, menacing, terrifying.

My sister stood outside our sanctuary, and the sword was back in her hands, drenched crimson with blood. My mother's orders had overridden mine, and somehow, June had bypassed the iron boundary and taken back the sword.

Cedar made a strangled noise. "She killed the guards." His voice was faint.

"Stay here," I whispered to Cedar. "You're in no shape to fight. Tell the horse to stay."

I hit it with another blast of hypnotic magic for good measure, jumped down, and ran to confront June.

"Sister," she said. Her nose was bleeding, her hands raw and ungloved, but grasping the talisman tight.

"What the hell *is* that thing?" I asked.

"Mine," said a voice that wasn't hers, and she lunged in a deadly swipe.

I dodged, skirting around her. "Stop," I said. "I command you to—"

The blade came perilously close to decapitating me. I dropped to my side and rolled over, feeling the cold kiss of the sword's presence against my bare neck. It hadn't felt like she was controlling it at all.

Since when could a talisman take control of a person? She couldn't be under hypnosis, being immune, unless she'd run into Aspen's pan pipes. No... somehow the weapon had overpowered her will. My vow should still be working.

I dug frantically in my pocket for my knife, which splintered in my hands. I yelled aloud as the fragments sliced my hands open, achingly cold. The sword's laughter echoed in my head. If ever I'd doubted it was a living thing, malevolent, evil, I knew it now.

With a whistling noise, the sword cut the air, dragging June along with it. I fired magic at the ground and turned the earth to ice, and her steps slowed, but didn't stop. She moved elegantly, gliding over the ice. Like a dancer, even carrying a sword with a mind of its own.

We were the same… so close to the same. And yet she'd been steered down a different path.

"Put it down," I warned. "Put the talisman down."

Her mouth twisted, and she raised the blade. A current of icy air hit me like a whip, slamming me onto my back.

"Is your talisman controlling you?" I gasped. "Put it down. Try."

She leaned over me, not smiling. Her mouth was cracked and bleeding, as was the skin on her hands, and her breath came out in gasps.

I am ancient, mortal, and you will bow to me. The voice rang out, echoing like a scream against the metal walls of a cage. Devastating, ancient, and more deadly than any Sidhe.

My sister screamed, as though she felt the voice inside her head, too, and held the sword over my heart. "Die, sister, before it kills both of us."

I am ancient, mortal… the voice came from the sword, thrumming like a beating heart. The heart of the talisman's magic.

I reached for that heart, searching for the deep knot that showed me where magic held its grip on her soul. The sword's evil presence was everywhere, binding it to her. I shoved my transformative power at her with everything I had.

Laughter echoed. "Did you seek to displace me, you fool?"

"Go to hell," I snarled at the voice, and pushed harder, harder. Magic exploded from my hands, fracturing the air in shards of ice, a whirlwind engulfing the pair of us.

And then Cedar's hand was on mine, his healing power reducing the pain as the clash of magic threatened to burn me out. His magic brushed against mine, entwined with it— and burst out of my own skin in a torrent of turquoise light. My—*our*—magic swamped hers, pushing until my body shook uncontrollably.

But unlike last time, I didn't feel death's cold touch. Only the sword's fury as its voice was stamped out, piece by piece.

Because of Cedar's magic and mine, as one.

I screamed as the sword emitted a piercing shriek more like an animal than anything. My ears rang with it, and blood trickled down the side of my neck. I felt myself falling, and Cedar fell with me—and we stopped, skidding to a halt on the ice.

The sword dropped to the ground with an echoing clang, and my sister fell to her knees.

"You—you're not strong enough to…" She choked. "You should have died. Like… Lady Hornbeam. You should be dead."

"She told you, did she?" I looked up at her, where she lay sprawled on the ice. "Well, if that's the case…" I glanced at Cedar, whose eyes were slightly glazed and carried a hint of bright green from the magic he'd used… and blue.

We did that. I crawled over to the sword and picked it up. No cold, angry voice spoke in my head. No dark impulses stirred in my blood. Green and blue light shone on the sword's hilt. I pointed it at June.

"Don't kill me," gasped my sister. "I didn't want to fight you again."

I lowered the weapon. "I'm giving you the benefit of the doubt only because I know that thing had a hold over you. Did she tell you before she gave you the sword?"

"It's not mine," hissed June. "You—you *stole* my magic. Where is it? Where's my vow to Lady Whitefall? And what did you do to the sword?"

"Seriously?" I asked. "No *thank you for ridding me of the creepy talking sword.* Some gratitude."

"You *destroyed* my magic," she gasped. "You poisoned my talisman. I won't bow to you. She'll take your talisman's power away from you soon enough."

I raised an eyebrow. "You'd seriously rather serve her than me? All right, then. When she and Aspen are dead, you're welcome to do whatever the hell you like. If you think I care, you're seriously overestimating your own importance."

She scanned me, as though searching my face for clues. "You're not the same kid who took the talisman."

"Thanks for noticing the obvious. Give Lady Whitefall the memo, if you see her again. But don't tell her what I did."

June pushed to her feet, her body trembling. "She'll know. She'll sense her magic in me, when I come back."

"The magic," I said, "is *mine.*" On the last word, I swore I heard an echo of another voice entirely. The sword glowed faintly blue. *I put my magic inside it.* Not just mine, but Cedar's.

Beyond all shadow of a doubt, Cedar *was* the source of power my mother sought out. The other half of the magic she'd wanted to use to take over the Courts.

And my magic was within June, too. I had a hold over her deeper than a vow, just like the control my mother had had over Viola. *Where is my vow to Lady Whitefall?* she'd asked.

Had I obliterated it? Or—was it because I'd replaced her magic?

"June," I said. "Tell me honestly. Do you still sense the vow binding you to me?"

She shook her head hesitantly. "Not exactly... I sense your magic. Not the same. Worse. Get it *out* of me."

"No chance," I said. "Tell me if you took anything else when you stole the sword back."

She shook her head. "I didn't."

I made a mental note to check the Summer security talisman anyway, and said, "Good. Now, I command you to stand outside the territory in the place of the guards you killed. If anyone asks, you're here because I commanded you to guard the territory. You are not to touch, speak to, or injure anyone unless I tell you to, until I decide to release you from your vow."

Which meant never, if I had anything to do with it. If my mother showed up—my wayward sister was the least of any of our concerns.

"She'll get to you first," said my sister. "She still wants your magic, and she wants you at her side. Or dead."

"Same old. You are not to speak a word to anyone about what happened today. On pain of death."

She nodded, her eyes clouded.

"Good. Go and guard the gates. I'll wait here for the others to come back."

She walked away. I closed my eyes, taking in a deep breath, then looked for Cedar.

He lay on his side where we'd fought, and he didn't move.

"Shit." I grabbed Cedar's hand. "Don't you dare die," I growled. "Don't you fucking dare. Not after this—not now." My voice broke. I didn't have healing abilities, but he did. And it wasn't enough, not for iron poisoning.

Wait. Our magic had connected before—and he'd used mine, at the same time as me. Somehow, we'd *exchanged* abilities, for a brief second there.

I let blue light flow over my hands, mingling with his, turning to healing light. Blue and green became turquoise. His hand locked around my wrist and he gasped, his eyes flying open.

"Thank the Sidhe." I grabbed his shoulders and wrapped my arms tight around him.

"I don't think they're who you should be thanking," he murmured against my shoulder.

"No, I guess not." Sidhe's blood, what had our magic done? And knowing that—what were we supposed to do to stop Lady Whitefall finding out?

I released him. "My delightful sister broke your security."

"I can fix it," said Cedar, but his expression darkened when he saw the fallen guards. "We need to make sure the others are safe."

———

What with rebuilding the defences, helping the injured, and getting everyone safely back into the palace, Cedar and I didn't get another moment alone all day. I wasn't sure if he knew any more than I did about what our magic had done, but I *was* fairly sure he didn't know the important talisman my mother was looking for... was him.

"Hey!" Viola waved a hand in front of my face. I hadn't noticed her sneak up on me while I'd been pacing around the perimeter to check on the iron barrier. "The barrier's fine, Raine. You've walked past the same spot six times."

I rubbed the back of my neck. "Just checking it's secure." I wanted to ask if she'd seen Cedar, but I wasn't sure what to say to him. After all, he was hardly Lady Whitefall's only target. She wanted every talisman, not only his magic. For all I knew, we weren't that important to her.

But he *was* important to me. The battle had driven it home for me, as sharply as a spear lodged in my chest.

"You haven't sat down since the battle," said Viola. "Come on, Raine. Let's get something to eat."

She was right, of course. I walked with her to the cafeteria, and chose a table away from prying eyes. Aside from Volt, her pet sprite, who flew happily around our heads and chased the ceiling lights.

"What's wrong with you?" she asked. "You're wandering around like you saw Lady Hornbeam's ghost. Was it June? Why leave her alive, anyway?"

"She wasn't exactly acting under her own power." I gave

her a brief run-down of the events, including what Cedar and I had done to the sword. Her eyes widened when I reached that part, and even Volt the sprite stared at me, though I wasn't sure he could really understand.

"Let me guess," I said. "You didn't know it was possible either?"

"Of course I didn't. My magic's the same as yours, remember?"

"Shit, yeah. You can't do the same, can you?"

She shook her head. "No. Not with Rose, either, but we were together before Lady Whitefall replaced my magic. We're not magically compatible like that, but it never mattered."

"I don't think it does," I said. "Believe me, if I've learned anything, it's that compatibility with magic doesn't necessarily mean you're good for one another."

I'd meant Robin and me, but she said, "Cedar. What does *he* think?"

"He doesn't know," I admitted. "And—I think she's looking for him. He's the talisman she's after."

"No," she said. "Surely not. How could that be possible?"

"He inherited his magic from Lady Hornbeam," I said. "And to think he thought his magic isn't worth anything."

We both fell silent, picking at our food. I felt Cedar join us without looking at him, because my magic sprang to attention when he came near. Maybe because his magic had been inside me, and mine in him, when we'd exchanged powers. A type of intimacy I hadn't known was possible.

"Raine?" Cedar asked. "Are you feeling okay?"

Apparently he couldn't sense the connection as intensely as me. Then again, we were in a public place. "I should be asking you that," I said. "You nearly died."

"I'm fine. Are you going to leave June outside?" asked

Cedar. "The guards are asking questions. Isn't she still vow-sworn to Lady Whitefall, technically?"

I shook my head. "No. What we did to her... undid that. She's on the other side of the iron barrier, besides. If she goes back to Lady Whitefall, she'll find out we destroyed the sword's magic. I highly doubt June wants to be on the receiving end of her anger."

"Maybe," said Cedar. "Nobody knows where Aspen fled to, though there are patrols searching the forest."

"Damn," I said. "I'm sorry. I made things worse by getting so close to him. The vow..." *Nearly made me kill my father.*

As much as I'd desperately wanted to believe it wasn't him, that the man I'd taken care of for most of my life hadn't morphed into a stranger, I knew in my heart it'd really been Dad. Not the person I knew, but the man who'd fallen into Lady Whitefall's hands and somehow ended up in the mortal realm as a human.

Thanks to Aspen's vow, I might never see the real him again. And I'd done what I said I'd never do. I'd turned my magic against my father.

"It wasn't your fault," Viola said. "None of us expected Aspen to know our army was coming. On the other hand, he wildly overestimated the hold he had over the Sidhe. He won't make the same mistake again."

"No, he won't," I said.

I didn't mention the obvious—that the hypnosis I'd used on my dad wouldn't last forever, and he'd be back in Aspen's hands at the first opportunity.

Viola yawned. "I'm off to find Rose. You two should get some rest. It's been a rough day."

I nodded in acknowledgement, rising from my seat to follow her, but Cedar laid a hand on my shoulder. "It really wasn't your fault," he said in a low voice. Even here in the corner, people darted looks at us from all around the room.

I shrugged. "Maybe not. I should go and check on June again."

"There's no need," Cedar said. "I asked some of the guards to watch her. They've set up an iron barrier around her so she can't attack anyone. We've lost too many people today."

No kidding. They were *his* people. The way the soldiers looked at him said it all. He was their leader, a Lord in all but name, and I'd never felt so alone in his presence. Nor so aware of the light humming sensation when my magic brushed against his.

"Yeah. We have." I began to walk away, and a moment later, he followed.

He spoke in a low voice. "What you did for me out there…"

"You mean the healing magic?" My heart rose into my throat. This was it. I didn't know if my mother was actively seeking him out—after all, she'd need to have me on her side before she could use his magic in conjunction. And that would never happen. *Never.* "I don't know how I did it," I said quietly, turning down the nearest corridor away from overly curious observers.

Cedar kept pace with me. His hand brushed mine, our fingers interlocking. "I don't either, but the Sidhe don't claim to know all magic's secrets."

"I took on your power. I doubt I can do that to just anyone. I think it's the link between our magics. They complement one another."

Cedar shook his head. "I've never heard of anyone being able to trade magic with another person. Not even from Lady Hornbeam. She had a large number of talismans, and nothing of that nature ever occurred, here or elsewhere. I think there's more than one reason Lady Whitefall left her sceptre behind when she fled."

"Yeah, about that," I said. "She got it from the Vale. Same

place the sword came from. They're not your run-of-the-mill talismans, but hell if I know *what* they are, exactly."

And what did that make *his* magic? The sceptre was a legend, a talisman which magic couldn't be removed from unless its wielder met with its equal, and our combined magic unlocked it.

Cedar squeezed my hand. "Whatever they are, it's not to do with our own magical compatibility," he said. "I know my own magic. Even when we traded powers, my magic behaved the way I expected when you used it."

"I still can't say I know everything about mine," I said. "Except yours charges it up to max power."

Cedar let go of my hand. Without my noticing, we'd walked all the way to the tapestries beside the corridor leading to his room. "By the way, I don't think the guest room is particularly suitable accommodation for someone who just won a battle. There's a proper bath in my room."

"Was that a polite way of saying I look like shit?" I enquired.

"No, but I expect you know by now that the guest rooms don't come with warm water. Besides, I'm concerned about your arrow wound."

"You got shot too." I'd expected him to see the lies in my face, but instead, he was inviting me into his room. No promises. No regrets—yet. I took in a deep breath. "All right."

The door at the back of his room did lead to a bath—or rather, in place of what I'd thought was a normal sized bathroom was what amounted to an indoor pool, an artificial replica of an outdoor pond, complete with real trees growing from the wall.

"You said 'bath', not 'swimming pool'," I said. "This is probably a bad time to say I can't swim."

A smile curled his lip. "I'll make sure you don't drown."

"So reassuring." The water looked nice, though. Really

nice. Almost enough to make up for my reservations about stripping in front of him. Court faeries had different ideas about modesty to those of us who'd been raised human, and besides, it wasn't any use hiding my attraction to him. I just didn't think my heart could take another betrayal.

I stripped off my clothes, relieved to be rid of the sensation of wearing someone else's blood, and sank into the water, groaning as it soothed my battered muscles.

"I can help with that." Cedar padded over to me. He'd removed his coat, too, and his shirt. Green light shone from his hands, and my tense muscles unknotted as he massaged my shoulders. "Nice trick." I let the heat and warmth of the water wash away the dirt from my skin. If only it'd wash away my misgivings as easily.

"The wound's healed better than I thought," he said, running a hand over my shoulder. There was a faint grey circle where I'd been shot, but it didn't hurt. His healing magic had reached me in time. His own scars gleamed under the light of a thousand fireflies which flitted about the ceiling. Band-shaped scars on his toned arms and chest indicated the places where iron had left its permanent mark on him. The newest scar still had a ring of grey around the edge. A reminder of what we'd faced, and what remained to face.

"Aren't you going to get in?" I asked.

"I'll have considerably more difficulty keeping my hands off you if I did."

I stiffened, almost unconsciously, and he withdrew his hand.

"Tell me what you want from me, Raine, please," he said, in a low voice. "If I've done something wrong—"

I twisted around to face him. "Cedar, this… our magic… it would never have happened if I hadn't picked up the talisman. If I hadn't come here. What you think you feel for me— it's a magic trick."

"You really think that." He frowned. "I think I fell for you long before I saw you use the talisman's magic. Maybe the first time I saw you."

I shook my head. "You're joking. You didn't know me then."

"I'm not," he said, seriously. "And I wanted to know you, even if you thought I was someone I wasn't."

"You used me to get your hands on the talisman," I said quietly. "I was nothing more than a means to an end. You might have changed your ways and decided you want me now I stand a chance against the Sidhe, but don't try to fool me with that."

"Have I ever given any indication that's what I think?" he asked. "I can swear a vow on my life that I will never use your magic against your will."

"No, you'd bloody well better not," I said. "I'm not being responsible for any more vows, here or otherwise. I'm not her. And if you think I'd do that to you—"

"I'm sorry, Raine." He closed his eyes, then opened them again. "I didn't mean to imply you were. I feel responsible for pressuring you to look at things the way the Sidhe do. In the beginning—I approached things all wrong. You're better than they are. And that's not why I want you." He leaned over me in the water, green light flashing across his eyes. "I want you because you're kind and caring in a way the Sidhe will never understand. And," he leaned closer, his magic sparking against mine, "you are far more to me than a means to an end."

Prove it, whispered a selfish voice in my head. But he had, a thousand times over. I just hadn't been willing to accept it. Betrayal had hollowed me out, making me forget how hope, even joy, felt. The spark of his magic on mine was only one part of it. I leaned forward and kissed him in answer, hard.

"That was a yes," I said, "in case you were wondering."

Light from the fireflies overhead sparkled in his eyes as I kissed him again. I buried my hand in his soft hair and he made a half-strangled noise deep in his throat, kissing me back with enough passion to send fireworks to my fingertips. Our magic brushed against one another, sparking, igniting, Summer and Winter, light and shadow, day and night. Not opposites, but something else.

"Cedar," I gasped. "If you don't take the rest of your clothes off now, I'm going to pull you into the water."

He laughed and pulled me *out* of the water instead, straddling me on the bank, soft grass cushioning my back. "Isn't this easier?" he asked, his voice a low purr.

Trees shrouded us, blocking off the world outside, muffling the noises we made as we explored one another, slowly at first, teetering on the edge of control. Threads of magic swirled around us, but I paid them no attention. When he finally slid inside me, I moaned against his neck, my fingers digging into his skin.

His hands gripped my hips, my name falling from his mouth like a curse or a prayer. We moved together, the friction gathering as we found our rhythm, as surely in sync as our magic. I let go, my back arching, and light exploded from our hands as we climaxed as one.

I collapsed onto the soft grass at the poolside, my head pillowed on his chest, skin tingling pleasantly where we touched. He kissed my shoulder, tracing a path to my ear and nipping the skin delicately. "You were worth waiting for. Every second."

19

My sister's vow wasn't the nicest alarm clock. I woke with a jolt when my magic reacted and nearly fell off the bed. I dug my hand into the side of the mattress and poked Cedar in the arm. I didn't remember how we'd ended up back in his room, but we must have stumbled in sometime around dawn.

Cedar's eyes cracked open. "What is it?"

"I think my sister tried to leave our territory." It wasn't Aspen, otherwise I'd have felt a stronger pull.

Cedar ran a hand over his face. "*Our* territory?"

I poked him again. "What, do I have to ask permission, *My Lord?*"

He grinned, though his brow furrowed. "I thought she couldn't leave."

"So did I. Her vow to Lady Whitefall's supposed to be gone. Maybe she got past the iron, or it was moved." I scrambled for my clothes, cursing inwardly. If Lady Whitefall had reached her, she must have come back into this part of Faerie overnight. Weariness from yesterday's battle made my hands clumsy. Cedar put a hand on my arm. Green light and warmth spread over my body, soothing the ache in my bones.

I moaned as the sensation moved down my legs. "I didn't know you could do that."

He smiled. "There are more perks to our ability to exchange powers. I could teach you later."

"Wish we had time to explore them."

He kissed me lightly on the lips. "So do I, Raine."

I'd have given anything to spend the day with him, but if my sister was on her way to join my mother's latest scheme, I'd rather ambush her first. If Aspen could drag me over to him using the vow without speaking aloud, maybe I could do the same with June.

I pulled on my clothes, transforming them into armoured ones, and stocked up on weapons. The sceptre lay on top of the cabinet where I'd left it. There was no power remaining inside it, but I distinctly remembered the bait-and-switch Cedar had pulled last time we'd faced Lady Whitefall. Maybe it'd work as a good luck charm, if nothing else.

Once the two of us were outside the palace, Rose ran up to us, despair and terror shining in her eyes.

"What's going on?" I shot an alarmed look at Cedar. "Where's June? And—Viola?"

Rose shook her head. "I didn't see June, but someone rode a horse past us in the forest, grabbed Viola, and took her. It was so *fast*—I can't find her anywhere. I don't know where they took her."

"The Vale." My heart sank. "Which direction did the horse—?"

A horrible screeching noise drowned out her response, followed by the beating of wings.

"That's... not a horse." Rose stumbled back, gaping at the sky. As did I.

The dark outline of wings blotted out the sky, passing

overhead. *The Morrigan...* Impossible. She'd been chained up in iron nobody could break. But I'd felt her magic before, sensed it through the chains. The earth shook, and the trees shed their remaining leaves as the torrent of darkness trailed into the sky, leaving shadows in its wake.

My mother had awoken the goddess of death.

"I think," I said quietly, "Lady Whitefall might be in the Death Kingdom."

Which meant Viola was there, too.

"How?" Cedar stared at the sky. Of the three of us, only I had met the Morrigan in person. I'd thought the Sidhe had permanently chained her up. How could my mother have set her free?

"I should have known she planned to go there," I said. "Even the horses—they were from the Death Kingdom, too. I should have guessed she'd steal a minor throne before aiming for the main Unseelie Court."

"You think she's there?" asked Rose. "But—then, where's the Morrigan going?"

"I don't know. But I don't see any horses." I began to walk forwards. "There are redcaps and worse in the Death Kingdom and with the Morrigan gone, I don't even know what's waiting for us."

Rose shook her head. "I can't leave her."

"We don't know for sure she's there," I said, with a glance at Cedar. "But I've been there before. I can find the way. This might be a ploy to lure me away from the Hornbeams' territory. Someone has to warn the soldiers. Cedar—"

"I'm not staying behind," he said. "I have enough guards watching for trouble around the palace."

"And they know an attack is likely," Rose added. "If she's hurt—I need to get her out of there."

We had no time to waste. "All right," I said.

I took the lead, walking swiftly through the woods. I'd

begun to learn my way around the Hornbeams' territory already, and once we passed into my own territory, I knew the route into the Death Kingdom well. Only now did I appreciate how close to the Grey Vale it was. The mist-wreathed paths were virtually identical to the Vale's. It and Death weren't so different. After all, nothing could die in the Vale. In the Death Kingdom, though… the Morrigan was the last true immortal. And my mother had been dead set on preserving her own life.

What did she do?

"Wait," Cedar said from behind me. "What exactly is the Morrigan's power? Why would Lady Whitefall target her first?"

"She can't die," I said. "Lady Whitefall wants something bigger than Faerie. What's bigger than the Courts?"

There was a long pause.

"Death," he said. "Immortality. The Morrigan… she's one of the last true immortals in Faerie."

"Exactly," I said. "I can't say I know what that means for us, except for a shitload of trouble if she's allowed to roam free."

The Morrigan's territory announced its presence with the foul stench of rotting meat and blood. Blood-soaked snow covered a sloping path to moat surrounding the Morrigan's palace. Shaped like a domed tent, it loomed over a river of blood, and the only way in was to cross a bridge above the dead bodies heaped around the moat.

"Lovely place, isn't it?" I muttered to Cedar. "Watch out for low-flying birds."

He glanced at the sky, carrying a blade in one hand. "I think they're the least of our problems."

Added to the corpses were fresh ones—the ogres which had once guarded her palace. The way inside lay clear. Even the horde of ravens had vanished along with their mistress.

I walked ahead, Cedar and Rose behind me. I'd only seen the palace once and it was enough to give me nightmares, but most of the horror lay in the beast whose giant talons were chained to the throne.

This time, Aspen sat on the Morrigan's throne, Viola at his feet. I heard Rose gasp behind me.

Aspen yanked me forward without a word, the vow working its magic. I spat out a curse, but my legs continued to move of their own accord, carrying me towards the throne. In front were the Morrigan's iron chains, lying in a heap between me and Aspen. Broken or not, the iron instantly dampened my magic. He'd put them between us like a shield.

"You?" I said, injecting as much derision into the word as possible. "You think you're a good replacement for a terrifying death goddess? I've seen trees that are more frightening than you are. You're nothing."

"I'm a future king," said Aspen. "I like this throne, but I think I'd like the Seelie Court better."

"What're you skulking around in the Death Kingdom for, then?" I glared at him, hoping he kept watching me—I might not be able to move, but Rose and Cedar could. "Is she sending you between thrones while she fights the real battles —or does she not trust you to handle anything else? Looks to me like she forgot about you." He wasn't the one calling the shots, unless my mother truly had entrusted him with everything, which I doubted. No—she'd never have told him the full extent of her plan. At least there were no signs of my father. Which meant he wasn't shielded.

Aspen needed to die. I'd take away his magic for good, like I'd done with my sister. And by doing that... *maybe I can undo that vow.*

He smirked. "Don't bother."

A transparent shape rose behind him, the shadowy form of a wraith smothered in blue magic.

"The dead don't rest easily here," he said softly. "I think I'll kill you first, brother. I have to admit, I never thought Lady Hornbeam's pet thief would be the one to try to take her crown."

The wraith roared, and icy magic slammed into me and Cedar. I stayed on my feet, but Cedar hit the wall, his body freezing. The wraith's blurred hands rose, and a second torrent of power aimed at Cedar.

I jumped into the way, and Cedar swore as I took the attack head-on. Pain racked up my spine, vanishing almost immediately as he transferred his healing power over to me. We moved forward as one, both calling on magic at the same time. Blue light came from my hands, green from Cedar's, and collided with the wraith in mid-air. Screeching, it exploded into smoke and ashes.

"So it's true," Aspen said. "I did wonder what I saw when you healed her, brother, but those traitorous Sidhe drove me away before I could be sure. Lady Whitefall's going to be very interested to know the power she seeks is in the blood of a weak half-blood—my brother, no less."

"You're no brother of mine," Cedar said, deadly quiet.

Oh Sidhe's blood. I should have told him. I shouldn't have assumed Aspen wouldn't have noticed. *Cedar.* I didn't want to see the betrayal on his face when it dawned on him I'd guessed what he hadn't... the enemy needed both of us—or our magic—to complete her plan.

Aspen rose to his feet. "Give me the power, brother, or your girlfriend dies."

I lunged forwards, but the vow slammed me to my knees before him. Another wraith rose where the first had died, icy magic streaming from its hands.

Cedar intercepted its attack, and cold Winter magic

swamped him, freezing him in place. Aspen laughed at both of us, then snarled when Cedar broke free from the magic.

Winter magic slammed into me, and I tasted blood as my head struck the cold floor. Gasping for breath, I lifted my head, struggling to move.

Warm healing magic rushed to my fingertips—from my own hands—soothing my bruised bones and broken skin. *Cedar gave me his magic.* That meant I could do the same to him.

I pushed to my knees and met Cedar's gaze. I'd been pretty clear about not letting anyone use my magic again, but this was different.

Use my magic. Knock him off his damn throne.

My magic exploded outwards from Cedar's hands, striking the wraith in the chest. With a screech, it exploded into fragments, leaving Aspen wide open.

I struggled to my knees and the vow pushed me down almost immediately. I pushed back, calling on Cedar's healing magic to numb the pain. Fresh agony shot through my bones as I resisted, but the healing ability repelled the vow's magic. I climbed to my feet and grinned at Aspen. He couldn't use the vow to knock me down when I had two people's magic at once pushing against him. *Take him out, magic. Destroy his power and the vow along with it.*

I stumbled towards the throne, and he held up the pan pipes. With a laugh, he tossed them from one hand to the other. "The dead themselves dance to my tune. As does she. But she's a little absent at the moment." He gave a dismissive glance downward.

Viola.

She rose at his command, stiffly. Her body moved, but her eyes were blank. Not the sort of blankness of someone who'd fallen under a vow, but worse. No life shone in her eyes, and cold emptiness filled her pale grey gaze. She was…

"Dead," he said, with a laugh. "Her spirit left her body, at any rate, but her heart's still beating. I debated finishing the job, but I thought it'd be fun to play with her for a bit."

Bile burned my throat. "You sick bastard."

"Bastard I might be, but I'm here on a throne, and you're in the dirt. Your servant is gone."

Rose made a choked noise from behind us. She'd been pushed back against the wall during our fight, her magic powerless against the dead.

My knees hit the floor and Aspen laughed at me again. Viola wasn't dead. Her body lived—and without the Morrigan, she couldn't move on. That'd buy us time, if it was even possible to bring her back. We were in Death's own kingdom, but for all my magic, nobody could cheat death. Except my mother, apparently.

"Kneel before me, Raine," Aspen crowed.

I snarled, pushing magic at him, but met a wall of iron. Those blasted chains. Even my talisman's magic couldn't outdo iron.

"You can't rely on iron," Cedar told him. "It'll poison you, too."

Footsteps came from behind us. Cedar's magic lessened the pain in my knees, and I straightened up.

Aspen's eyes narrowed at the person behind me. "You're on *their* side now?"

I risked a quick glance, not expecting to find June standing defiantly beside Cedar.

"No," said June, jerking her head in my direction. "*She* vow-bound me. But I'm still loyal, and I came here to remind you of your true purpose. Stop playing games with these people. Lady Whitefall is counting on you for a lot of reasons."

"Yes, including getting the power off my dear brother—"

The vow loosened as his attention slipped, and I moved.

Fast. I threw myself at the throne, kicking the iron chains into the air with the edge of my boot. The iron rose, smacking him in the face.

Aspen screamed in pain, momentarily stunned, and I tackled him off the throne, conjuring gloves to my hands and grabbing the chain. It burned me through the gloves, but I didn't care. Cedar shouted at me, words I couldn't hear. The iron scorched a sharp line down Aspen's face to match Cedar's own scar, and he roared in pain again.

A flock of birds flew over my head, along with a current of air that knocked me flat. I landed on my side, rolling to my feet. Aspen twitched at my feet, moaning.

And the Morrigan herself sat in the entryway.

"Are you fighting over my throne?" she croaked, looking around. June stood frozen near the door. Rose crouched over Viola's motionless body. Cedar stood apart, ready to leap in and help me fight Aspen. I looked for Lady Whitefall, but she wasn't there. Just the Morrigan, a hulking bird-shaped shadow.

"We're deposing this prick," I said loudly. "He took your throne. I didn't think you'd like that."

"Lying does you no favours, mortal," said the Morrigan. "I can rip out your soul, like I did to her."

"Her? Lady Whitefall?" My heart skipped a beat.

"Not her. The girl."

Viola. *So that's how...*

"Can you put it back?" I asked desperately.

"Not when the soul is lost." The Morrigan shuffled into the cave. She was in her more human-like form, but somehow looked younger than last time I'd seen her. Her face was wrinkle-free, her hair glossy black, but her eyes were ancient as the sun, dark and terrifying. Cold fear traced down my spine and I looked away to avoid falling under her magic's thrall.

"She's not dead," I said to the Morrigan—everyone else seemed to be too terrified to speak. "Her spirit hasn't gone far. You know. Right?"

She laughed. "There is one who can retrieve it, who can walk between the spirit realm and here. Otherwise, unfortunately, your friend is lost. I rather think that's the last of your concerns, mortal."

"Are you here to kill us?" My heart raced. *Viola.* Who could bring back someone whose spirit was gone? And why had the Queen of the Death Kingdom come back herself?

"No," said the Morrigan. "You have no interest for me. I'm here to reclaim my throne."

I stared at her. "But—does Lady Whitefall not want it? I thought you'd joined her, or she'd captured you."

"Captured?" she laughed. "Nobody can capture me, fool. The Sidhe saw to that. But I can be temporarily freed... under the right circumstances. I have no desire to help the Sidhe dig themselves out of the latest mess they have created. In the end, only I will remain, eternal."

"What did she ask you for, then?"

Instead of answering, the Morrigan prowled over to the iron chains, lifting them in a claw-like hand. Instantly, her face wrinkled and her body hunched up as the iron's effect came on. Yet it didn't kill her, like it would us, despite the magic shining in her primal gaze. She was another creature entirely.

"You're taking the chains back? Why?"

Again, she didn't respond, looking down at Aspen instead. He groaned quietly in pain. "This is the one she had guarding her throne?"

"You can tear his soul out," I said. "I thought you ate souls."

"Unfortunately, it goes against my orders," she said. "Lady Whitefall compelled me not to sever another soul before I put the chains on again. In case I decided to destroy her forces, I suppose."

"Damn, she covers her tracks well." She must have used a specific vow to get exactly the right amount of help from the Morrigan, then dismissed her without allowing her to go free.

"That she does," said Lady Whitefall from behind me.

I froze. So did everyone else, except the Morrigan, who tilted her head on one side as though fascinated to watch the carnage unfold. Lady Whitefall was there, clad in battle armour, cold and resplendent.

"What are you doing, Aspen?" she said sharply. "And—*you*. I knew you'd interfere, daughter."

Aspen moaned, "She attacked me."

"He deserved it," I told her.

"What a waste. Heal him," she ordered Cedar.

"I'm not yours to command."

My breath stuck in my throat. I didn't dare move. She stood too close to Cedar, and the knife in her hand was the one she'd nearly killed me with when I'd been in the Vale. The real thing this time, not a fake.

She turned to Cedar, eyeing him coldly. "You will be, or you'll be dead. Morrigan?"

The ancient faerie gave a coughing laugh. "I'd rather not bring the forces of death on your tail, Lady Whitefall. I gave you what you asked for."

For a heartbeat, I expected the two goddesses to erupt into battle. But Lady Whitefall herself laughed. "Yes, of course you did. Those Court bindings are certainly an inconvenience."

There was a snapping noise as the iron chains repaired themselves around the Morrigan's clawed hands. I'd never seen iron obey magic before, but it was clear that what contained the Morrigan was no ordinary spell. It felt almost like a spell from the mortal realm, but a thousand times stronger. She'd fought on the wrong side in the last war, so the Courts had taken pains to stop the same from happening again. Someone needed to warn them she'd been freed—assuming my mother wasn't about to storm on the Courts now. But again… nobody was coming to help us.

"Aspen, June, you can leave," said Lady Whitefall. "I wish to speak with you alone, daughter. Let's put an end to this childish game."

"I'm not the one screwing around in the Death Kingdom," I told her. "We'll meet on my terms, not in the Vale."

"Very well." Lady Whitefall smiled broadly, beckoning me to follow. I glanced around, hoping at least the Morrigan's flock of giant crows might help us, but it was hopeless. She had no stake in this fight. The Sidhe had bound her, and she didn't give a crap about the rest of us.

Cedar gave a slight nod, indicating he was about to follow us. I wouldn't get a better shot at Lady Whitefall than this. As she beckoned me to follow, I ran after her, out of the Morrigan's cave.

The instant I reached the threshold, the world warped around us, and ice froze my limbs into place.

"Now," she said softly. "Tell me about the talisman's magic."

20

Ice crept up my arms, pinning them to my sides. We stood in an unmarked clearing between snowy trees, one I didn't recognise, and my friends were nowhere in sight. Nor were Aspen or June. She'd moved us somehow, trapping me in her magic. For the first time, a spasm of fear shook me, faced with her raw power. I'd been afraid around her before—for my own life, and my friends'—but I'd never been hit with the same blast of pure terror the other Sidhe projected. Because she hadn't used it against me.

Apparently, her patience with me had snapped.

I held my breath, refusing to speak. I didn't know what she wanted me to say, but if she questioned Aspen, she'd know what Cedar and I could do.

You don't deserve my fear.

"Well?" she said. "What can you tell me?"

I licked my dry lips. "The talisman took less than five seconds to choose me over you," I told her.

Her mouth curved down at the corners. "That's not what I meant, daughter, and you know it."

"No, I'm afraid I don't. If you want the magic, you can

duel me for it. Unless you're afraid you'll lose, or having second thoughts about finishing me off after all."

"Oh, I don't *need* you," she said. "I merely wanted to know the nature of your connection with your friend's magic. The limits. Whether I'll need both of you, or just one."

"For what? You have all the power you need without either of us."

"You're too dangerous to leave unchecked," she said. "Your power is mine, one way or another. You gave it to me yourself."

I twitched my hand, willing the ice to melt. Nothing happened. "What?" Did she mean June? I had given her my power, after all. Part of it. Like Viola. But that wasn't the same as the magic I possessed myself, because she could still use magic independent of me.

"The magic you use is somewhat volatile," said Lady Whitefall. "It destroys all other magic it comes into contact with. Enough traces remained in the sceptre before I gave it you back, Raine, for me to test it through my useful new tool, in conjunction with some other magic inside it. But I can't wait to see what you can do by yourself. You... and Cedar."

My blood froze. *The conduit...* somehow, it'd been *my* magic which had caused the explosion, when put together with some other Summer power.

My mother had found a way of using my magic by proxy, putting it into the conduit and *then* using it, rather than making me do so. The power was raw and uncontained and had nearly destroyed me when I'd used it in its wilder form to kill Lady Hornbeam. *But I thought there was nothing in the sceptre left.*

"You're lying," I whispered.

"I think we both know I'm not, daughter," she said. "What's interesting to me is that the sceptre's power's equal belongs to a Summer faerie. Don't look so alarmed. I haven't harmed him."

Cedar. "Leave him out of this."

"Not until I find out how it's possible." She tilted her head. "Aren't you curious where I got the sceptre from in the first place?"

"The Vale. Everyone knows."

"Do they really?" Her mouth twisted. "And did you not think it odd that the talisman was legendary in the Courts, who possess power enough to rule a world? That there were many who'd kill to possess it, even here where murder is forbidden?"

"No. You people have been killing one another for centuries. None of this is news."

"Oh, but it is." She smiled. "Daughter, I only possessed the talisman for a short while before you found it, but immediately knew it for more than a regular magical artefact. Normally there are written records, but that particular talisman... none. It wasn't even a legend—there were no records of it at all."

"So? Is that what this is about? You want to be the villain in all the scary stories they tell to children in Faerie?"

Rather than answering, she looked at me pityingly. "There are certain talismans," she said, "which contain... let's call it less than conventional magic. All magic belongs to one of the two types."

My heart beat faster. *Shit. She's way ahead of us.*

"Everyone knows that," I said. "Summer or Winter. It's basic stuff."

"Not Summer or Winter," she said. "Life or death. Beginning or ending. All are two sides of the same coin, and one and the same. The seasons chosen by their respective territories are nothing more than an attempt to maximise their power. Summer is where life thrives, and winter where it lies dormant, cold, dead."

"Your point is?" But I knew. The witches had told me enough.

"Some talismans have power that belongs to neither Court." A smile played on her mouth. "I heard of them a long while ago. During my trips to the Grey Vale, I made a point of seeking them out."

So that's why she had the entrance to the Grey Vale. Not to build a secret Court, but to search for those talismans.

"The sword," I said. "You found it in the Vale, right? That's why it seemed like it was… alive."

She smiled. "Yes. Certain talismans contain a piece of the gods themselves, and that one remained conscious."

"I take it these gods aren't the nice sort." The Morrigan was a death goddess and even *she* hadn't creeped me out as much as the sword did. As the Hemlock witches had told me… my talisman was more than a Sidhe one. Its magic was something else entirely. A force more ancient, and dangerous.

"No," she said. "The Sidhe cast them out, after all."

I raised an eyebrow. "Cast out their gods? *Why?*"

"You won't find many people here who'll willingly speak of it. It's ancient history, but the Vale never forgets, nor is their power dulled with time."

So talismans thrown into the Vale might stay there for an eternity, and their power would never fade like ordinary ones did.

But… what did it mean for the sceptre? And for me?

"It's not alive," I said. "I think I'd know if it was."

"There's one way to rid yourself of the burden," said Lady Whitefall. "Wouldn't it be simpler to hand the power over to me?"

"And watch the Courts die?"

"The Courts have lived long past their time," she said indifferently. "You haven't been here as long as I did. The Courts have always been tedious, static. We are not made to live in peace."

"Sounds like they earned that peace, if they cast out their gods to do it," I said. "And you wanted their power? The talismans?"

The sceptre's power… damn. Not only could it replace the magic in a regular talisman, it could replace the magic of the *gods*. Like the sword. Because it *was* one.

Viola had said that when my mother had replaced her magic, *the connection of our magic gave her a hold over me that went deeper than a vow.* I'd done the same to my sister. If I let Lady Whitefall get hold of my power, she could replace the magic of a thousand lesser talismans, and turn their owners into her slaves. There would be no more Seelie Court, and the Unseelie Court as it was would cease to be. Just one Court, hers, a Court of exiles and death. The true Death Court—where its rulers were forever undying.

That was the power inside me, the power she intended to hijack for her own gains. And if Aspen could use the conduit to do so without me even being present…

Not on my watch. Not ever.

I met her eyes. "I'm not handing my power over. It's *mine.*"

Blue light surged to my hands, but didn't break through the ice. The god—or what was left of it—had apparently chosen me for a reason. Whether it was a good reason or not, I didn't care. Anything was better than handing her my magic.

"That's a pity. I hoped we might come to an understanding, daughter, now you know the truth."

"Too bad," I said. "We're not on the same page, mother, and we never will be. You're despicable. And I will *never* forgive you for what you did to the people I care about."

"If you mean your father, he's never suffered at my hands. I removed his memories to protect both of you."

"And stealing his magic? What was *that* in aid of? Aspen's using him as a human shield. Don't think I don't know about it."

She frowned. "Your father will not be harmed. I had to put his magic to good use, since the alternative was to allow him to join you against me. Then I'd be forced to remove both of you."

"Nobody's forcing *you* to do anything," I spat. "You brought this on yourself. And you still haven't explained why you kidnapped a half-blood from Summer and made him think he was human by stealing his magic."

"I didn't steal his magic," said Lady Whitefall. "I sealed it away. Can you imagine how the Courts would have treated a Summer half-blood with a Winter child?"

"Don't try to fool me into thinking you were looking out for my best interests," I snarled. "You violated both of us against our will, and you never do anything but for your own selfish goals. If you loved him, which I sincerely doubt, you'd have left him the hell alone. Thanks to you, I've lost *both* my parents."

"Believe it or not, I did care for him," said Lady Whitefall. "He was nicer as a human, more pliable, as mortal fragility brings. In this form he's nothing but trouble."

Anger scorched me from the inside, yet my magic still couldn't break down her icy prison. "You hypnotised him, wiped his memory, and turned him into someone else. And me, too. There's such a thing as allowing the other person the choice."

"I allowed you the choice, did I not?"

I glared at her. "There are no choices for exiles. But you're not one. You walked away from the Courts willingly. You don't know shit. And unless Aspen takes the vow *off* me, I'm going to be forced to kill my own father. I take it that was your idea, too?"

Her mouth turned down at the corners. "No. I wasn't aware you were bound to Aspen in such a way. In any case, it'll be irrelevant when you hand over your magic to me. The binding between the two of you will be undone. It's better this way."

My heart jolted. *Hand over your magic.* So... when June's vow to Lady Whitefall had come undone, it hadn't been because I'd replaced her magic with mine. It'd been because I'd totally obliterated it. Vows didn't exist independently of magic at all. They were dependent on it.

If I gave up my magic...

"Well?" my mother asked, a smile playing on her mouth.

"I was bound to Aspen when he forced me to act as his entertainment for mortals," I told her. "No wonder he looks up to you so much. I literally exist because you were twisted enough to decide wanting someone was enough excuse to bulldoze through every life that stood in your way—unless it was just my father's magic you wanted."

She looked at me, her face pinched, and for the first time, looked older than she had before. "You were the end goal. It's impossible for a Summer and Winter Sidhe to conceive a child together—and almost impossible for a higher Sidhe to have any children at all. There have been very few, in the last several centuries—but half-bloods are a different story. Suppose I were to conceive a child with someone of as strong a Summer bloodline as my own Winter one... then the possibilities would be endless."

I stared at her a moment. I'd heard what she'd said, all right, but the words were slow to work their way into my head. "You can't—what the hell are you talking about? Nobody can inherit more than one kind of magic, not if they're half-blood. Even if they're both Winter and Summer. Unless you have a talisman, it isn't possible."

"Correct," she said. "I made a deal with someone who could have corrected that little mortality problem of ours. Unfortunately, the person in question disappeared before he could fulfil his end of the bargain. When the mortal realm fell under attack by the Vale, the borderlands became incredibly volatile. The other families didn't know I had a husband and child, you see. If they'd found out, they would have taken you away to get their hands on my treasures. So I did the only thing I could think of— I sent both of you away to the mortal realm as soon as it became clear I would never be able to make you into a true immortal."

"Make me into an immortal? That's not possible."

"It isn't now," she said, a touch sadly. "You would have been able to join me, a being of both Courts and ruler of everything. You would have been a goddess."

"It's not possible." Because whatever had made the Sidhe immortal had been destroyed. "If that's the case, why not bring me back to Faerie later?"

"The source of immortality went missing at the time of the invasion," she said. "I was forced to find other means of securing my reign."

"The Morrigan."

"Yes, daughter. Immortality will be mine. I will break the chains of mortality and rule this realm and others. And if you will not stand at my side, then you will forever be my enemy."

I gave her my darkest look. "I'd rather be your enemy than your subject. And I'm glad the talisman chose me."

She reached out a hand, grabbing me by the throat. "Then you choose to die, daughter."

"You—need me," I warned, choking as she squeezed tighter. She was going to take my magic by force after all—

tear it out of me like she'd done to Lord Hornbeam. And in doing so, the vow compelling me to kill my father would be destroyed.

All I had to do was hand over my magic.

"No, daughter, I do not."

Darkness encroached on my vision. However badly I wanted to be freed from Aspen's vow, giving her my magic would cost more lives than it saved. And however easy it seemed just to let go… to give into the pain and let her remove the magic warping my soul…

I'll give up the magic on my own terms, or not at all.

I wrenched myself away from her, power rising to my fingertips—healing magic, restoring my breath. *Oh no.*

"But you need me," said a male voice. Cedar.

"No!" I gasped. "Get out—"

If she took *his* magic, then she'd be able to use it to take down the Courts. With the conduit.

She threw back her head and laughed. "You'd trade your own life for hers?"

"Only if you agree to a vow."

Cedar.

No.

My throat was too raw to speak, and shock roiled through my bones as my magic objected to the near-miss. Cedar approached her, crossing the clearing. He must have searched the territory to find me.

"Tell me more," she said. "What kind of deal will you offer me, Cedar Hornbeam?"

"I will come with you, if you swear not to bring Raine into the Grey Vale, or wherever you plan to attack the Courts and put your plan into action. Leave her and her family and friends alone, including her father, and release her from her vow to Aspen."

She gave him a smile. "I'll see what I can do, Lord Hornbeam."

She's scheming. She might not need my magic in the short term, thanks to the conduit, but she'd come after it eventually. Maybe she'd send someone else, or find another way to trick it out of me. But the only way to keep her promise was for me to give it up to her.

"Don't," I said warningly. "Cedar—"

Lady Whitefall turned her back on me, took Cedar's arm, and the two of them vanished.

21

I stared at the spot where they'd vanished, horror rising in my throat. "Dammit, Cedar."

"Raine!" shouted Rose's voice.

I spun around, looking for her. Now my mother's spell had worn off, I saw the paths leading out of the clearing, and the faint fog that suggested we were close to the territory's edge. Rose approached, carrying Viola over one shoulder. "She won't wake up." She looked at me desperately, tears spilling down her face. "I don't know how to fix her."

"It's not yet too late," said a male voice. A Little Person emerged from behind a tree. Not Moss Beard, but one of the identical bearded men who lived in the forest. I tensed automatically. Despite knowing the traitors had been arrested by the Unseelie Court, I still didn't trust him.

The Little Person looked at Viola's limp body. "I know how to get your friend back."

I glared at him. "Don't pull that one on me."

"You know the person who can help you," said the Little Person. "The only human who can walk into Death—*our* Death. She lives in the mortal realm."

Wait... "Who, Ivy?"

"Yes." He nodded. "If you desire, I will allow you free passage through the rift to speak with her."

It's true. Ivy said she can walk into the Vale... which leads to Death by extension.

Rose gave him a suspicious look. "Didn't some of your people get executed for treason?"

"I'm not going to betray you," he rasped. "The traitors died, and deservedly so. But if you want to get your friend back, you must act fast."

"I'll go," I said to Rose. "I can warn the others in the mortal realm while I'm at it, too. When someone messes with Death, it causes a knock-on effect. But you should take her back to the Hornbeams' place. Keep her safe until I can get her back."

Indecision fogged her features, but she nodded. "I—okay. Viola would want me to." She swallowed, blinking back tears. "I don't know how long we can hold Lady Whitefall off, if she attacks again."

"I think the Courts are her next target," I said. "I'll be quick." I turned to the Little Person. "Let's go."

He withdrew into the trees. I followed, and soon enough, we reached a rift.

Cold mist swallowed me up, mist clinging to my face and mingling with the tears that freely fell. I'd lost Cedar—after everything, I'd lost him to a vow after all. Maybe he had a plan, but he sure as hell hadn't told me what it was. But saving Viola... that, I could manage. *I hope.*

I appeared on the hillside, and collided with Robin. I caught myself in time, skidding in the wet grass, then carried on walking.

"Raine!" he called after me.

"I don't have time to chat." I walked faster, but he caught

up easily. It was so foggy I could hardly see him, much less where I was going, and drizzle soaked my clothes. "Seriously, Robin, unless you know where Ivy Lane is, I'm not interested."

"Ivy Lane?" he echoed.

"It's not like I have a phone. I don't even know her address." I dug my hands into my pockets and walked faster. "By the way, Lady Whitefall won. If you haven't worked it out already. I'm here to warn this realm, and then—then I get to choose whether to stay here and hope this realm survives, or walk to my death and possibly cause the apocalypse all on my own." I was babbling, but it didn't matter how much he knew. Not now. Nobody could stop her if she truly had conquered death.

"What?" Robin called after me. "I can call Ivy myself. Please hear me out."

I didn't turn back. "I gave too much of my life to you already. You won't take any more of it."

Despite my speed, he still remained just behind me. "Lady Whitefall has spies everywhere. Your magic—if she's telling the truth, it'll mean war if she gets hold of it."

"Tell me something I don't know," I said.

"Raine," he said. "I know what she asked the Morrigan for. She put the Death Goddess's magic in the conduit."

I stopped walking. "What? She can rip out souls?" But... how could that give *her* immortality? "Or—something else?"

"The Morrigan's magic *is* death," whispered Robin. "The Morrigan's very nature allows her to survive death, and she's reborn when she dies. Like the Sidhe used to. That magic..."

"Then she's truly immortal," I said. I'd guessed as much already, but futility sank its claws in me again.

"No, she's only borrowing it," Robin said. "The conduit's the source of her power. If you got it away from her—"

"I'd have to stop her tearing my own magic out first," I muttered. "Besides, Aspen has the conduit, and he's got me ensnared in a vow. So I don't give a fuck if you decide to go and tell her everything, including where I am. She knows she's won."

"I can't tell her," he said. "I'm trapped here. Raine…"

His subdued tone sounded unusually faint. My spine prickled. *Something's wrong.* Wait… he was bound to her with a vow, so how could he tell me so much? She couldn't have freed him.

As I turned to face him, the fog shifted, but he remained, semi-transparent and hovering above the hillside.

He was dead. I'd been speaking to a ghost the whole time.

"How?" I whispered.

"She knew I was immune to her magic," Robin said, his eyes downcast. "She found out, and used the Morrigan's magic on me as a test subject. But—she killed my body to make sure I couldn't return from death."

I just stared, lost for words. He'd done so much to screw my life up, but having your soul ripped out wasn't a fate I'd ever wish on anyone. It was pointless—cruelly pointless to kill him that way. She'd wanted to get to me. No way could Robin have been around her so long without her guessing some of our history.

"Raine. You're not responsible for—"

"Damn fucking right I'm not," I growled. "This is all on her. And if you're stuck here—how does it work? Didn't she kill you in Faerie?"

"She killed me in the Vale, then pushed me out here so I wouldn't interfere in her plans. But there—it's impossible to move on."

Of course. Because the dead didn't truly die in a realm cut off from Death itself.

"I can find Ivy for you," he added. "I can move anywhere now."

"Of course you can." I looked past him, squashing any lingering guilt that I was in any way responsible for his predicament. Lady Whitefall might be my mother, but he'd brought this on himself. "Tell her to meet me at the witches' forest as soon as possible. And," I added, as he began to fade out, "find Denzel, too. Ask him to meet me at the same forest in half an hour."

I was all out of ideas, save for one last, wild scheme. One that might backfire horribly. Desperation was all I had left. I'd keep my magic out of Lady Whitefall's hands, at any cost.

I left Robin behind, quickening my pace. It was impossible to tell if the drizzling rain signalled any change from my mother's interference in Death, or just normal weather. I walked fast, taking every shortcut, and by the time I reached the entrance to the forest, I found Ivy waiting outside.

"Ghosts are following you this time?" she asked.

"One ghost. She killed him." One thing I appreciated about Ivy was that she didn't waste time with pleasantries. I got to the point quickly, summarising everything she didn't already know.

"The Morrigan?" Her eyes widened. "Impossible. Not again. The Courts bound her."

"From what I can figure out, Lady Whitefall gave her a specific set of instructions. The Morrigan left the chains, went to do some small job for her, then flew right back and tied herself up again. She was also forbidden from clawing anyone's soul out afterwards."

"Good. That's the worst part of her powers."

"What she did is still pretty bad," I said. "Lady Whitefall took some of—her essence, I guess. She made herself immortal."

"You can't *make* yourself immortal," said Ivy. "The

Morrigan and a few death faeries, like banshees, are the closest to immortal you get these days."

"But—when I was a baby, Lady Whitefall planned to use the Sidhe's old immortality source on *me*. I'm part Summer and Winter faerie. She wanted to make me a queen, apparently. It might have been a lie. I mean, the source of immortality was destroyed a year ago. Even when you take into account Faerie's messing with time, I lived there for at least three years."

Ivy's brow furrowed. "The source was abandoned after the invasion... long story, but nobody could use it until a year ago, and it was destroyed immediately afterwards. If your mother did plan to use it before, she might not have had the chance. The Morrigan, though, the Courts themselves couldn't destroy her. Her soul's stuck on a loop. The miserable old bat."

"She took someone I know," I told her. "My best friend. Her body's still alive, but her soul's somewhere in Death."

"She's not dead?" Ivy frowned. "Someone told you that I can find her, didn't they."

"I—can you? I don't want to ask, but I can't lose her as well as Cedar."

Ivy nodded. "Vance won't be happy about me taking another trip over the veil again, but I can handle it because my magic feeds on death and lets me leave my body without dying. Like a necromancer, basically, except my magic's originally from Winter... sort of."

"Wait," I said. "Feeds on *death?*"

"Death energy," she corrected. "So does all Winter magic, come to that. Like Summer feeds on life. But mine's bound to the death realm itself, both human and faerie. It's sort of complicated."

Complicated... like a god's. Her talisman came from the Vale, too.

"Ivy," I said. "Have you ever spoken to the faerie gods?"

Ivy stepped back. "Who told you that?"

"Nobody. It's… my magic. I'm told my talisman's not from the Courts at all."

"Of course the bloody gods would be involved," Ivy said under her breath. "Your talisman's one of them?"

"Apparently," I said. "According to the Hemlock witches. So is it possible to speak to whoever's power it is? I mean, talk to the god?"

Ivy's mouth pinched. "No. I mean, it's possible, in the Vale, technically. If you try to speak to a god, you'll need its name, at the very least, but I'm told there aren't any of them left. The talismans only contain fragments of their power. I really wouldn't try it."

"Damn." I sighed. "Just wanted to be sure."

"I'd concentrate on stopping Lady Whitefall first," said Ivy. "I'll be back here, once I've got your friend back. Then if you need me to fight with you, I will."

Even with her talisman sheathed, she carried herself like a warrior. With Ivy on my team, maybe there was still a chance.

I nodded. "Sure. Thanks for helping me out."

"Any time."

As she left, I stayed on the path, but walked deeper into the forest, away from any listening ears.

"Hey," I whispered to the sceptre, pulling it from my pocket. "I need to talk to you."

My throat was dry. I didn't know its name—didn't know *whose* power filled the sceptre. Only that it wanted me to wield it, and all that remained of its consciousness lived here… within me.

And it'd be really pissed off with what I'd chosen to do.

A chill raced down my back, a response. Conscious… but not exactly like a voice. More a presence. Magic shivered up my arms, and a faint blue glow ignited at the sceptre's end.

"I'm trapped," I said in a low voice. "Either my mother will get you, or the Summer Court will. You don't want either, do you?"

The talisman's magic rose around me in a cloud of blue light.

I took a deep breath. "I want to make a deal."

22

As I'd arranged with Robin, Denzel met me at the forest's entrance after Ivy had left.

"This had better be good," he said, clip-clopping over the undergrowth. "This place is creepy as hell. What do you want?"

"You to hang onto this," I told him, holding out the sceptre. "Give it to Ivy when she wakes up."

"What?" He blinked, his brow furrowing as though he thought I was mocking him.

"Take it," I repeated. This time, his jaw dropped, like it'd sunk in that I was serious. "Don't steal it or try to sell it. I'll know."

"What...? I don't even know who this Ivy person is."

"Robin will take you to her."

"Robin's a *ghost,*" he said. "You didn't want to mention that part? How did he die?"

"Lady Whitefall," I told him. "My evil mother wants the talisman, so you won't tell anyone you're holding it. Ivy's off on important business, but you'll give her the talisman. If you don't… Let's just say some of the legends about faerie talismans are true."

"You're creepy as they are now," he muttered.

"Believe me, I'm not," I said. "Think of it as a favour for all those shiny trinkets you swiped from my room when you thought I wasn't looking."

"Hey—I didn't. Raine, I swear I never—"

Too late. I'd left him behind, hurrying through the trees to half-blood territory. Robin would watch him—I'd ensured that, at least. But it was time for the less-than-fun part of my trip.

The part where I handed myself in.

I still didn't know if I was making the right decision. But life didn't come with dress rehearsals. You had to hope that if you made the wrong choice, you could handle the fallout. Even if the best-case scenario prevailed, I'd be kicked out of Faerie. I had little left to lose.

Sure enough, three figures on horses were patrolling half-blood territory. I'd figured there was a possibility the Summer Court had sent a patrol here on the off-chance I'd show up.

They were on me before I got within ten metres of them. As the three horsemen turned around, their magic rippled through the air, wrapping around my legs, holding me in place.

Justice—what passed for it in Faerie—had come for me at last.

"Well," said the first messenger, a bronze-skinned male knight riding a jet black steed. "What do we have here?"

Green light swirled around all four of us. The messenger Sidhe didn't move—instead, the world came *towards* us, the fields of Faerie replacing half-blood territory in a mere flash of green light.

I coughed on the smell of burning as we landed in the

meadow the explosion had wrecked—*my magic* had wrecked. Of course I wouldn't recognise its unique scent, because I'd been carrying the magic inside me for weeks.

Vines appeared from the air, binding my hands, leaving my legs free so I could walk. I didn't resist, as much as I wanted to. This was part of my plan. And without my magic, *her* plan would fall apart.

A chill raced down my back. My power… or the world.

My connection with Cedar… or the safety of the people I loved.

I'm sorry, Cedar. I'm so sorry.

He'd handed himself over to the enemy. And now I was about to take away the one advantage we had left.

With the others, I headed for the Summer Court—and my fate.

The Summer contingent summoned up another flash of magic, which took us to a path fringed with leafy plants. A gate at the end made of thorny stems opened at a command from one of the messengers, and a grassy hill blurred around us as though the world had spun into fast-forward.

The assault of Summer magic on my senses pressed against my body, and we landed in front of the doors to a vast palace. Oak doors opened into a hall shining with opulence—golden ornamental flowers seemed to be the main feature, though there were a fair few banks of real flowers growing inside, too. A piskie flew past, pulling my hair, as the messengers pushed me to my knees on the doorstep.

A tall Sidhe warrior walked out from behind a tapestry on the wall, eyeing me coldly. "What's this? A Winter half-blood?"

I remained still. The warrior wore golden armour that matched the hall. His skin was deeply tanned, his eyes bright green. A noble Sidhe with powerful magic.

"Whitefall," said the messenger, in disgusted tones. "We finally caught her."

"Indeed," said the Sidhe. "One of you inform the Seelie King's advisers. I'll deal with her myself."

"Excuse me, Lord Kerien," said the messenger. "Don't you want us to assemble for a trial?"

"We have more important things to concern ourselves with."

"Finally one of you sees sense," I muttered.

A sharp silence. "What was that?" said Lord Kerien. "Another insolent half-blood, of course."

My body lurched forward of its own accord as a wrenching tug dragged me to my feet. *Aspen's vow.* "He's here —" I cut off in a gasp.

Dad stood behind Lord Kerien. He stepped towards me, staring like I was a ghost, and the vow clutched at my chest, demanding I kill him.

"Get him out!" I shouted. "I'm under a compulsion—I can't stop—"

My body froze. Green light shone from the floor, locking my limbs in place. "No magic enters here without my permission," said Lord Kerien. "*You* didn't mention this, half-blood."

"She's my daughter," said Dad.

He *knew* these guys? Of course he'd been from a major Seelie family, but of all the times to show up, he just had to pick now.

"Dad," I said through gritted teeth. "Get out. You know if they let me go, the vow will make me kill you."

He looked at me sadly, then at the others. "I wish to plead on my daughter's behalf."

What? No. What he was playing at, I had no idea. He was essentially a stranger to me, a stranger who looked like a more polished version of the father I'd taken care of all my life. My stomach twisted with guilt for wanting him to leave, for cursing him for showing up now rather than letting me go ahead with my plan before Lady Whitefall found out.

"For what?" queried Lord Kerien. "She broke our laws and killed a Sidhe. You might have our blood in your veins, but you are still half-blood. You will not speak for her."

"Lady Whitefall kept me captive and made me forget who I am," said Dad. "She stole me from the heart of your Court. She's been stealing from you for a long time... as has Lady Hornbeam. She was not guiltless, and had her own designs on your Court. My daughter stopped her."

"Lady Hornbeam is not the one who is on trial," said the Sidhe.

"But would she be? You let her live, out of fear, knowing what she was capable of. It wouldn't have been long until she staged a coup."

"Because of my magic," I said. "She could have used it to take the Court—exactly the same as my mother's plan, if she'd taken my magic from me." I willed him to take the bait.

"You needn't concern yourself with that," said Lord Kerien. "Magic will be stripped from you at exile."

"Then let me offer my own magic," said Dad.

I shook my head. "No," I said. "Take mine—I'll willingly give it up. But—I want to bargain with you about exile. It seems pointless to send me into the Vale when my mother's waiting there to recruit me to fight the Courts. Send me to her and it won't change a thing. Kill me, and you're doing her job for her."

"You think you're in a position to bargain?" said the Sidhe in a soft voice.

"I saved your necks. That means you owe me a debt—all of you. I saved you from Aspen."

I was sure at least one of them had been there in the battle. Lord Kerien looked coldly down at me, then at the others. "She is correct. We cannot kill her, and as for exile—her mother might be counting on that very outcome."

"She's a criminal," said one of the others. "A murderer."

"Her magic is the cause. Take it from her and it will not cause any problems. She's a lowly half-blood, doubtless not long for this world anyway."

Despite myself, a flicker of anger stirred. I tamped it down. *Play along...*

"So be it," said the messenger. "She's not worth calling in the whole Court. Just another pathetic mortal."

"Very well," said Lord Kerien. "You will not be exiled from the Courts… but the price I ask for is your magic. If I'm right in thinking the same magic is what destroyed our territory?"

I swallowed. "Yeah. It was." My heart fluttered. They'd—unintentionally—offered me a lifeline. Did they know? With the Sidhe, it was impossible to tell. If I was exiled… I had a backup plan.

And it relied on the Sidhe being as oblivious to my real magic as almost everyone I'd met had been.

"I have one question," I told Summer's representatives. "When you remove my magic, will it remove the vow I'm under, too?"

"Vows are a different type of magic entirely," said Lord Kerien. "But vows are also sealed in magic, and when yours is removed, it'll reset you to the human you should have been."

Should have been, huh. I barely concealed my smile. I'd been right. *Thanks for giving me the idea, mother.*

Then he spoke, loud and clear, words I didn't know but that resonated with me on some deep level all the same. My father shouted my name.

Magic roared in my veins, objecting to being torn free, and I screamed, too. *Mine. Mine. Mine.* The voice pounded in my head, no longer sounding like mine but something else's —a scream of pure rage, echoing through an abyss. Pain splintered up my arms, and I screamed my throat raw, certain I wouldn't survive the pain.

I'd been spared death, but losing my magic was going to kill me anyway.

Cold emptiness beckoned, and I fell into the dark.

———

Dad was holding me when I woke up. We lay on a meadow of soft grass under a sky of periwinkle blue. Definitely a dream. Nothing like this had ever happened in my mundane mortal life. He'd never looked at me like he was the parent and I was the child. For as long as I could remember, I'd had to take care of both of us. He'd never stroked my hair and told me bedtime stories to make the demons—or faeries—go away.

The smell of Summer, though… that was new.

Reality crashed on me like a freight train, and I jumped away from him. My body didn't feel like mine, my legs clumsy, my hands shaky. If I'd been reborn when I'd picked up the talisman, I felt like I'd been reset to factory settings. And everything hurt.

Cedar's healing magic was gone. So was our connection. Maybe forever.

I squeezed my eyes shut. *It was for the best.* She couldn't use us as a double-edged sword. And she'd never see me coming.

"Raine." Dad looked at me. "I'm sorry—I can explain everything."

I sank onto the meadow next to him. "I'm okay, Dad."

Without the sceptre's magic, my body felt… lighter. Like a weight had disappeared from my shoulders. Of course, it might have been the absence of the price on my head. Summer and I were square, for all the good it did.

"That awful magic," he said. "I'm glad it's gone, but you can't go back to her. If she finds out—"

"That's exactly what I'm hoping for." I looked at him. "It's okay. They didn't take anything I didn't intend to give away."

I looked him in the eyes, willing him to see the truth. My hypnosis magic. The default magic binding me to Faerie, which made me who I was, and helped me survive this pain. The magic I understood now, more than I had before.

The magic I could hide. After all, I'd gone so long without knowing it existed, letting it fade to the background was second nature. No vow I'd made was bound to this magic. It was mine.

"It's like hers," he said softly. "Of course."

Those simple words hurt me more than they had a right to. I stood again. "Sure I am. Just like her."

He rose to his feet, catching my sleeve. "Raine, that's not what I meant. You're not like her—you're better, the best parts of her, and I'm so sorry I couldn't give you the life I wanted to." He blinked, tears in his eyes. "I can't go with you. This is the only place where Aspen can't use my magic. It's thanks to you that he left without me."

A lump grew in my throat. "Dad, no offence, but I'm still not a hundred percent sure I'm actually talking to my father. I feel like I don't know you."

"I'd like to know you," he said, with a tentative smile. "And I do. I remember how brave you were. How much you risked to help me. I wish I could have been the father you needed."

"I don't understand why she made you human," I said. "And—you never had magic in my visions of our past."

"I agreed to it," he said. "For you. I didn't need anything else."

I closed my eyes, then opened them again. "She brainwashed you. You know that, right? She took you away, put you under her spell, and abandoned both of us when it suited her."

"She did," he said. "But I think she was misguided. She loved both of us."

"She's an amoral power-hungry Sidhe," I said, my voice rising. "She doesn't know or understand love, not the way mortals do. She left me believing my whole life that she broke you. You nearly *died* when your memories almost came back. I blamed myself for it all. I can't—I can't accept this is real. I just can't."

He stood awkwardly. He looked younger, as though the weight of years had fallen away with his humanity. With the years of living a lie. I'd thought the invasion was the reason he had no family, no photographs in the house.

"I'm real, Raine," he said, softly. "I'm your father. And I'm so very proud of what you've achieved."

"What, murdering a Sidhe?" I dropped my voice. "You nearly ruined my plan. Besides, I don't understand what unlocked your memories in the first place, much less why you decided to walk into Faerie and not tell me."

"I wasn't in my right mind, not at first," he said. "Something compelled me to walk into the witches' forest. I came to half-blood territory myself to seek you out, after some disturbing dreams. I believe they were the result of the witch concoction wearing off…"

"Shit." I clapped a hand to my mouth. "I only used that because the memories were killing you. I guess the dosage must have worn off earlier than I thought."

"Don't blame yourself for it, Raine. You couldn't have known. *I* didn't. But I saw… visions, in the woods. Those visions led me to remember enough that I knew I couldn't stay in the mortal realm while Lady Whitefall was out there. I ordered the mercenaries watching the house to leave, and I set off for the half-blood territory's forest again." He drew in a breath. "I was told to find the faerie known as the memory-eater if I wanted my past back intact, so I did. And once I had, I made for the Summer Court. Lady Whitefall's people ambushed me on the way."

So he'd been under Aspen's control for only a short time when I'd run into him. That would probably have saved his life.

"The memory-eater? You spoke to *her?*"

"I did," he said. "And my past is mine again."

"But… you're not under Aspen's control?"

"I swore a vow to serve the Seelie Court," he said. "There's a reason Lady Whitefall can only get exiles and half-bloods to serve her."

I blinked. "I never thought of that. So you have a Court's vow… but I don't. I need to go and find her, right away. Without her magic, I can't be used as a weapon against the Courts."

But I had a weapon of my own. In my blood, waiting to activate.

"I want to keep you safe," he said. "Raine… she's too powerful. No Sidhe could beat her alone."

"This isn't my Court," I said. "Nor is Winter, nor the mortal realm. How long do we have to wait before the rest of the Courts decide the situation's urgent enough to offer their help? Where'd Summer's messengers go, anyway?"

"To inform the Erlking that you've been taken care of."

I snorted. "At least they didn't exile me. I was about fifty percent sure they would."

"You planned this," he said. "Why?"

"Because it was my magic she wanted, and as a bonus, I'm not bound to Aspen any longer." I smiled. "Where's the way out."

"Any direction. This is a pocket dimension near the borderlands. It belongs to my family." He spoke with a quiet sense of resignation. "If you're sure… I'll be waiting for you, Raine. I want to be the person who should have taken care of you." He leaned and hugged me. I stiffened, trying to quell the wariness like I was interacting with a distant relative, someone I only vaguely knew. Then familiarity settled over me, like a distant memory slowly coming back.

"You'll win this," he said quietly. "My girl."

My breath hitched, and I let him go. "Bye, Dad," I choked, and half-ran downhill before I broke down in tears.

Within a few metres, the world went fuzzy, and the next thing I knew, I was on the path linking Summer and Winter territory. When I turned around, the meadow had vanished from sight. *I hope he stays hidden.* Because my dad wouldn't be a victim of her again. I'd lost too many people already.

I'm coming, Cedar, I promise.

I nearly turned and walked into the Hornbeam family's territory, but something held me back. With Viola and Cedar gone, their army wasn't as powerful as usual. We needed more than one army.

Time to call in my favour.

I walked along the path, towards the edge of Winter territory where the conduit had exploded. Stopping beside the gutted house, I called out Lord Lyle's name.

He melted out from behind the nearest tree, his eyes narrowed. "You. I heard you'd been caught by Summer."

"They let me go, and I'm going to stop my mother invading this realm. But on the off-chance that things go horribly wrong, I think I'll ask for that favour you owe me."

"That's not how it works," he growled. "Your favour was for us to protect you—and besides, it was your friend who made it, not you."

"Then we'll make another deal. My mission is to get a dangerous instrument away from her, one she stole from your territory. Heard of the conduit?" I looked pointedly at the ruined house.

His face paled, though he didn't speak. *So he did guess.*

"And the Morrigan?" I said. "Somehow she got the information on how to free her from the heart of *your* Court. Summer and I have a special arrangement. You wouldn't want that information making it over there, would you?"

He growled, "No. I will bring my forces to assist you in this fight. Assuming you survive the war, mortal, we're equal."

And he vanished into the trees. *He actually said yes.* If I had to guess, he didn't want to be indebted to me forever. Which was fine by me.

I left the house behind and returned to the path, heading for the Hornbeam family's territory this time. The whole forest seemed eerily quiet, and when I reached the palace gates, I stopped. Two bodies lay inside, unmoving. *Dead?* I'd ordered June not to attack anyone. Had someone else been here? The guards didn't have any visible injuries, and appeared to still be breathing. Were they asleep, or drugged?

"June!" I shouted. "Get out here."

"Sorry, sister," she said, emerging from behind the fence. "Your vow forbade me from harming them, so I had to improvise. I don't want to kill every half-blood in the borderlands, believe it or not."

"So you choose her. Pity. I gave you the chance to walk away."

Facing her without my magic wasn't ideal, but I needed to get her out of the way before she realised she wasn't bound to me any longer. From her lack of reaction, she hadn't guessed. After all, there was no way to remove a vow, save death—or the removal of the caster's magic.

"She's going to win, one way or another," said June. "I

don't want to be here when she tramples the borderlands flat."

"Keep telling yourself that. I'm going to find her. She wasn't lying about her hideout being underneath the palace, right?"

She looked at me suspiciously. "There's something different about you."

I shrugged and walked past her, through the gates to the Hornbeam territory. I half expected her to attack me, but she didn't. The absence of a tugging sensation confirmed the vow binding us had collapsed when my magic had been ripped away from me. The same would be true of the one linking Aspen and me. But before I went to confront Lady Whitefall, I had one last stop to make.

Several soldiers confronted me inside the palace. "Where's Lord Hornbeam?" they asked as I passed by, thoroughly confusing me for a second before I remembered that was Cedar's title.

"With Lady Whitefall," I told them. "Prepare for battle. I'm going to confront her alone."

Voices followed me, but I shut them out, running in the direction of Cedar's rooms.

I already wore my armoured coat. Without the talisman's magic, I couldn't transform my clothes nor disguise myself. But I didn't need or want to play masquerades with her this time. I'd face her as me, and knock her off her damned throne.

I retrieved the false sceptre, replaced the weapons I'd lost when the Summer Court had captured me, and stopped at Viola's room to check on her.

"Raine," said Rose, on her feet the instant I entered the room. "I thought you went after her."

"I am now," I said. "Is Viola—"

"She hasn't woken up yet. She's still breathing, but..."

It's been over an hour, at least. Ivy said it wouldn't take long. I hoped nothing had gone wrong. Ivy was the only person left with a talisman which might be powerful enough to beat Lady Whitefall. Taking her off the battlefield might hurt us, but letting Viola die wasn't an option.

"Ivy's on the case," I told her. "But we're going to war with Lady Whitefall. I need to get Cedar away from her."

"Of course." She dipped her head. "I'll relay instructions to the soldiers on your behalf, if you like. You think she'll attack through the palace, or the forest?"

"Best prepare for both," I said. "This place isn't on her radar, so she's more likely to attack the main Courts. Get the soldiers to stop her, in any way possible."

"Got it. I'm glad I spent so long hanging around army quarters with Viola." She looked down at her body on the bed, her mouth pinched.

"She'll be okay. I need to go, anyway. Good luck."

"See you later," she said.

I retraced my steps out of the palace, finding June waiting outside the fence. She eyed the fake sceptre questioningly. The real thing was with Denzel—hopefully with Ivy soon, if she got Viola back. If not, and word reached Lady Whitefall of what I'd done… then we were screwed.

"You're not staying here," I told June. "You're coming with me, to find our mother."

For a split second, I thought the truth would dawn on her. But she followed me without speaking. I bit back a smile. Most likely, having magic so similar to mine herself made it impossible for her to tell if it was being used against her.

The palace drew nearer, just as quiet as the Hornbeam family's territory. The gates were open, an invitation. I strode ahead, expecting to find her waiting inside the grounds, but nobody seemed to be about. "Interesting." I pulled out the key, hoping it'd still work though my magic was no longer bound to the palace. To my relief, it did.

My footsteps echoed off the polished floor. Not only was my mother not here, but a door to her suite lay wide open. She'd made it easy for me, leaving the path into the Vale ready for me. Perhaps she really had thought I'd join her in the end.

I walked into my mother's suite, June at my heels. The wardrobe was open, too, but the tunnel no longer looked like a dingy hole in the ground. Instead, a gold-plated corridor waited ahead.

I rolled my eyes at it. "Of course she redecorated."

There was a single door at the far end, identical to the one which had appeared in the old dungeon. That lay open, too, revealing a foggy path. *Here we go.*

I led the way out into the Vale, and emptiness flooded in. Not as intense as before, but the muffled sensation was enough to remind me my magic still existed.

Mist swam around a grim, square building. Not a palace, more like the Hornbeams' old prison, minus the iron.

"She's not even making an effort anymore, is she?" I shook my head, eying the construction. The building seemed to have no defences, and a single door in front, which opened before we reached it.

"Daughter." Lady Whitefall strode out, looking me up and down. "I didn't think you'd be self-centred enough to let your lover's sacrifice go to waste. He came with me so you didn't have to."

"I'm aware of that," I said. "It's his choice. And this is mine. You want my magic: it's yours. And so am I."

23

Silence fell for a brief moment, as my mother and I looked at one another.

"You've given up your chance already, daughter," Lady Whitefall said. "You mistake me if you think I'll invite you to join me again so easily."

"I'm not asking for an invitation. I'm asking you not to attack the Courts." Where was the conduit? Surely Aspen didn't have it, if it contained the key to her newly minted immortality. But she held no visible weapons. Of course, she might be hiding anything—and the Sidhe alone knew what other magic she possessed. The building had no windows, preventing me from seeing where Cedar might be. Or Aspen. June, at my side, didn't speak a word.

She tilted her head on one side. "Leave us, June. Raine, come with me. Leave all your weapons at the door. *All* of them."

Figures. I pulled the knives I'd grabbed from the palace out of my pockets. All I had left was the fake sceptre. "Want that, too?" I asked.

She gestured to the corridor ahead, which was lined with

tapestries depicting scenes of slaughter. "Bring that with you."

I followed her, unarmed and magic-less, into a small room hidden behind a tapestry.

"So," she said. "What have you come to mock me with this time?"

"Nothing." I held out the sceptre. "It's yours, if you want it." My hands shook, betraying the real fear lurking beneath the surface. Honesty was my new mask, and hope that she didn't see through the cracks until it was too late.

"You…" She paused for an instant, betraying no emotion. "There's no magic left."

"That's because the Seelie Court took it from me, in payment for killing Lady Hornbeam. They left me the talisman as a souvenir. Now you can see why I throw myself on your mercy. Even the palace isn't mine anymore."

I held my breath. I didn't need to will my magic not to give me away, because it was barely visible anyway.

Fury brimmed in her eyes. "I see. In that case, you're going to tell me *exactly* where the real sceptre is, and I'm going to assign my pet thief to steal it back."

I blinked. "Excuse me?"

"You think I wouldn't recognise this false one?"

"Fine," I said, having figured she wouldn't fall for the ruse. "They took it. It's no use to me now the power's gone."

"And your lover's army?"

I flinched. "*She* took care of them. June. You still want her, even though her talisman is useless now?"

"You certainly pulled a nasty trick," she said. "That's why I believe you're lying to me."

"I'm not." I held up my hands. "No magic. No weapons."

"If you do have anything up your sleeve, I'm beyond Death, so killing me will cause little harm. Except to your conscience, maybe."

I nearly snorted aloud. Conscience. She'd probably never had one.

"Though I have to say, daughter…" She looked me up and down. "You certainly don't act like someone who's lost her magic."

I met her stare. "Want to know why? Because I spent most of my life believing I didn't have any. It's less of a shock when you never expected you'd ever have anything to lose. I'm *glad* I gave it up. I thought you never wanted me to have it anyway. I'm your daughter. Can't I just be that? I'm not a little kid, but…" I broke eye contact, trying to look cowed. "My father's gone. My friends are dead. This game's not worth it. I'm off the playing field."

"You know, daughter, you need to work much harder at deceit if you want to fool me. Contempt is in your very countenance."

"You know where I got it from." I shrugged. "If you won't believe my words, make me a deal. Give Cedar back to me, and we'll leave."

"Him," she said, her mouth twisting with distaste. "Lady Hornbeam's offspring. You might have chosen better."

"Aspen's hers, too."

"Yes, but you know very well that I have need of Cedar's magic. Would you want to put him through the same pain you experienced, stripped of his magic?"

Ice trickled down my spine. I hadn't even considered that option, and it repelled me. "No, because it should be his choice."

He'd do it. The fool would jump in boiling lava for my sake, or give up his magic to her. But why offer me an option at all? She must know that with my magic gone, he was no use to her. Not in her eyes, anyway.

She raised an eyebrow. "I see. That's where you stand?"

"Yes, it is. Can I see him now?"

"I would prefer to ask you to swear a vow to me," she said. "In order to ensure you won't make things difficult for me in the upcoming battle."

"I'd prefer not to. That wasn't part of your conditions. You promised Cedar."

"I can always dispose of him."

My throat went dry. "Try it and I'll rip out every shred of magic you possess with my bare hands."

"Well, now." Her eyes glittered. "It didn't take long for you to show your true colours, daughter, did it? You truly gave up your magic to come after him. How disappointing."

"Actually, I gave it up so you can't use me to annihilate the Courts. Whichever you'd prefer."

"So you guessed. As for your friend, I may have to revise my plans for that one. He's a little *too* obedient."

My stomach twisted. What had she done to him? "You said you'd consider—"

"I said nothing, daughter. Your army is pitiful, though I'll see to it that it's broken one way or another. I'd like to thank you, however, for taking another problem off my hands." She smiled. "Your human friend, the one you so foolishly sent into the spirit realm on a pointless quest. Her talisman is the one thing that might have prevented me from winning this war."

My heart sank like a stone. It should have stood to reason that Ivy might have had a chance of challenging my mother with her talisman. But Lady Whitefall and the Morrigan had conspired together after all. Ivy was stuck in death, as was Viola, and it was too late for me to do anything about it.

"And she had this," said Aspen, from behind me.

I spun around. Aspen grinned at me, holding the real sceptre.

"Your friend was begging me to finish him off by the end,"

he said. "I knew you'd sneak out of this realm, so I waited. Your attachment to the mortal realm will be the end of you."

"You killed Denzel?"

"Naturally."

A sick taste rose at the back of my throat. "And Ivy?"

He scowled. "No. She has some mages protecting her, but she'll expire soon, if she doesn't get out of Death. I did as you commanded, Lady."

Lady Whitefall stepped forwards. "Then hand over the talisman."

He walked past me and held the talisman out to Lady Whitefall. My hands itched to reach out and take the sceptre, to feel its magic once more. I knew beyond all shadow of a doubt it was the real thing. Even the echo of its power called me, demanded I take it back. I dug my nails into my palms hard enough to draw blood. But he *shouldn't* have known about it. I'd covered my tracks. Either I'd seriously underestimated Aspen's intelligence, or he'd forced Cedar to tell him all my potential plans. Even the ones I hadn't admitted to myself.

"Go," she said to Aspen. "Prepare the soldiers for war."

He left silently, and I was alone with her, the sceptre, and my secret.

I held my breath as she turned the talisman over in her hands, searching for clues. She wouldn't find them. Anticipation burned inside me. *Go on. I knew you'd take it back. But you gave it up. I remained loyal to it, in the end. I promised.*

Her brow furrowed. "You unlocked its magic the first time by using it in conjunction with your little friend, didn't you?"

"It's dead," I told her. "No magic left."

"I'll be the judge of that." She waved a hand, and the small room disappeared, to be replaced by an empty hall. Wooden floor, high ceiling. Like the true Sidhe, she could make the world bend to her whims. "Thief," she called. "Come to me."

Nobody answered. I held my breath.

"Aspen," she said sharply. "I know you're here, too. Come and stand where I can see you."

Aspen swaggered over to us from an open door. "I told the soldiers to be ready. They're waiting for you to give the word, Lady."

"Let this be dealt with first," she said. "Thief, there's no use resisting. Come here. *Now.*"

I couldn't sense the vow binding them, but a similar ache caught at my chest all the same. Aspen and I were no longer bound. He didn't even seem to have noticed. It'd be so easy to strike him down—

"I wouldn't, daughter," she said. "In fact—Aspen, you make sure she doesn't."

He grinned again and held the pan pipes. "My pleasure."

As he played the first note, Cedar appeared in the doorway where Aspen had walked in. His eyes were glazed and he stared ahead without speaking, without looking at me.

The pan pipes' notes jammed in my head, and I bit down on my lip, tasting blood. My hands swayed, and so did my feet. *I won't let it control me. I can't. Not again.*

But for all the notes, I remained in control of my own mind, watching Cedar approach Lady Whitefall.

"I need you to unlock this talisman," she said, holding it out. "I don't need to tell you what will happen to you if you try to take it for your own."

Cedar took it from her without speaking. Green light flared, and my heart sank again. If it worked—if his magic forced the god's magic to awaken again, and she could claim it… then it was over. I'd lost.

"Give it back." She all but snatched the sceptre away from him. "No… it's not working. Why?"

"Might I suggest using the conduit instead?" said Aspen. "She's clearly messed with that one."

She flashed me a glare, pulling the thin glass rod-shaped contraption from her pocket. *There it is.* The source of her immortality, the power of the Death goddess contained within. I tensed, ready to throw myself at her and snatch it from her hands, but I'd expected the talisman to reject her, and then her to turn on me. Instead, we were stuck in a weird standoff. Aspen winked at me.

What the hell is going on? Cedar wasn't looking at me, but Aspen was, and not at all like he was angry I'd broken his vow. Something was messed up here—and my mother wasn't in on it.

Aspen turned to face me again. Wait… he didn't look right. His eyes hadn't been hazel last time I'd seen him. They were Sidhe green. Not like…

My breath caught. *Cedar.* Cedar was pretending to be Aspen. It didn't even take much glamour. Aspen must be under a compulsion spell. Or a vow. No wonder the pan pipes hadn't worked on me.

He did have a plan after all. Or the beginnings of one. But he didn't know *my* plan, and chances were, we'd unintentionally sabotage one another if we made any sudden movements. Lady Whitefall held the conduit over the real sceptre, eyes narrowed.

Then I threw myself at her. We hit the wall in a crash, and Lady Whitefall screamed in rage. A word burst from her lips, forcing us to our knees—the invocation, Ivy had called it. Except not-Aspen was already behind her, and magic arced from his hands, not aimed at my mother, but at the weapon in her hands.

A jet of blue light poured from the conduit and my

mother hit the wall with the force of a car collision. Dust stung my eyes, and someone slammed into me, knocking me away from the explosion. My hands burned, scraped raw, only for healing magic to seal the wounds as they opened. Cedar—wearing his own face again—looked down at me, and mouthed, *you shouldn't have come.*

Like I'd leave you with her, I mouthed back.

Cedar pushed to his feet, colliding with the real Aspen. Now I looked into the false Cedar's eyes, I saw his eyes were definitely the wrong colour. She hadn't noticed… because she didn't need to. He wasn't on her radar as a threat, even when she realised he had the magic she needed.

"I'll take that," I said, and grabbed the sceptre from where it'd fallen to the floor.

"It'll wear off," said Cedar. "We need to move before the army realises—" He cut off in a choked gasp as Aspen lunged and seized him, one arm wrapped around his neck. The two were within inches of one another in height but Aspen was bigger, trained as a soldier rather than a thief.

"Hey!" I leaped at Aspen, wishing I had a better weapon than my own fist. I missed his jaw but hit his neck, giving Cedar the chance to break free.

"Stop there," growled Aspen. He didn't look remotely like Cedar anymore, his own glamour gone. "Take my knife, and cut your lover's throat."

He still thinks I'm under the vow.

Aspen's mouth twisted in a smile. "Take the knife, Raine."

I took it. And he was still grinning at me when I plunged the blade to the hilt in his chest. Blood dribbled from the wound, and from the corners of his mouth. He gasped something—maybe my name—and I yanked out the knife and I cut his throat for good measure.

An alarmed shout drew my attention to Cedar. He backed away from the place where the blast that'd hit Lady Whitefall had blown out a chunk of the wall. *Get back,* he mouthed at me. *Run.*

The hole in the wall shimmered oddly, and my skin prickled at the sensation of an unfamiliar magic. The sceptre vibrated in my hands, alarmingly. As it had when I'd 'spoken' to it in the witches' forest, pleading for help.

It's been a while... It was more a sensation than a voice. The sceptre vibrated so hard my teeth chattered, drawn in the direction of the shimmering void like a magnet.

Then the shimmering light shifted, revealing a dark shape. Like a shaggy black dog, a bigger form than a hell-hound. Its magic hummed in the air, in a realm where magic wasn't supposed to function at all.

Lady Whitefall didn't do things by halves. She'd woken one of the gods.

24

T he beast looked at me, eyes brimming with dark intelligence. Barely leashed rage churned inside those dark depths. Hate, too deep to comprehend. Lady Whitefall stood at its side.

"So I take it your plan to take down the Courts without bloodshed is in ruins," I said.

She rested a hand on the creature's head. "That was never the plan, daughter. And your talisman was merely one option."

No kidding. She had a backup plan, all right. "I knew I didn't mean that much to you."

"No," she said, "you didn't. Kill her."

The sceptre's magic rushed through me, claimed as mine once more. Magic arced from my hand, but bounced off the beast's hide.

"No!" June screamed. "Stop—*please.*"

The god-creature lunged, slapping June sideways into the wall. She hit the stone hard, falling to the ground. "Please," she moaned. "I'm your daughter."

"Believe me," said my mother icily, "I regret the pair of you. Your father, too. His magic did come in handy, but he ultimately proved more of a hindrance than a help."

Your father. He must have been half-blood—like mine. She hadn't seduced humans alone, but had kidnapped half-bloods to steal their magic and use it. How many ruined lives had she left behind?

Before I could move, she spoke a single word: *Kneel.* All of us fell under her command—all of us but the god-creature. Cedar shouted my name, and the world burst apart as blackness exploded from the gaping hole in the world behind her.

Warm blood trickled down my back. I'd hit something hard, but my vision was too blurred to see. I tried to move, and pain racked my body. Agony spiked, then disappeared in a warm rush of magic. I twisted around to thank Cedar, but found myself face to face with a wall of stone and dust. There was no sign of the god-creature... or Cedar. I couldn't sense his magic anymore, even with the sceptre back in my hands. The remaining piece of the god's consciousness rested within it, where I'd persuaded it to hide while I'd been in the Summer Court. Of course, Summer wouldn't be pleased if they knew, but I'd suspected the odds of me surviving this fight were low. And now, with another god on the loose... even Lord Lyle's army wouldn't be prepared.

Cedar climbed out of the wreckage. Blood spattered his armoured coat, but he was alive.

"Thank the Sidhe." I ran to him, wrapping my arms around him. "I thought it was too late."

"That creature—it vanished. It went with her to the borderlands. Or the Courts."

"Sidhe's blood." I cursed. "I warned Lord Lyle to be prepared for another attack on Winter, and the Hornbeam army will be ready, but none of them are prepared for *that.*"

"What is it?" Cedar drew back from me. "You *know* what that creature is? It isn't fae."

"No." I swallowed. "I don't know exactly what it is, but I'll bet I know where she worked out how to summon it. And being immortal, it can't harm her. That's the probably the only reason she's keeping it leashed. Her hypnosis can't work on something like that forever."

"It's a Vale beast," said June, staggering into view. Blood covered her arms and she didn't appear to be carrying a weapon. "A *true* Vale beast. I heard her talking about them, but I never—I never thought she'd go ahead and summon it. They were kicked out of Faerie for a reason."

"Shit." I looked at Cedar. "Wait—speaking of power. Where's the conduit?"

"Dead," he said, holding up two pieces of the glass rod. "Her magic, though—whatever the new magic she got is, she took it out first. I saw her do it."

"Oh hell. It was the Morrigan's magic. No wonder she didn't fight hard enough to keep hold of the conduit. She took it into herself."

"She would have killed you," Cedar said softly. "I can't believe you followed me here."

I folded my arms. "I'm not going to attempt a counter-argument after what you pulled. You almost gave her the real sceptre."

"I had it covered. I trusted you."

I scowled. "You played a major gamble. And is Denzel alive? If you were the one who went after him?"

"He's alive," Cedar confirmed. "He's cowering in half-blood territory. And help is on the way. She might find us first, but we need to get off this territory if we want to track her down."

"Who... wait. Not Ivy Lane?"

"Got it." He gave me a faint smile. "She didn't buy my act at first. Even as a spirit without a body, she was deadly. But she's on our side."

"Damn right she is," said a voice.

I spun around. "Looks like I got here just in time." Ivy lowered her sword. And beside her, very much, alive, stood Viola.

"Hey," said Viola, with a grin. "Guess who came back from the dead?"

I gasped. Then I ran to hug her. "I thought we were too late."

"You almost were," Ivy remarked, stepping up behind her. "Where's Lady Whitefall?"

"Gone into Faerie." I let go of Viola. "I'm sorry I left you."

"Not your fault," Viola said. "I was rude to the Morrigan. She tricked me into thinking you were dead, and I lost it."

"You've no idea how glad I am that you two made it out." I looked at Ivy. "I thought I'd doomed both of you."

"Happy to help," said Ivy. "I don't know about you, but this place gives me the serious creeps. What do you say to a change of scenery?"

"Definitely," I said, and Cedar dipped his head in agreement.

"What about her?" asked Ivy, jerking her head in my sister's direction.

June said, "You can't leave me behind."

"I could." She'd done more than enough to merit being left here with the other exiles forever. But I had enough enemies. "Let her come. If she turns on us later, I'll take care of it."

Ivy nodded. "Right. Let's move. You mentioned a way into Faerie from here? I can take us into the mortal realm, but I'd need an invite to whichever Court's territory you need to get to."

"I think we're too late for pleasantries," I said. "But I know the way. It's my palace, too." With the talisman mine again, it was, anyway.

I took the lead out of the ruins. As it turned out, the path remained where it was, as did the door itself, sitting alone between the trees.

I held my talisman tight. *Ready?* I asked the magic. *Want to fight with me again?*

The talisman hummed in agreement, and I opened the door.

"Nice," said Viola, eying the gold-plated corridor inside. "I did wonder how she crawled up that tunnel."

"One mystery solved," I said, with a glance at Cedar. "Watch it. She might be in the palace, waiting for me."

We stepped into the corridor, and I turned to Viola. "By the way," I said. "There's something you should know."

"What is it?"

"You're free," I whispered. "I gave up most of the talisman's magic to the Seelie Court, and it caused every vow tied to my magic to reset. I know it doesn't make a difference to the battle, but I wanted you to know."

Her eyes widened. "But I just saw you use magic."

"It's not the same magic," I said. "Not really. It's sort of a long story, but I gave up my magic to remove the charges against me. So the Whitefall vow is gone now. I won't force you to serve me. I wish I could say it lets you off the hook, but there's a war on the other side of the door. Are you sure you want to join me?"

"I wouldn't be anywhere else." She grinned at me. "Bring it."

We walked the short distance in silence. At the corridor's end, the door into Lady Whitefall's suite lay open, and beyond that, the entrance hall. Of course, she hadn't come back this way, so the palace remained the way I'd left it.

I crossed the entrance hall and opened the front door. Outside, not an inch of snow had been disturbed, but the sounds of fighting carried through the trees. Ivy took the lead, pulling her sword out, and we ran through the gates into pandemonium.

Giants tore up trees, and wild fae ran for their lives. Ivy stepped out, cutting down a hobgoblin, while Viola ran past, wielding her own magic. Wraiths began to appear in the trees, fighting against… Sidhe. Lord Lyle's army.

Ivy carved her way through the fighting. Her talisman cut down the dead as easily as the living, relentless and deadly. But the forces kept on coming, and there was no sign of my mother. If she'd taken the Morrigan's magic into herself, then the only option was to tear it out of her —but it was a goddess's magic. Could mine stand up to it, considering all her other abilities? Maybe. After all, the Morrigan hadn't given her all of her magic. She'd loaned her a kernel. A small sliver that might be stolen like any other magic.

Cedar and I fought back to back, fending off any enemy who came near. We'd lost track of the others, but a humming sensation drew me forwards, almost unconsciously. The air itself sang with power, drawing out the magic in from my talisman.

I cut down a shrieking hobgoblin and turned to Cedar. "It's close. That creature. I can sense it."

He grimaced. "Your magic didn't work against it. I'm not certain mine will. Are you sure you don't want to leave it to the Sidhe?"

"Little late," I said, raising my sceptre.

The god-beast appeared in a haze of shadows, gliding between the trees like a wraith. Its magic stirred mine, making my teeth chatter with the force of its power. My sceptre buzzed angrily, its rage rolling through me, but I held onto my own will, my gaze trained on Lady Whitefall. "Nice, mother. Hiding from the battlefield?"

"Certainly not. The Courts are running scared." She moved to the beast's side, power rippling the air. A dark glow surrounded her body, and coldness radiated from her very being. Raw, metallic fear rose on my tongue. The same fear I'd felt when I'd been near the Morrigan. She and the creature stood side by side, a goddess and her pet, wreathed in primal, deadly magic.

"I assume you've guessed the nature of the power which resides within that talisman of yours," Lady Whitefall said. Even her voice sounded different, having cast its melodic cadence aside for a bone-deep, chilling whisper.

"Yeah, I have." I swallowed against my dry throat. "I prefer it in this form. That thing is ugly as hell."

The creature hissed and stomped its feet. Its huge shapeless form exuded dark, terrible power, like standing next to the talisman sword all over again. *Maybe it's a relation.*

I kept my gaze on a spot near Lady Whitefall's feet, fighting the instinctive fear. It was just magic—ancient, terrifying magic, but a spell all the same. She was still my mother, with as many foibles and petty weaknesses as any of the Sidhe, however much they preferred to claim otherwise.

"I have *your* magic to thank for its revival," she said. "The talismans are a mere shadow of these creatures' powers. And now I know how to get them to obey my every command."

"Because you failed to do the same for me," I said. "You can't win over human allies any more. You're alone, Nessa."

Her expression didn't change, but something in her demeanour shifted. Perhaps my words had broken through. Maybe deep inside her rotting core, some small part of her cowered at my harsh words. Nobody could hurt you like the ones you loved.

"Daughter," she said. "I'm terribly sorry about this, but

your lover here still belongs to me. The stunt he pulled doesn't erase the vow he swore to serve me." Her gaze passed to Cedar, and a smile curled her lip.

Cedar didn't move, didn't contradict her words. How had I managed to overlook the obvious? I'd given up my magic. Cedar hadn't. And now…

"Kill Raine Whitefall," she said to him.

Cedar didn't move. I prepared to call on magic to defend myself, but Cedar merely smiled.

He's not under her control? But nothing could undo a vow. Nothing except…

Losing her magic.

"What?" she said, eyes narrowing.

"I'm not beholden to you," Cedar said. "Our vow has gone. I'm surprised you didn't notice."

"You're lying," she said. "I let you keep your magic."

"But you gave up yours."

I knew it. She'd taken in the Morrigan's power, and it must have erased her own. Including vows… and including the hypnosis.

Hey, I thought, trying to catch the god's eye. *Fight her.*

It didn't move. I wasn't sure it could actually read my thoughts—the talisman and I went more by feeling than anything else—but maybe it *wanted* to fight at her side. Against the Courts. She'd freed it, after all. But if her magic didn't hold it… her grip on the creature was less secure than she'd thought.

That's what happened when you had the hubris to take power from a god. The Morrigan must have known. I almost wanted to run back to the Death Kingdom and hug the evil old bird.

"You're lying, mortal," said Lady Whitefall. "I have more power than the Courts."

Branches snapped as she raised her hands, raw fury

pouring off her. Her white hair streamed behind her, and the trees bent and swayed. My legs locked into place under a torrent of fear—and the spell broke when June swung a knife at her from behind.

The blow should have struck. Instead, power exploded from my mother's hands in a shower of darkness, and June collapsed, unmoving.

"You're next, Raine," she screamed.

I raised the sceptre, called on its magic, and pushed it at her. My magic bounced off an invisible shield. Damn, the Morrigan's magic was strong. She was a shield all on her own, surrounded by a rippling current of energy similar to the god-creature's.

The beast no longer stood at her side.

Oh hell.

Darkness shifted beside Cedar and me, forcing us back. The god-creature appeared in a wave of shadow, teeth snapping. It wasn't quite solid, but definitely wasn't a ghost either. Or a wraith. I danced out of the way of its bite, one eye on my mother, who was still shielding. Attacking both of them at once was impossible, and my hypnosis had apparently had no effect on the creature. From the way its bites targeted me and not Cedar, I'd probably just pissed it off.

I swung the sceptre through the air, calling my own god's magic, and icy energy whipped from my hands, smashing into the god-creature. On sheer brute strength, it had me outmatched, and while I was forced to keep shielding, dodging its attacks, it was impossible to get another hit in with the hypnosis. Lady Whitefall raised her hands, and another dark current of energy slammed into Cedar and me.

His healing magic slowed my fall, and I rolled out of the god-creature's way again. Dark intelligence and wrath shone from its eyes, and its teeth snapped, nearly snatching the sceptre from my hands.

Oh. It wasn't *me* the creature was mad at. It was the god—or what was left of it.

I rolled to my feet, yelling at Cedar—"Hold her off! I've got this."

If my plan didn't work, I was dead. Backing away from the god-creature, I flung the talisman aside.

Its path diverted, teeth snapping at the bushes where I'd thrown it. Drawing on all the hypnotic magic I could, I blasted it full in the face. Its dark eyes momentarily blanked, then their intelligence—and anger—came roaring back. It wasn't enough. Whatever dark power had brought it here, the being was too much for this realm.

Wait. It'd been *my* magic which had brought it here—mine, in the conduit, in conjunction with Cedar's.

I backed away, continuing to blast the creature with magic, until I reached Cedar's side again. Lady Whitefall and he were locked in a stalemate, shield crushing against shield. Taking the Morrigan's magic had also robbed her of her natural magic, and it didn't appear to be made for direct combat. We wouldn't have a better chance than now.

I caught Cedar's gaze, and pushed the slightest hint of the sceptre's magic into his hands.

His hands glowed green. Blue light shone from my own. And our magic dispersed as my mother's death-magic lifted me off my feet. She snarled, mouth twisted, face warping, more like the Morrigan than my mother. But of course—she'd pretty much signed over her soul to become a death faerie, and essentially turned into a second death goddess.

The Sidhe had successfully trapped the Morrigan once already.

Our magic pushed against her, forming a net—frozen pieces of ice mingling with the shield Cedar created. Even the god staggered back, its eyes clearing.

I pushed my magic towards Cedar, and let go.

Magic burned from his hands, both Summer and Winter. At the same time, I used my other power and shoved every ounce of hypnotic magic possible in the creature's face.

"Go home," I roared. "Get back into the hellish place you came from, and *take her with you.*"

My mother screamed. The god-creature leaped at her, and its shimmering darkness engulfed the pair of them. The darkness shifted, becoming a shadowy hole in the world. My mind spun as it struggled to comprehend what I looked at—a realm not Earth or Faerie or even Death, but some kind of hellish between place, darker than the Vale.

My mother's hands latched onto the edge of the dark pit. "No!" She screamed, pulling herself half out into the forest. Her eyes met mine, dark where they'd been blue before. Pleading. "Daughter," she gasped.

"Let that magic go," I told her, "or die."

She did. Magic spiralled from her in thick black tendrils, drawn into the pit. Her eyes paled to blue once again, and the hole closed around her as her hand let go—

And I grabbed it, pulling her free in one wrenching tug. The darkness blinked out, and was gone.

I laid her down on the forest floor, my whole body trembling.

"You know," I said, "a simpler way to live forever would have been to stay in the palace and not open secret doors to the Grey Vale. Just saying."

Nessa Whitefall didn't answer. She appeared to be unconscious.

"Raine." Cedar crouched down next to me. "We need to get her out of here. To the Unseelie Court."

"That was my next plan, once I got my breath back." I pushed to my feet, and ran to the bushes to retrieve the sceptre. "The dungeons will hold her until then."

The moment I put my hands on her shoulders, a current

of magic shot through me, almost like the grip of a vow. I opened my mouth to shout a warning, and my breath was snatched away, my senses flaring up. *What in the world—?*

Tremors racked my body, but Cedar stumbled, too, and the whole earth shook as though under the force of an earthquake. Ahead, the Whitefall palace trembled. The doors flew wide, and power washed through me, reaching the foundations of the earth. I felt it, every inch of it, and knew I could control and reshape it to my will. Lady Whitefall must have had some magic left after all. *And now it's mine.*

I lifted my mother's limp body and moved almost without thinking first, warping the world around me the way the Sidhe did. I landed in the dungeon, throwing Lady Whitefall into one of the cages, and disappeared a heartbeat later.

I didn't need to open a door, not when I could extend my magic to anywhere in the palace. I found her suite, the wardrobe still open, and willed it to collapse into nothingness. The corridor winked out of existence in a heartbeat, and the door to the Vale along with it. I yanked the power back into myself, and brushed against something conscious. In the entrance hall. *Aha.*

Her magic unravelled around the statues held captive for who knew how many years, and I pulled it away from them, willing them to wake up.

"I am your new queen," I told them. "You're free now, but there are some who wish to take this territory from you. If you want to stay here in Winter, you'll have to chase them off."

They woke. Hobgoblins and trolls, fae and half-bloods, even some pure faeries. With war cries, they ran from the palace, screaming for blood.

As for me… I willed myself to reappear beside Cedar, on the battlefield where Lady Whitefall had fallen. The palace's magic trembled through my body, and all around, the sounds of fighting raged on. The freed creatures ran, tearing into any remainders of Lady Whitefall's army. They were merciless, and furious, and their combined strength ripped through the Vale's forces. The trembling stopped as the palace came to a halt, and so did I.

I turned to Cedar. "Looks like I just inherited a court."

25

Unsurprisingly, things weren't that simple. For one thing, the court in question had been happy to take my orders in battle, but afterwards was a different story. Half of them had wandered off by the time Cedar and I had searched the forest and confirmed that Viola, Rose and the others were okay. After all, they'd sworn no vow of loyalty to me, and considering they'd been stuck in the palace for so long, I didn't blame them for taking off.

Once the injured had been returned to the Hornbeams' territory and everyone accounted for, I left for the Unseelie Court. Lord Lyle's army had vanished once the battle was done, having fulfilled their end of our bargain. Cedar had disappeared, too, and I hadn't been able to find him, so I figured I'd send a message to the Unseelie Queen that the former Lady Whitefall was currently detained in her old palace, magic-less and awaiting a trial.

As I reached the path connecting Summer and Winter territories, Cedar walked along the path from the Seelie territory to join me.

"Hey," I said, somewhat surprised. "Where have you been?"

"Replacing Summer's security talisman."

"Oops. I never thought of that," I said. "Did they assume Lady Whitefall stole it?"

"Ivy distracted them by asking for a lift back to the mortal realm," Cedar said. "I think they're a little preoccupied."

"No kidding." I stopped walking, and hugged him properly for the first time since the battle. "Thank you. For everything. No thanks for scaring the shit out of me and scheming behind my back."

He rested his forehead against mine. "I couldn't think of anything else to do. Is she still in the dungeon?"

"Yeah. I was on my way to tell the Unseelie Court to pick her up," I said. "They might kill her, but letting her live without magic is worse."

"The Morrigan knew," Cedar said. "I'm sure she did. She agreed to loan out a piece of her magic knowing it'd obliterate her other powers."

"Yep," I said. "The Morrigan makes the Sidhe look like amateurs at their own games. Anyway, I'm leaving her fate up to the Courts."

"And if they exile her?"

I shook my head. "She has allies in the Vale. They have more sense."

Cedar looked at me. "Considering their history, you might be giving them too much credit."

"You have a point," I said. "But don't worry. I'm going to her trial in person to advise them, in case Lord Lyle forgets what we did for him."

"Good," he said. "And then?"

I shrugged. "I don't know. Claim a court… or not. I'm not keen on the whole ruling thing."

"You got a round of applause from the Hornbeam army."

"So did you." There was no question he'd take leadership, but now I was unquestioningly Lady Whitefall, did that make us rivals? The borderlands didn't follow the same cut-throat rules as before, but we still belonged to opposing Courts. And there was one slight issue. "Cedar... I guessed that our magic was compatible—more than the usual—and I didn't tell you. I knew she was looking for you, and that you'd give yourself up to her if it meant I'd go free, and I didn't dare risk it. I should have known she'd have figured it out anyway. It might have cost us the battle."

He looked at me, a flash of green appearing in his eyes. "I proved you right, didn't I?"

"I guess, but I'd have done the same." A moment passed. "Does that mean you forgive me?"

"Of course it does," said Cedar. "I knew there was something different about our magic the first time we used it in conjunction."

"Yeah, that's what I don't get," I said. "The sceptre was from the Grey Vale, and its magic doesn't even belong to the Courts. Yours does."

"It might not," he said. "The magic I used isn't the sort I was born with. Lady Hornbeam gave me the magic herself. Directly from a talisman."

"What? Seriously?"

"She was paranoid someone was going to steal it, so she chose to give it to someone nobody would suspect of wielding powerful magic," he explained. "I didn't realise the magic must have come from a talisman—honestly, the thought didn't cross my mind until recently. Thanks to the iron she made me carry, I didn't figure out my magic was different for a long time. I think the gods' magic isn't all that different from the Sidhe's, when it comes down to it."

"Damn." I shook my head. "You have no end of surprises, Cedar Hornbeam. Or should that be *Lord?*"

"I'll consider it," he said. "It's only fair to ask my people first. I was taught only to serve, not rule. I'm a thief, not a soldier."

"And I'm a thief and a noble. You can be both. You've accepted leadership in every way short of taking the title."

"And a talisman," he added.

"You do have one. Besides, who's saying we have to stick to the Sidhe's rules? Not me." I leaned in and kissed him, thoroughly.

"Remind me to ask for your advice more often," he murmured against my neck.

I grinned. "You're welcome."

———

Dad showed up at the Hornbeam family's palace on the second day after the battle, dressed in the finery of the Summer Court. I almost didn't recognise him in resplendent green and gold, a crown of thorns on his head, when the guards at the gate parted to allow him inside.

"Hi, Dad." It felt weird calling him that, when we were almost strangers, though maybe less so since we'd spoken in the meadow. "Is the Summer Court treating you well?"

I'll bet they want me to see them. I'd been expecting as much, considering reports of how I'd defeated Lady Whitefall would have reached Summer by now, but I hadn't expected them to let him come near me.

"They've asked me to invite you to attend a Gathering tonight," he said. "At the house of a noble of the Seelie Court."

"What?" I blinked at him. "If they want me dead, there are more subtle ways of going about it."

"They don't want you dead," Dad told me. "The offer extends to your court—and the Hornbeams', if you wish."

"I don't think so." I frowned. "Even if you ignore the fact

that I duped them, they don't like half-bloods. You know that."

"You saved Faerie," he said. "They know."

"So what? The Sidhe are the definition of ungrateful. And the first time I attended a Gathering of the borderland families, someone tried to shoot me to death."

"That won't happen," Dad said. "They're extending an offer of peace, both to you and the borderlands, for aiding them in the fight against Lady Whitefall."

"They do know I'm not even from Summer, don't they?"

"You have their blood. I'd hazard a guess that they may wish to take advantage and win your loyalty over the Unseelie Court, but they are prepared to swear not to harm you. Unlike the borderland Sidhe, they don't make a habit of murdering one another. I think this is the best way to ensure peace, and clean up any former misunderstandings."

"They'll hate me," I said. "For what I did."

"Some might," he admitted. "Others would admire you. The new Lord Hornbeam is also invited, and the Seelie Court would like to welcome the Hornbeams amongst their allies again."

Pretty words, and most likely lies. But being allowed to see Dad again, and walk freely in Faerie without fearing retribution from the Sidhe of Summer... it tempted me, however unlikely it might be. "I'll see," I said. "But are you really staying there? In Summer?"

A wistful look entered his eyes. "I don't think the mortal realm will have me back."

"I know that feeling, but... you lived there longer than I did." I couldn't think of him as belonging to the Seelie Court. I wasn't sure he did, either. The double memories must be confusing. Technically, we *could* go into the mortal realm now the rifts were re-opened, but I had nothing more to do there. My friends were here.

"We have time enough to think about it, Raine," he said. "Consider accepting the invitation, anyway. It's a chance to mend things between the borderlands and the Seelie Court."

"All right, but I won't make any promises."

———

Cedar said yes, to my intense surprise.

"They won't try anything," he said. "It's not like Lady Hornbeam. If they wanted you dead, they'd have already come for you. I can't say they'll forgive your deception, but if they want us to come to a Gathering to which other half-bloods are invited, it suggests they're willing to recognise us as part of the faerie courts. Thanks to the constant wars between families in the borderlands, we never had that option before."

"Hmm. I'm not Seelie, though," I said. "A quarter, technically, but I'm more Unseelie. And I thought they hated us."

"I wouldn't go as far to say they'll invite the Unseelie Sidhe to one of their parties, but half-bloods are different. There are more than you'd think who straddle two Courts, especially from the mortal realm."

"I know," I said. "But I'm taking a wild guess that if they don't want me dead, they want a favour. Dad hinted that they want me on their side over the Unseelie Court."

"You're probably right," Cedar admitted. "But I've worked rather hard at keeping up the appearance of running a stable court, and I think the Gathering will work to our advantage."

"For you, it might. I'm only going because I want to see the Sidhe's faces when they have to be polite to me."

He smiled. "There's that, too. Did I ever mention that I think it was a masterful plan?"

"A fair few times, but I'll never get tired of hearing it."

———

Ivy Lane, of all people, met us on the way through Seelie territory on the way to the Gathering.

"Nice to see a familiar face," she said. "I promised not to drag any of my human friends into this realm, so I'm stuck waiting for their messengers to take me back to the mortal realm. Faerie meetings are tedious as hell."

"Sounds fun," I said.

"They hate me," Ivy confided. "All of them. They don't know I'm the one who messed up their immortality, but by walking in here and disrupting the peace…"

"Peace?" I raised an eyebrow.

"Status quo. Whichever. They want to carry on kidnapping humans for fun and throwing all responsibility for their actions out the window. I made it impossible. They won't forgive that, even if I saved their lives."

"Some gratitude."

Ivy smiled. "You know, they're not so different from humans."

There was a flash of light, and three Seelie messengers appeared from thin air.

"Ivy Lane," one of them said tonelessly.

"Hi, Lord Raivan," she said. "I'm more than ready to go home, thanks." She gave me a nod. "I'll see you around, Raine."

All the messengers vanished in a second flash, except Lord Kerien, who turned to face me. As before, he was tall and intimidating, his handsome face creased in a scowl.

"Raine Warren, the deceiver," he said softly.

"It's Whitefall, and I never broke my word."

And I hadn't. They'd hate me, true, but I'd never come here to make friends with the Sidhe. Like Ivy, I'd deal with them by necessity.

His eyes narrowed. "If not for your actions in service of the Courts, you would face punishment as severe as your mother's. I trust the Unseelie have that in hand?"

"Yeah, they put her in jail for the rest of her life," I said. "Tell me why you called me here. If you harm me, Cedar, my father or anyone else, you'll face the wrath of the borderlands."

"The borderlands," he said, "have always been neutral. This is a problem, when two Courts are too close together. Summer and Winter are not meant to coexist."

"Tell that to everyone living in peace in the mortal realm and here," I countered. "There are no Sidhe left in the borderlands, right?"

"Why do you ask?"

"I want to petition to make the borderlands into Half-Blood Territory," I told him. "They're mostly abandoned anyway, and I think most half-bloods would feel more at home there than in the Courts. You clearly don't need them, and neither does the Unseelie Court."

He arched a brow. "You'd willingly give up your territory?"

"Not giving it up." I smiled. "Expanding it. My neighbour's, too. The new leader of the Hornbeams is all about second chances."

"I would support this," Cedar added. "A large number of half-bloods reside in the Courts when I think they would prefer the borderlands."

His forehead creased in thought. "The borderlands are a lawless wasteland, under constant attack by the Vale. We have no need of them. Are you prepared to defend your territory, Hornbeam?" He addressed Cedar, ignoring me. Apparently he was fine with someone who hadn't duped him taking over the borderlands. Too bad for him, because Cedar and I came as a unit, and wherever he went, I did.

"You mean *Lord* Hornbeam," I added, and Cedar gave me a look. I shrugged innocently as Cedar answered Lord Kerien's question in the affirmative.

"Hey, you *are* a lord. Own it," I whispered to him, as Lord Kerien turned to converse with another Sidhe knight who'd appeared at his side.

"Maybe I'll take another name," he muttered back. "The last Lord Hornbeam was hardly a stellar example of good leadership."

"Suppose not. It's your choice. Maybe I'll go back to Warren."

Like Dad. I wanted to know him—the real him, the person my mother's magic had tried to take away—until he was no longer a stranger to me. For that, I wanted to stay here in Faerie. At least for now.

"It's up to you," said Cedar, when the knights had gone. "I like the idea of keeping the borderlands for half-bloods. I guessed you were about to make such a suggestion."

"It's the obvious solution," I said. "But the Sidhe won't take my word alone, not after what I did."

"You beat them at their own game. They have to acknowledge that, at least."

"I think it'd kill them to admit it," I said. "And to think I hoped I'd get through this Gathering without anyone dropping dead."

"You never know," he said. "This might well be the first non-violent Gathering in a century."

"Would you bet on that?"

He briefly turned to me and stroked my face. "Yes, I would. Ready to join the party?"

I took out my talisman, and felt the sceptre's magic humming inside me in conjunction with Cedar's. "Maybe I'll give the Sidhe a performance. Wait, do you reckon they remember I can hypnotise them?"

"Why do you think I'm so confident I'll win the bet?" he asked. "Unless—unless you don't want to use that power anymore."

"Are you kidding me?" I frowned. "I didn't just adopt that magic for the battle with Lady Whitefall. It's mine." More than the sceptre was, really. It'd take a while to disentangle the magic—and dancing, for that matter—from what Robin had done, but maybe I already had. I'd left that life behind, and with the last threads of Lady Whitefall's influence gone, I had a lifetime to use the magic to carve out my own path.

"Good." He smiled. "I'm glad."

I held the sceptre and faced the path into the Summer Court. "The Sidhe won't know what hit them. It's show time."

ABOUT THE AUTHOR

Emma is the New York Times and USA Today Bestselling author of the Changeling Chronicles urban fantasy series.

Emma spent her childhood creating imaginary worlds to compensate for a disappointingly average reality, so it was probably inevitable that she ended up writing fantasy novels. When she's not immersed in her own fictional universes, Emma can be found with her head in a book or wandering around the world in search of adventure.

Find out more about Emma's books at
www.emmaladams.com.